Pitch Dark

Also by Paul Doiron

Dead Man's Wake
Hatchet Island
Dead by Dawn
One Last Lie
Almost Midnight
Stay Hidden
Knife Creek
Widowmaker
The Precipice
The Bone Orchard
Massacre Pond
Bad Little Falls
Trespasser
The Poacher's Son

Pitch Dark

Paul Doiron

MINOTAUR BOOKS
NEW YORK

First published in the United States by Minotaur Books,
an imprint of St. Martin's Publishing Group

PITCH DARK. Copyright © 2024 by Paul Doiron. All rights reserved.
Printed in the United States of America. For information,
address St. Martin's Publishing Group, 120 Broadway, New York, NY 10271.

www.minotaurbooks.com

The Library of Congress Cataloging-in-Publication Data is available upon request.

ISBN 978-1-250-86442-0 (hardcover)
ISBN 978-1-250-86443-7 (ebook)

Our books may be purchased in bulk for promotional, educational, or business use. Please
contact your local bookseller or the Macmillan Corporate and Premium Sales Department at
1-800-221-7945, extension 5442, or by email at MacmillanSpecialMarkets@macmillan.com.

First Edition: 2024

10 9 8 7 6 5 4 3 2 1

In Memory of Hayden Anderson

Part I

No one is so sure of his premises as the man who knows too little.

—Barbara W. Tuchman, *The March of Folly*

I

I'll buy the test tomorrow," Stacey said from the sofa. She had kicked off her moccasins and stretched out across the cushions with her stocking feet inches from the woodstove, and she had a book of Rick Bass's essays tented on her chest. "But honestly, I'm not *that* late."

"You said it's been two weeks."

"Which has happened before. I've never had the most regular cycles in the world. And the odds of my being pregnant—"

"But you switched up your birth control after our honeymoon."

Stacey had long brown hair and almond-shaped green eyes that made some people wonder if she might be Eurasian. She'd always been rail thin, and lying down, her body looked the same as ever.

"And we were extra careful during that time. Mike, I know you hate not knowing. But we'll have an answer tomorrow. Besides, I thought we agreed we wanted kids."

"But now doesn't seem like the ideal time."

"There is no ideal time. All my friends have told me that. Besides, I'm sure this is a false alarm. I don't know why you're freaking out."

"I'm not freaking out."

At which point, Shadow glanced up from the rug with his sulfur-yellow eyes and growled at me. It was not a sound I took lightly from the 145-pound wolf dog. Hybrids are unpredictable, which was why I had a special permit to own this coal-black brute. I was

3

under no illusions about the wildness lurking in his unknowable heart.

That said, Shadow had been getting more indoor time since Stacey had moved in. Prior to our marriage six months earlier, I'd kept the half-wild animal in a fenced pen with supervised visits inside the house and occasional sleepovers if he was well behaved. But some ineffable quality in my new wife seemed to soothe the savage beast. Frankly, I was a little jealous of how quickly they'd bonded.

"Well," she said softly, "Shadow seems to think you're 'exercised a mite,' as my dad might say."

I did my best to calm my voice. "Sorry about that, buddy. Everything's chill here."

It was a lie, of course. Because I was indeed freaking out at the possibility of Stacey being pregnant—in my experience, anyone who claims not to be freaking out is, by definition, freaking out.

I'm not even sure I should have a child, based on my own warped upbringing.

Fortunately or unfortunately, I was prevented from blurting out my cri de coeur by the ringing of the phone in my home office, down the darkened hall.

My state-issued cell identified my caller as the game warden assigned to the Rockwood district—a remote area of commercial timberland and nature preserves northwest of Moosehead Lake. Brandon Barstow was twenty-six and had recently graduated from the Advanced Warden School. I was the investigator who'd done his background check prior to his hiring.

"Hey, Mike," he said. "I think I might possibly have a missing person case maybe."

Might? Possibly? Maybe?

"That sounds serious, Brandon. Should I marshal the entire search and rescue team?"

I hadn't bothered to turn on the desk lamp. I listened to the downpour outside. It had rained all through April and now into the first week of May. The raindrops were coming down as hard as hailstones.

"You're being a wiseass," he said after a pause.

As in nearly all law enforcement agencies, it was part of the culture of the Warden Service to haze rookies, but I realized I was taking out my anxiety about Stacey on poor Brandon. He might well have an emergency on his hands and was looking to me, as an experienced game warden investigator, to provide guidance, not jokes.

"Tell me what's going on, Brandon. How can I be of help?"

"Well, OK. There's this guy, he's rented a cabin up at Seboomook Farm. His name is Hammond Pratt, and I guess he's from Idaho, according to the license he showed Ivan Ivanov when he checked in."

Ivanov was one of those oddball characters who populated the North Woods: a Russian emigree who'd chucked his career as an aeronautical engineer to buy a hunting lodge that stirred his nostalgia for his childhood in the wilds of Karelia.

Brandon, meanwhile, was rattling on: "Pratt's car is a rental out of the Bangor airport, nothing special, full-size Toyota sedan. And anyhow, when he checked in, he asked Ivan if he could arrange to rent an ATV."

Maine game wardens are responsible for finding anyone who goes missing in the woods—the trick is determining whether someone is truly missing or not. Lots of folks are bad at informing others of their half-baked plans. Wardens waste tons of time searching for people who aren't lost at all but merely noncommunicative and inconsiderate.

"Something tells me Mr. Pratt doesn't have a lot of experience with all-terrain vehicles."

"Why do you say that?" Brandon said edgily as if he thought I was mocking him again.

"It's been raining for a week," I explained, "and Pratt wanted to go mudding alone in some of the roughest country in Maine? Also, the fact that you're unsure if he's missing or not means he didn't leave a trip plan with Ivanov. Most of the logging roads between Moosehead and Jackman are gated and off-limits through mud season—even the roads normally open to four-wheelers. Not to mention that the designated ATV trails in your neck of the woods must be impassable after a long winter followed by a month of rain. There's been no time for the crews to clear away the deadfalls."

"That's all true! I mean, like, one hundred percent."

The young man couldn't suppress his astonishment at what, to me, were basic deductions.

"How did you guess all that?" he asked.

"I've had a lot of experience."

The last time I'd seen Brandon Barstow had been at his graduation, when the commissioner of the Maine Department of Inland Fisheries and Wildlife—the agency that oversees the Bureau of the Warden Service—had sworn him in, along with seven classmates. What I remembered most vividly was how impossibly young he'd looked in his red-and-olive dress uniform: wide-eyed and beaming, with an ill-timed case of acne on his forehead and a smooth chin that probably didn't require shaving more than twice a week.

Has it really been ten years since I've taken that same oath?

"My first question," I said, "is why did Ivanov agree to rent this Pratt character an ATV, knowing there was nowhere to ride it?"

"I guess the dude's pretty intimidating," said Brandon. "Ivanov told me he's huge with a shaved head and lots of tats and a gray beard. Middle-aged, but you wouldn't want to mess with him. I'm also thinking Pratt slipped him something under the counter for the ATV? He paid for his room in cash, which is why Ivanov doesn't have a credit card on file."

The story was intriguing me, I had to admit. Whatever Pratt had in mind coming to Seboomook Farm during one of the worst weeks of Maine's most godawful season, I doubted recreation was involved.

"How long exactly has he been unaccounted for?" I asked.

"Tonight would be the second night."

I squeezed my eyes shut from exasperation. The temperature had been freakishly warm in the North Woods, but a person soaked to the skin could succumb from hypothermia in hours.

"And Ivan only got in touch with you now?"

"The folks at the farm didn't know what to make of him. There's barely anyone staying at the lodge on account of the weather, but I guess Pratt was asking the staff if they knew anything about a man living with his young daughter in the woods nearby. He said they'd be keeping a low profile, this father and daughter. He was offering a hundred dollars to anyone who'd point him in the right direction."

Like the home offices of many game wardens, mine was decorated with taxidermy. An eight-point deer head gazed down with marble eyes from the wall. A mounted pine marten held a mounted red squirrel in jaws secured with wire and cement. Being morbid by nature, I normally found nothing ghoulish or disturbing about these objects. But there was enough weirdness in Brandon's story that I felt unsettled by their deathly stares.

"*Are* there a father and daughter living in the woods near Seboomook Farm?"

"Kind of."

"That was a yes-or-no question, Brandon."

"There's a man from Alaska named Mark Redmond building a cabin for Josie Jonson on Prentiss Pond, near the Canadian border. I've never talked with the dude, but I've seen him come into Maynard's a few times to gas up this monster vehicle he owns. It looks like a freaking tank, and Redmond carries himself like he's ex-military. He has a little girl, people say. But no one's ever seen her except Josie. You must know her, the bush pilot?"

"Josie Jonson is my wife's godmother."

"No shit?"

"I want to get back to the daughter—you said Redmond never brings her into town."

"Never."

So he leaves her alone in the woods? Why would someone do that to a young girl? In addition to being negligent, it seems unfathomably cruel.

My loud mention of Josie's name caused Stacey to appear in the open doorway behind me. I heard the floorboards creak and, turning, saw her tall, slim silhouette against the golden light of the hallway beyond.

"*Who is it?*" she mouthed.

I raised a finger, promising to answer.

"Have you been in touch with this Redmond to see if he knows anything about Hammond Pratt?" I asked Brandon.

"Prentiss Pond is way off the grid. I mean, like, I wouldn't even trust a satellite phone to reach that place. Other than driving out there—and I doubt I could make it tonight in this rain—I wouldn't know *how* to reach him."

"Have you tried calling Josie, then? She must have a way of communicating with her builder other than flying to the building site. Maybe she talks with him via sat phone or radio?"

"I was going to call her next—if you thought it made sense."

Of course calling Josie Jonson made sense. And Brandon should have known to contact Redmond's client before he called me. I had to take a breath and remind myself that I, too, had been a rookie, although my problem had been—and perhaps still was—arrogance rather than indecision.

"I'll handle it, Brandon."

"You will?"

"But I want you to call Ivanov back. Tell him that if Pratt hasn't returned by first light, you're going to drive up to Seboomook Farm and stand watch outside the door while the housekeepers clean his room."

"Isn't that illegal?"

"No, it's *inadmissible*. If they find evidence that suggests Pratt's engaged in a crime, the prosecutor won't be able to use it. But we're not conducting a criminal investigation into the guy. We're trying to determine whether we have a missing person on our hands."

"But the maids aren't allowed to search through his personal possession, right?"

"No, but if they happen to see a map 'in plain view,' for example, and decide to take a picture of said item—"

"I don't know about this, Mike."

"If you get blowback from your sergeant or lieutenant—which you won't—you can blame it on me. The district attorney has my number on speed dial."

"I'm sure he does," the young warden muttered.

"Oh, and take a few photos of the rental car—inside and out. There's no prohibition against your doing that. And you never know what might end up being useful."

Stacey leaned against the doorframe with her arms crossed, eavesdropping. She wore my old Colby sweatshirt over jeans that flattered her runner's legs, and had on buckskin moccasins, handmade by a friend of ours who belonged to the Passamaquoddy Tribe.

Looking at my beautiful wife, an image of Brandon Barstow at his graduation ceremony flashed through my memory. He was married himself, with an infant daughter.

"I've been meaning to ask, how's your wife taking to life in the North Woods? You two are originally from York, right? Winter in Rockwood must've been a new experience for a couple from southern Maine."

"Wendi's trying to adapt. But she says it's hard living in the boonies, not having anyone to help with the baby." He hesitated before he continued, worried how the admission might sound to a senior officer. "I sometimes wonder if I made a mistake."

I knew by "mistake," he meant accepting an isolated posting in the North Woods with a wife and young child.

Nevertheless, I couldn't help but hear his uncertainty through the echo chamber of my own worries. I glanced back at the hall to look at Stacey. But she was gone.

2

By the time I returned to the living room, Stacey had spread out across the couch again, but she had put aside the book and had folded her hands over her lower abdomen. I wondered if the posture meant she was reflecting on the odds of being pregnant.

The room smelled of the birch fire in the stove and the balsam pillow beneath her head—and of the wolf dog, of course. Every room in the house, even the ones he seldom visited, carried his earthy scent. That is what it's like to live with a good-size canine.

Shadow cracked one baleful eye but kept the other closed tight. I had no idea how to interpret this watchful gesture. Was I safe with him now or not? Genetically speaking, he was almost entirely wolf, which was how I always thought of him, forgetting the dog part.

Slowly, carefully, I took a seat in a rocking chair where he could see me and I could see him.

Stacey interlocked her fingers to make a cradle behind her head. Then she crossed her ankles. "Why does Brandon Barstow need to get in touch with Josie?"

I told her what he'd told me.

"Josie isn't really my godmother," she said when I'd finished. "She just likes to call herself that. Jo's more like an old flying buddy of my dad's. She's a strange bird—raunchy as hell—but I do love the woman."

"But I was right about her having a two-story cabin built near the

Québec border? Didn't you tell me she posted pictures of the work in progress? Remember? Because you were so impressed. It was only half-done, you said, but—"

"It's going to be a spectacular place. Redmond is a legit cabin master." Stacey sat up and reached for her phone on the mug-ringed coffee table. She clicked an app and thumbed through a chain of posts. "That's weird. It looks like she deleted the album of pictures."

When I leaned forward in the antique rocker, it offered a complaining creak that attracted Shadow's displeasure. "Do you remember what she said about Redmond?"

"She called him a genius. But she wouldn't share his name even when people were begging in her comments. She said he's a very private person."

Stacey continued opening and closing social media apps, searching for the phantom photographs.

"You'd think he'd want to advertise his work, if it's so spectacular, to get more commissions. Building a real log cabin is a lost art. People would pay big money for the genuine article."

She shrugged. "Maybe that's why she took the pictures down—because she was worried about losing him to a better-paying client."

"Maybe," I said. "Did she mention anything about Redmond having a daughter with him on-site?"

"I would have remembered if she had. It was strange enough that the guy was living up there in the mountains all winter. That's hard country even during the warm-weather months."

"Try googling him," I suggested.

Stacey tied her hair in a loose knot to keep it out of her face. Then she set to work. She had a job as an EMT now but had once been a wildlife biologist and still possessed a scientist's enthusiasm for doing research.

"The first Mark Redmond who comes up is a rheumatologist from Sherman Oaks, California. I doubt that's our guy. There are literally dozens of people with that name, and none of them is showing up as a Maine cabin master. Let me try adding Alaska as a filter . . ." Her thumbs tap-tap-tapped the glass. "As far as the World Wide Web is concerned, this particular Mark Redmond doesn't exist."

"Is it possible these days to have no footprint on the internet?"

"I imagine it would require living in a very deliberate way." She gazed at me with a sly smile; her pale green eyes were alive now with the thrill of the hunt. "Let me try Hammond Pratt. That's such a bizarre name. Surely, there's got to be . . ."

"What?"

"Nope. Nada. Nothing."

"So we have one cypher searching for another cypher."

"One cypher searching for two cyphers. You're forgetting the daughter." She cocked her head to get a view of the weather station on the wall. The digital display showed the time and temperature, as well as the wind speed, rainfall, and barometric pressure: all of which were dismal at the moment. "It's late, but you should call Josie. Pratt sounds creepy to me, and she may want to alert the Redmonds."

I had been rocking in the rocking chair, forgetting how much the wolf disliked the back-and-forth motion. He reminded me of his displeasure with a curled lip that showed his rear fangs.

"I need to go up there," I said. "This whole situation is so weird. Pratt sure sounds like he may be dangerous. But there's something off about this builder's story, too."

"Not everyone who chooses to live off the grid is hiding from someone or something. And how will you get in if the roads are blocked and washed out?"

"Tomorrow morning there's supposed to be a break in the rain. Do you think I could get Josie to fly me to Prentiss Pond by helicopter?"

"No."

"No?"

"She hasn't met you yet, babe, and like I said, Josie can be strange."

"How so?"

"She gets into moods and takes things the wrong way. Like, we were flying together once in her floatplane—it's a de Havilland Beaver—and I asked about it, and she snapped at me that hers wasn't for sale. I told her I didn't want to buy it, but she was snippy the rest of the flight as if she didn't believe me. She knows you're a warden investigator and may get it into her head that you want to arrest her builder for some reason."

"That's crazy."

"No, that's Josie."

"How do I persuade her, then? If she's already mistrustful and super protective of Redmond?"

"Get my dad to do it. In fact, I think he should call her tonight and tell her about Pratt. She might want to let the Redmonds know he's been asking about them. I'm sure she will, in fact. Of course, if you do drive to Jackman, Dad's going to insist on tagging along."

"That's a given."

"It's too bad he's getting the gyros replaced on his Skylane," Stacey said. "You could have zipped up there in the Cessna instead of having to spend three-plus hours on the road, listening to your father-in-law spin yarns the whole time."

My father-in-law.

Charley Stevens had been my friend and mentor for years—the closest thing I had to a real dad—long before I'd married his daughter and made the relationship official. Every time I thought of the old fart as my *father*, I felt an upwelling of joy in my chest.

"I never mind listening to your old man," I said, smiling.

"That's why he loves you," Stacey said. "But I don't get your suspicions about Redmond. Beyond his being a deeply private person, what's really bothering you?"

"The fact that he may have a young daughter with him. That area is beyond remote. And logging is the most dangerous profession in the nation. It makes policing look as safe as library science by comparison. Brandon said he never even brings her to Jackman or Rockwood, either. Why is he hiding her from the world? Is there an ex-wife wondering where she is?"

"You once told me good investigators don't jump to conclusions."

She was right; I had said as much. But now I waved away my own doctrine. Literally waved it away with my hand.

"But we listen to our intuition," I said. "And something feels off. Even assuming he's cleared everything with the state and is homeschooling her, and the child welfare people have blessed the situation, which I doubt they would, it still rubs me the wrong way. I don't think a kid should be deprived of the company of children her own age—"

"We don't know a thing about what he's doing or not doing. And judging other people's parenting decisions is always a mistake."

The comment was a blatant callback to the disagreement we'd been having before Brandon had interrupted us.

"You'll buy the test tomorrow?" I said.

"After my shift." Stacey drove an ambulance based in the nearby city of Belfast. "Do you want me to take it immediately or wait until you get home?"

"Can I give you my answer later?"

"Oh, Mike."

Still seated, she reached for my hand across the black ruff of the sleeping wolf. Despite the cozy heat from the stove, her hand felt cold. I clutched it between mine to warm it up.

3

When I got Charley on the phone and told him what Brandon had told me and what Stacey and I had subsequently learned—or not learned—about Mark Redmond and Hammond Pratt, and after I had explained my plan to ask Josie to fly us to Prentiss Pond, his response was exactly what his daughter had predicted.

"It's better if I call her. Jo's wicked protective of those Redmond folks. She's kind of adopted them, it seems. The man's daughter especially. Let me give her a ring and see if I can persuade her to give us a lift to the pond after the rain clears."

I'd returned to my office to call him and this time had turned on the lights to avoid the chiaroscuro menace of the stuffed-and-mounted animals watching me with their unseeing eyes.

Listening to the rain, my thoughts bounced back and forth between the reclusive Redmonds and my own personal preoccupation. My biological father had been an emotionally abusive womanizer and dangerous criminal who'd left my psyche scarred in ways I was still discovering nearly ten years after his death. Charley had provided me with a role model of what real fatherhood could be, but I didn't possess his patience or generosity of spirit. I could barely take care of the wolf in my charge.

I was letting my worries run away with me and needed to knock it off. My wife was one of the most intuitive people I had ever met, almost scarily so. Surely Stacey knew what was happening inside her own body. I needed to trust her.

Charley phoned back within minutes.

"Josie can't reach them on the radio, but that's not unexpected with the terrain and the storm. Her Uniden can barely reach them in good conditions. But I spooked her, I have to say, and she says if we're not up there when the rain stops, she's going in alone in her helicopter."

"Great."

"Why are you so convinced there's something shifty about this Redmond, Mike? In my experience, there are flocks of odd ducks roosting in the Maine woods. And most of them are harmless. This cabin master sounds to me like just another coot."

"It's not just him. There's Pratt—what's he up to? And where is he?"

"The man could be lost on a dirt road or have sunk his tires in a mud pit."

"True."

"It'll be a long haul up and back by truck," Charley grumbled.

He offered to borrow a bush plane, since his own was undergoing a major repair. But I wanted the control, autonomy, and freedom that came with driving my own state-issued truck: an unmarked GMC Sierra that, despite its anonymous exterior, announced me as a game warden to every veteran poacher I passed on the road.

"You can keep me entertained by telling me the old warden stories you've told me dozens of times before," I said.

"Oh, I have a few tall tales you haven't heard."

There was humor in his voice now, and I knew that whatever doubts he was harboring about my plan, he was smiling at the prospect of our father-and-son road trip.

I hung up and went to join Stacey in bed. I tried to sleep, while outside, the rain continued to hit the house like buckshot.

Charley Stevens, being Charley Stevens, arrived before dawn, having driven down the coast from the cottage he and his wife, Ora, owned on

Little Wabassus Pond in the pine forests of eastern Maine. My father-in-law had a long, weathered face that was mostly chin and a shock of white hair that bristled when Ora ran a clipper through it each week. He greeted me with a hard clap on the back: his standard greeting.

"I have news from Josie," he said with a grin. "She spoke with Cady half an hour ago—"

"Cady?"

"Redmond's daughter. She's twelve. Her dad was already up and out trying to clear the deadfalls blocking the only road out of Prentiss Pond. But she says everything is fine there, except for being permanently drenched. She's never heard of this Hammond Pratt."

"Josie told the kid his name?"

"I thought it was a mistake, too, but Jo claims the girl is mature for her age and she didn't want to lie to her."

"I wish she hadn't done that."

"I agree, but that's Jo Jonson. The woman's got a long history of making questionable decisions, but that never seems to stop her from making new mistakes. Anyway, she's willing to fly us in if you have your heart set on it."

"More than ever."

"Glad to hear it. It's been ages since I've taken a ride in a whirlybird."

While I finished loading my truck, Charley went into the house to say hi to Stacey. The sound of the flood-swollen Ducktrap River, down the hill, was louder than I'd ever heard it. A raven was calling in the near darkness.

If anything, Josie's news had only deepened my foreboding. The thought of a child, alone and vulnerable, living at a construction site far from town gnawed at my still-empty stomach.

Overnight, the driving rain had become a faint drizzle. It seemed a promising sign. The National Weather Service was predicting there would be an interval of clear skies between this departing low-pressure system and a brief storm arriving from Canada. I hoped this window would be sufficient for Josie to fly us to the cabin.

Stacey was up and making coffee when I went inside. She was wearing the worn flannel bathrobe she had permanently borrowed from me. I didn't mention the pregnancy test in front of her father. I had a long day ahead and needed to put the matter—and my fears—out of my head.

"Have you checked in with young Brandon yet?" Charley asked as we set off in my truck.

"He's supposed to call me when he's had a look around Hammond Pratt's cabin at Seboomook Farm."

The earthbound pilot was dressed entirely in green: rain jacket, nylon flight suit, and baseball cap. Aside from the bone-handled pocketknife I knew he always carried—a retirement gift from his fellow wardens who'd teased him about taking up whittling as an old man—he had brought nothing but a thermos of black coffee. He sipped from the screw-down cup at fifteen-minute intervals, rationing the caffeine, trying to make it last.

As we drove westward, the drizzle turned to a light mist that saturated the air. Fog emanated from every stream and pond. We saw turkeys pecking in the sodden fields, as if they knew no hunter would venture out in all this wet. Then we crested a hill between two blueberry barrens where Charley had once seen a young bear dart across the asphalt. As often happened, this memory prompted another memory, which, in turn, led to a story I had somehow never heard from him before.

I practically swerved into the shoulder when he reached the plot twist. "You didn't tell me you were mauled by a bear!"

"More like swatted around. I'd gotten between a mama and her cub, and she eased me aside. Sadly for me, this happened about a hundred miles from the nearest hospital. But it's amazing the uses you can find for a barbless fishhook and some monofilament. It didn't take more than a dozen stitches to close the wound."

This was my father-in-law in full: offhandedly recounting a death-defying encounter that, for anyone else, would've been one of the defining moments of their life.

Before I could pepper him with questions about the incident, the phone rang. It was Brandon Barstow. I put him on speaker and told him that my father-in-law, the retired chief warden pilot, was riding shotgun and had been fully briefed on the situation.

"So, I'm up at Seboomook Farm," Brandon said.

"Has Hammond Pratt returned?" Charley asked.

"No, he hasn't. I told Ivanov about having his housekeeper look around the cabin, and he got all cranky and obstinate—"

"Put Ivanov on the phone," I demanded. "It's a damned welfare check, not a gross violation of his Fourth Amendment rights. Let me talk with him."

"That won't be necessary. I told Ivan that Mike Bowditch would be making his life miserable if he threw a fit. You should have seen how fast he folded when I mentioned your name."

Charley leaned over the center console and whispered, "Your reputation for being a pain in the derrière is finally paying off."

"Did the maid find anything helpful?" I said, waving away the old man.

"Pratt takes good care of his teeth. He has one of those electric toothbrushes, and there was floss in the wastebasket. He also packed condoms."

"For a visit to the North Woods in mud season!" said Charley. "The man is an optimist. I'll give him that."

"Any indication he might be armed?" I asked.

"Besides the two empty boxes of ammo?"

"Two!"

"Yep. Both handgun calibers: .45 ACP and 9mm. Hollow-point rounds."

"Where did Mr. Pratt think he was headed?" Charley remarked. "The O.K. Corral?"

Brandon continued his report. "I looked in the car, like you said—a silver Toyota Camry LE with Maine plates. There wasn't anything in plain sight except four empty cans of Red Bull scattered in the back seat."

"Send me all the photos you took," I said. "Maybe we will see something you missed."

"What else do you want me to do? It seems like we should begin a search for him, don't you think?"

"We're getting close to making that decision," I said.

"How much more information do you need?" The young man's voice tended to go up an octave when he was peeved.

"You'll know when I know. It matters why Pratt is looking for Mark Redmond. Answering that question helps us understand the kind of a man we're dealing with. Who drives up to Seboomook Farm with two guns and a packet of rubbers?"

"Don't forget the dental floss," added Charley.

Brandon responded with a sniff, "I'm glad you two think this is funny."

"Call the car rental company with the plate number," I said. "Start with the counter at the Bangor airport."

"Won't I need a subpoena?"

"Not if you can convince them we're dealing with exigent circumstances. The company will want you to put in a formal, written request before they consider releasing information. But if you emphasize that their customer might be a missing person engaged in potential criminal activity, they should come through with his name, date of birth, address, and a photo of his license, if we're lucky."

"Make sure the agency understands how important it is we have as much info as possible on the man we're looking for," added my father-in-law.

"Except we're *not* looking for him," Brandon protested. "We haven't initiated a search."

"I'll be in touch from Jackman after I finish my interviews. And I might want to meet you later at Seboomook Farm. Keep your schedule open this afternoon and evening."

After we'd signed off, I cast a look at Charley. "What do you think?"

"About Brandon? That he's exceptionally hardworking and thorough for a young warden. Has a bit of an attitude, but that's just his youth showing."

"What I meant was, what do you think we're going to find at Prentiss Pond?"

"I have decided to withhold judgment pending further investigation."

I wished I had that gift.

4

Our route almost perfectly bisected Maine, taking us via country roads and logging highways from the rocky coast to the forested highlands that bordered the province of Québec.

Three hours after we'd left my home on the coast, we crested the height of land above Jackman.

In 1842, surveyors had drawn a jagged line along the watershed of those hills and mountains. Where the streams flowed south and east, joining and gathering in volume, and where they turned finally toward the Gulf of Maine, lay the United States. Where they coursed west, spilling in cataracts into the St. Lawrence River, was Canada. You could stand astride Slidedown Mountain, as I had done, with one foot in one country and the other foot in another and feel very much like the Colossus of Rhodes in miniature.

Now the entire Moose River Valley was spread before us, the lakes deep blue and almost entirely ice-free except in the coves. There, the shadows of the mountains kept the sun from touching their stubborn gray crust. I knew I was looking into Canada from this vantage—that the arbitrary, invisible border zigzagged along the farthest peaks—but I didn't feel as if I had approached the edge of anything, not the way you recognize upon seeing the ocean, for instance, an absolute division between one thing and another.

"Have you ever seen this country so freakishly green the first week of May?" Charley asked.

"No, but I think we're looking at the new normal."

He pointed west. "There's some nimbostratus beyond Burnt Jacket."

It took me a moment to spot the dark smudge of rain-bearing clouds above the shoulders of the mountain.

"Then we'd better not waste time taking in the view."

I eased my foot from the gas and let gravity pull the truck down the hill toward the village.

Jackman nurtured its reputation as a frontier town: the last stop on a very long, very wooded highway before you crossed into Canada. It boasted two mottoes: the one emblazoned on banners hanging from the light posts (THE SWITZERLAND OF MAINE) and the other printed on bumper stickers on the mud-spattered pickups parked outside Bishop's Store (MORE MOUNTAINS, LESS ASSHOLES).

It was hard to argue that Jackman was undersupplied with mountains, although none of them rivaled the smallest of Alps. To the south of town, snowcapped Sally Mountain rose from the cobalt waters of Big Wood Pond; beyond Sally, the dromedary hump of Attean climbed into view above the lake that shared its name; beyond the lower reaches of the Moose River loomed Number Five Mountain with its telltale fire tower, and its fraternal twin, Number Six Mountain. Beyond them, the next storm was gathering.

As for the paucity of assholes, well, I'd heard differing views from the wardens who worked the area. Whatever their opinions, all of my colleagues agreed that the locals were hard as nails. People who live along the rough edges have to be as rough as the land itself. And Jackman had always been a settlement in the wilderness.

Charley had once described the town to me as "the truck stop that time forgot." But seeing its half-empty streets again for myself, I thought we might well have returned to an era when river drivers spilled out of saloons to brawl in the streets, and the boardinghouses brought *prostituées* down from Québec, along with the bootleg whiskey that fueled the nightly melees.

"Take a right after that bridge," said Charley. "We'll follow the

Heald Stream Road to the River Road. Josie's place is on the north side of the stream, across from the airstrip. In the summer, she ties her de Havilland up to a float outside her door."

I followed his directions and found myself almost immediately confronted with what might best be described as a flash mob of white-tailed deer. The two biggest bucks vaulted for cover, but the does and yearlings reacted with varying degrees of concern, indifference, and lassitude. Some gave us long, dismissive looks before wandering casually off into the evergreens, disappearing instantaneously and absolutely into the trees as only deer can do.

"I take it the people in Jackman feed them after hunting season," I said.

"Yeah, folks put out corn, oats, barley, and such."

"The first day of hunting season must be a regular shooting gallery here, as accustomed as these animals are to humans."

"A blind man could bag one—and probably has."

The Moose River was so high with meltwater and surplus rain that it no longer had banks as such; the flood had crept into the forest, submerging the roots of the trees to form a bitterly cold swamp. Someone's aluminum canoe had floated off a lawn and was now wedged between two maples in the latte-colored water.

"Can't say I've ever seen the Moose this high," said Charley. "That's the farm, ahead on the left."

He didn't need to provide directions. The Robinson R44 Raven helicopter on the paved helipad outside the barn-turned-hangar told me whose home it was.

It was an impressive spread, dominated by a massive old farmhouse with a steep roof and smoke feathering from twin chimneys, a wall of stacked cordwood to feed the fires, a fenced chicken coop, and in back, a rocky pasture where heavy-uddered goats grazed with the same blithe indifference as the deer.

The only surprise—and I can't say the sight didn't give me pause—was the gleaming white pickup in the drive.

The vehicle was a Ford Explorer belonging to the Canada Border

Services Agency. I couldn't recall the last time I'd seen a foreign patrol truck on the American side of the Boundary, as locals called the dividing line between the two nations. Maybe I never had.

"Now, there's a surprising sight!" exclaimed Charley. "It seems one hell of a coincidence that Josie is entertaining an agent of the Services frontaliers this fine morning."

"Or no coincidence at all," I said.

5

The temperature in Jackman was at least fifteen degrees colder than at home. The rain might have pummeled the snowpack until the ground was mostly bare, but I spotted white pockets lingering beneath the shaggiest evergreens. I shivered and zipped up my Gore-Tex jacket as I stepped from the truck.

The cold air, blowing down the hillside, smelled faintly of goats.

Beyond the waiting helicopter, the double doors of the barn stood yawning. Josie had been forced to widen the entrance so that she could tow her Raven inside for the winter or ahead of damaging weather. Coming from within, I heard voices: a man's and a woman's.

I readjusted my belt, heavy with the tools of my trade.

Warden investigators are essentially plainclothes detectives. Even though I was dressed in civvies, I was carrying my SIG P226 service pistol on my belt, two magazines, a multitool in a sheath, and handcuffs in a leather case. The key to the cuffs was attached to the ring I used for my truck and house keys. But a fellow warden who used to be a Navy SEAL—trained to escape hostage takers—had advised me to cut a slit in my gun belt at a six o'clock position where I could hide a second key between the layers.

"You never know when your own gear might be used against you," he'd said in a syrupy southern drawl. "God willing, you'll never need that spare key, but if you ever do, you're going to kiss me for having taught you that trick from the Coronado handbook."

Inside the dark, drafty space, we found Josie gabbing with her Canadian visitor. The hangar was even colder than outside. The sunlight shining through the open doors didn't reach the straw-strewn depths of the former barn. The air smelled of oil, hydraulic fluids, solvents, and paint: aromatherapy for the mechanically minded.

Jo Jonson was that rare specimen in life, the person who looks exactly as you imagined they would: a woman in her late sixties, prematurely aged by weather and misfortune, but vigorous and erect in posture.

She threw her long arms wide. "Chuck Stevens, you handsome devil!"

No one, absolutely no one, called Charley by that nickname. Or so I had believed until that this moment.

"In the flesh, Jo."

She wore her silver hair cut short; I wouldn't have been surprised to learn she trimmed it herself with sewing scissors and a hand mirror. A pair of aviator sunglasses perched atop her head. She was dressed as if she'd planned on spending the day splitting hardwood to feed her stoves, wearing an oversize plaid shirt, flannel-lined jeans, and service boots stained with oil and tree sap. As a collector of North Woods memorabilia, I immediately coveted the hand-tooled sheath on her belt and the deer-antler hunting knife inside it.

"How do you manage to get sexier as the years go by?" She loomed over Charley as they embraced, but her kiss on his lined forehead was the definition of chaste. "You're becoming a regular Christopher Plummer."

My father-in-law, with his jutting jaw and deep wrinkles, bore not the slightest resemblance to the charismatic late actor.

"I hope we haven't interrupted an important confab," he said.

"The *officier* and I were just shooting the shit. Monsieur Nadeau, I'd like you to meet Chuck Stevens, the second-best pilot in Maine."

The Canadian was tall—six-three or -four—and broad shouldered. His hair was sandy, but his eyebrows had already turned white. His skin was exceptionally pale except where the capillaries flared along his cheeks and the bridge of his nose. His ears were an even darker shade of red. His eyes were the color of faded denim but without the softness.

He was dressed not in the green fatigues of a field agent but in the crisp navy uniform I associated with officers who staffed the fortified checkpoints at the border. Although he wore a dark blue ballistic vest over his shirt, his sidearm was conspicuously missing from his holster. He'd probably been forced to leave it behind when he'd crossed over from Québec. Whatever his rank in his home country, here in Jackman, he was no longer a law enforcement officer but a visiting foreign national.

"Good to meet you, Chuck." Nadeau displayed no Québécois accent whatsoever, but he was unusually hoarse, as if he'd punished his vocal cords singing at the top of his lungs the night before.

The two men shook hands.

Josie had called Charley "the second-best pilot in Maine," but I doubted anyone in the Northeast could surpass his skill in flying single-engine aircraft. My father-in-law's imperviousness to teasing was a virtue I hoped to absorb from him. Ten years on the job, I was still too easy to bait: a bull always on the lookout for red capes and rodeo clowns.

"Who's that with you, Chuck?" asked Josie, squinting at me as if I were a near-invisible wraith.

"Josie Jonson, I'm pleased to introduce my son-in-law, Warden Investigator Mike Bowditch."

She had a strong handshake and a mobile, expressive face with cheeks that glowed through skin permanently tanned from decades in the hot sun and raw wind. Her manner was light and unaffected. However apprehensive I might have been about what we'd find at Prentiss Pond, she seemed to be suffering from no such concerns.

"I was pulling your wiener, Mike. I recognize you from your wedding photos. Sorry I couldn't attend, but I had to fly some caribou hunters up to Labrador."

"You wouldn't happen to be Jack Bowditch's son?" interrupted Nadeau in a rasping voice.

On my deathbed, I wondered, *will the priest delivering the last rites ask me that same damned question?*

"I am."

I wasn't surprised that Nadeau recognized my name. My father had been the subject of an international manhunt before he died. At one point, the searchers had feared he'd managed to cross into Canada. Both the Services frontaliers and the Mounties—probably the Sûreté du Québec, too—had been put on high alert.

"I met your old man a few times along the corridor," Nadeau said. It strained his voice box to speak. "He liked to sneak back and forth across the slash for kicks. I can't say I was surprised to hear that Jack had finally become a murderer. He was always destined for it, in my opinion."

"And what brings you to Josie's door this morning, Officier Nadeau?" Charley interjected. No doubt he wanted to keep me from snapping at the man's casual rudeness.

Nadeau considered the old man's question, but his blue stare never left mine.

"I had a meeting with my counterpart at Jackman Station. Josie and I have met many times on my side of the border when she's assisted us with aerial searches—missing persons and the like. I thought the time had come to pay her a visit at home. With all this rain, Jo, I'd expected you to have the de Havilland in the water."

"The river's been too high to tie up the floatplane," she said. "I've got it in a hangar at the airstrip across the stream. I've been having too much fun flying the Raven."

"So your visit was a spur-of-the-moment thing?" I asked Nadeau, not quite believing this Canadian had decided to drop in on Josie at the exact moment a mysterious man was asking questions about her mysterious builder.

"I suppose you could call it that." Nadeau checked his watch: a gold Rolex that looked too expensive for a government employee. "I'm afraid I have a meeting back in Armstrong. If you'll excuse me . . ."

As soon as I heard his engine turn over, I addressed Josie. "Is it common for you to get unannounced visits from the Canada Border Services Agency?"

"What are you thinking, Mike?" Charley asked.

"I don't believe Officier Nadeau was here by accident. What did he want to talk with you about, Josie?"

"The Canada Border Services Agency knows Mark is building a cabin for me. It's not a big secret in Jackman or across the Boundary. Nadeau wants to build a place of his own and was curious how the job was going. He thinks he can lure Mark over to Lac-Mégantic after he's done working for me, but that's never going to happen. I tried to tell him the Redmonds are nomads."

"And that's all? Nothing else?"

Her bright expression went suddenly dark, like a light bulb had blown behind her eyes.

"He might've asked who else had been out to the pond to see the construction."

"Who else has been out there?"

"No one that I know of."

"And you didn't find the question unusual?"

She cocked her head. "In what way?"

"Why would Nadeau care about Redmond's visitors?"

"I have no idea. What does any of this have to do with your missing person?"

"Maybe nothing, but these are questions I'm hoping to ask your builder."

She advanced on me until I could smell the sickly sweet gum she was chewing.

"You wouldn't be misrepresenting to me why you want to talk with Mark, would you? Because if you are, I'm going to be more than disappointed—I'm going to be pissed."

I hadn't meant to offend her with my questions—I had mistakenly assumed she welcomed bluntness, given her otherwise gruff demeanor—but the protectiveness she felt toward Redmond told me I shouldn't look to Josie Jonson for objectivity in this matter.

"I need to make a decision whether the Warden Service will or won't initiate a search for this Hammond Pratt. Right now, we know very little about him other than he's been asking questions about the Redmonds. I'd like to ask Mark why that might be."

I considered telling her about the empty ammo boxes Brandon had discovered in Pratt's room, but her suspiciousness made me hesitate. I worried that if I pushed her, she might refuse to fly us. Stacey hadn't exaggerated how cantankerous the woman could be.

"I promise I'll make the conversation as quick and painless as possible."

She clutched her jaw for dramatic effect. "Every dentist in my life has used those same words. And every time I left their offices, I spent the next week sipping soup through a straw."

Charley again adopted the role of peacemaker. "How did you come to find Mr. Redmond in the first place, Jo?"

"Dumb luck—which is why I'm afraid of ruining it. I flew a client to New Brunswick last year, and he showed me a fishing cabin Mark was finishing on the Cascapédia River. It was the most beautiful camp I'd ever seen. The logs were so tight an ant couldn't have crept between them. Mark got to talking, and as it happened, he had never done a job in Maine and was intrigued by the project I had in mind. The fact that he could harvest the wood from the hills around the pond interested him."

"How long has he been working for you?" I asked.

"Started last fall, getting building materials on-site. He's been up all winter. Him and Cady. I thought they'd take mud season off, but he wanted to finish the interior: floors and cabinets, et cetera. The man is, like, the Michelangelo of cabin masters. I don't know how I got so lucky to find him, but I'm not letting him go. That's my worry here—that you're going to spook him, being law enforcement, and he's going to quit on the spot with my job half-done."

"I understand," I said.

"I hope you do!"

"Still," I said. "It must have been tough on his daughter, spending the entire winter in the woods with no one but her dad for company."

This statement seemed to affect Josie. Charley had told me she had been a mother herself. She blinked several times but somehow remained dry-eyed and responded with a smile that only bordered on the tremulous.

"It's true I felt sorry for the girl, living so far from kids her age, but Mark is about the best father I've met. I saw him one time with a Spanish edition of *Doña Flor*. He told me he was learning the language to teach Cady. She's not even a teen, but that kid knows more than most college grads."

Charley let out one of his signature guffaws. He enjoyed playing up his affect as an old Mainer. "I haven't even met Mr. Redmond, and he's already making me feel parentally inadequate!"

Josie cast a worried glance at the light angling in through the hangar door. "We should get moving while we can."

Again, I had to wonder if my unfounded suspicions were leading me astray.

The man Josie had described sounded quirky but no more suspicious than most North Woods recluses. And he seemed like a caring and attentive father, too. Was I inventing reasons to suspect him of being someone other than he seemed? Based on everything Josie had told us, Redmond was a decent man while Hammond Pratt was almost certainly bad news. What if we flew to Prentiss Pond and, instead of finding an idyllic cabin, discovered a blood-soaked killing ground?

6

The Robinson R44 Raven seats three: the pilot in front and two passengers in back.

After we'd taken off, Josie insisted on making a circle over her beloved Jackman even though we hadn't asked for a sightseeing trip and time was pressing. The meteorologists were forecasting that the next storm would come roaring out of Canada shortly before dusk. I glanced at my watch, an old Marinemaster. Noon had come and gone.

We were all wearing headsets, and Charley spoke through the mic connected to the intercom. "I see the lumberyard is a going concern."

"It's hanging on, yeah," Josie said. "Logs and maple syrup are our big exports. Teenagers, too. Most of the kids who grow up here can't wait to get the hell out of Dodge. My boys were the exceptions."

Charley had told me—*cautioned* might be the more apt term—that Josie wasn't just a widow. She'd lost her two adult sons, too. One was crushed by a tree he'd been felling with a chain saw. The other had run his pickup into a bull moose a few years later. The animal, amazingly, had ambled away into the resin-scented darkness where it had either died of its injuries or, if you were the superstitious sort, had transformed back into the evil spirit it had been.

Neither son had left behind children. Josie was facing her senior years knowing she was the last of her line.

"How a person can suffer so many intimate tragedies and still be capable of laughter is beyond my understanding," the old man had told me. "But some people are born survivors."

This was a subject on which he had some credibility; Charley Stevens had made it out of the Hanoi Hilton.

I liked to think I qualified as a survivor. But a pigheaded refusal to die wasn't what he'd meant. His definition was closer to Hemingway's famous quote about how the world breaks everyone, and afterward, some people are strong at the broken places. That description surely fit Josie and Charley. Whether it applied to me was for others to decide.

Charley made a throat-clearing noise into the mic. "It's been an age since I last flew a whirlybird, I must confess."

When Josie turned to address me, I smelled her gum again. Chuck Yeager had famously popped a stick of Beemans before every test flight. But Josie, it seemed, was a Dubble Bubble fan.

"As soon as your father-in-law called to say he wanted a chopper ride, I knew he'd ask to take the controls. How are you doing back there, Mike? Don't believe what people say about the R44s being death traps. This one hasn't crashed yet."

"That's reassuring."

I hadn't ridden in a small helicopter in years, and I had forgotten the nonstop jostling; I could almost feel the fillings shaking loose from my teeth. But so far, my breakfast—a convenience-store egg sandwich purchased en route—was staying down. Josie had also loaded the rear with supplies she'd been gathering for the Redmonds. I felt cramped for space amid the totes.

"I understand you spoke with the girl this morning," I said. "Did you ever get to talk with her dad about Hammond Pratt?"

"No. Why?"

"Cady couldn't possibly know all her father's acquaintances. And we learned something new about Pratt that's troubling. The man is armed."

Josie laughed into the mic. "So is everyone in Jackman."

"Not everyone in Jackman is waving around hundred-dollar bills for information about the Redmonds."

"If he's looking for trouble, I have no doubt that Mark Redmond can handle him," Josie said in an offhand manner. "But he's probably just some old friend from the military. Mark's never said so, but I'm pretty sure he served. He knows firearms and can fly a single-engine plane. Helicopters, too. I bet he has more time in choppers than you do, Chuck."

She kept dodging my questions. Before I could find one she couldn't duck, my father-in-law broke in. "How would you feel, Jo, about me taking the controls on the flight back from Prentiss?"

Whatever else we found at the building site, Charley Stevens wasn't going to be diverted from his goal of flying the Raven.

Josie gave me another amused, over-the-shoulder glance. "Gee, Chuck, I don't know. It's been years since you've flown an eggbeater, you say? Maybe I should give you a flight exam before trusting you with my honey."

"Two hundred forty kilometers per hour," he announced. "That's your max speed."

"Not fully loaded, it ain't. Although I've gotten close enough to two forty that I'll give you that one. What about max weight?"

"Twenty-four hundred pounds."

As the two seasoned pilots bantered, I kept my eyes focused on the waterlogged forest, partly to avoid vertigo but also because I was scanning the logging trails.

I didn't really expect to see Hammond Pratt, unseated from his ATV, stumbling along one of the muddy tracks, limping, drenched, and hypothermic. At the moment, I wasn't even convinced the mysterious stranger was lost. But being a career first responder had taught me that almost anything is possible.

We hadn't been in the air for five minutes before signs of human activity grew more scattered—just a few remote camps connected by muddy tracts—and then ceased altogether. Beneath us was a forest as impenetrable as any in Maine. While the lower reaches were unnaturally green, the highlands were mostly gray, except where the crags and summits were piebald with unmelted snowbanks. Here and there, swollen ponds shone amid budding maples and evergreens so dark they appeared black. And ravines flashed with iridescence where streams exploded into spray as they plunged downward toward the flooded rivers.

"Excuse me, Josie," I said. "Is it true Mark and Cady are from Alaska?"

Her voice sharpened. "Who told you that?"

"Brandon Barstow."

"It's true," she relented. "They're a hearty pair of sourdoughs. It's how they were able to spend a Maine winter in one of those outfitter tents with nothing but a box stove for heat."

Hammond Pratt claimed to be from Idaho—not exactly the next state over from Alaska. So what was the connection?

"And these days, they bounce around from place to place, building cabins in remote locales?"

"That about sums it up."

"Brandon told me that Mark never brings Cady to town. That can't be true, can it?"

"Of course not!"

"So you see her in Jackman occasionally."

"No, but . . . I'm sure he's brought her to town. He must have."

People who chose to live in the woods were often rebels and hermits, but I wondered how Josie would have responded if Redmond had been a city dweller who forbade his daughter from leaving their apartment. Never mind that there was no place less safe for a child to live than a construction site where trees were being felled and split to build a cabin.

"Based on what you told me, I take it he homeschools her?" I said.

Josie snapped her gum. "Are you a warden or a truant officer? Are you always this suspicious of people?"

I tried to make my tone light, but the subtlety didn't come through over the microphone. "I just know that anyone who chooses to live in the unorganized territories faces special scrutiny from both the Department of Education, as well as Child Welfare."

Josie seemed to feel the need to respond to a question I hadn't asked. "It's not like the Redmonds have been *stranded* all winter. Mark has a snowmobile and a four-wheeler that he takes to Jackman and Rockwood. He also has a Unimog, a big tractor-type thing he can drive out when the roads are passable to get supplies and building materials. And I fly in with groceries and goodies from time to time when the weather allows. In fact, I'm bringing Cady some of her favorite candy. Mackintosh's Creamy Toffee. I'd never even heard of the stuff before she asked for it."

"Do you happen to know where her mother is?" I asked.

"I can't see how that's either of our business."

"The young man is just curious," Charley said. "Curious to a fault, I often tell him."

"I apologize," I said after a long silence. "Charley's right that I sometimes let my curiosity get the better of me. It's just that I can't imagine spending the winter in such isolation."

"It's not like they're totally alone up there," Josie said. "The Stombaughs have their sugarhouse on the South Branch Road—past Wounded Deer and Dority Ponds. Have you ever heard of Moose River Maple Works, Chuck? There's a lot of people tapping trees these days. But Bob and Rose Stombaugh make syrup that'll curl your toes. Something about the casks they age the stuff in. Genuine Kentucky whiskey barrels."

"I can't say I've ever gotten sluiced on my breakfast," said Charley.

"The syrup only tastes of whiskey. I don't buy it myself. I'm not on the best of terms with Bob and Rose. It's one of those feuds we've got in Jackman where we don't even remember who started it or why." She snapped her head around. "And Cady visits them! She goes to see the Stombaughs sometimes. She's told me she does. She takes the snowmobile or ATV."

I considered this, reflecting on how it might mitigate my concerns about Redmond's closeting away of his daughter.

Josie sounded triumphant. "So you can't say Cady is being cut off from other people."

I wondered. But I would soon see for myself the effect living far from civilization had on the twelve-year-old. I had to consider the possibility that I really had fallen prey to the folly of prematurely indicting Mark Redmond as a father.

And yet . . .

The helicopter, dipping and rising on the wind, continued steadily to the northwest, into the wild.

7

Josie hugged the main road for the remainder of the flight. It was the two-lane highway that led to the twin border checkpoints: at Sandy Bay Township, Maine, on the American side, and Armstrong, Québec, on the Canadian side. The altimeter showed us at a mere 1,500 feet above the ground. Several times, she banked and brought us around for a closer look at something that had caught her eye; it wasn't always obvious to me what that something was.

A cleanup crew was taking advantage of the lull between storms to clear blowdowns from the Old Kelly Dam Road, where it joined Route 201. From our aerial vantage, we could tell the job would take days if not weeks. Dozens of trees had fallen across the gravel logging trail, rendering it impassable.

To make matters worse, where the road wasn't blocked, it had washed out. The restless Penobscot River had left its former bed below Little Canada Falls, cutting a new course through an alder swamp it had previously left unmolested. The flood had carried away tons of gravel and sand, exposing the rubbery black geotextile fabric under the road.

Beneath us now, a flecked and frothing stream came pouring out of a valley at the base of the mountains and passed under a bridge. The water had reached the level of the road and was spilling over the boards at such a ferocious rate it seemed likely the structure might give way at any second.

"I don't know if I'd chance crossing that bridge," Charley said, echoing my own thoughts.

Josie snapped her gum again. "That road is the only way out of my valley unless you take the ATV trail past Wounded Deer. I'll have to tell Mark about the bridge. He'll want to make sure it's structurally sound before he tries driving his Unimog over it."

"Even if he can cross the bridge," I said, "where can he go? The Old Kelly Dam Road is going to be out of commission for a while."

"There might be another way out," said Charley. "Isn't that tree line the South Branch Road? It connects to the Golden Road if I remember my geography."

Once again, he was only feigning ignorance; as chief warden pilot, he knew every nook and cranny of the North Maine Woods. He could have found the Golden Road at night, blindfolded, with his eyes shut.

"You remember right." Josie scanned the forest to the north. "See that thread of smoke yonder, Chuck? That's the Stombaughs' sugarhouse. They're done boiling sap, but there's always a shitload to clean up after the season. If they're at home, it means the way is clear to the Golden Road."

Above the stream, the road to the building site was blocked with deadfalls for about twenty yards. Then it showed signs of having recently been cleared. The muddy tract was tawny with sawdust and littered with boughs and branches. Redmond had been at work that morning with his skidder.

"Your man has been a busy bee," said Charley.

"He told me he doesn't like feeling trapped. But you're right about his work ethic, Chuck. Mark Redmond makes a dairy farmer look like a lazybones. He doesn't smoke, drink, or even swear. I thought he might be a Bible banger when we first met. But he hasn't tried to save my soul yet."

"Could be he saw what an irredeemable sinner you are, Jo."

"Could be!"

Flying low above the treetops, Josie followed the stream toward the valley above. The surrounding mountains weren't particularly tall, but they formed an unbroken wall of escarpments. Somewhere on the other side lay Canada, but these treacherous-looking cliffs seemed a more effective obstacle to crossing than any human-made fence.

"What's beyond those mountains?" I asked.

"Trees and more trees," Josie answered. "There's the usual cut along the border—a twenty-foot corridor through the woods—but if you're asking if there's a town on the other side, the answer is no."

"Sounds like your valley is a perfect cul-de-sac," I said.

"Mark says I should name my place Hole in the Wall, after Butch Cassidy's hideout."

No sooner had she uttered these words than a pond came into view. I knew at once that it must be Prentiss. In size, it looked to be something like fifty acres, with steep cliffs on its northwestern side where the mountains rose abruptly from the saucer-shaped valley. Loggers had cut the land hard, but not recently, and they had even left a stand of towering hemlock on the northern shore.

The cabin was set in a clearing above the pond, in the shadow of these conifers. A skidder trail ran from the construction site past the evergreen grove, before disappearing over the lip of the valley.

The earth around the foundation was currently a muddy expanse, but the messiness of the site didn't take away from the impeccable craftsmanship of the cabin-in-progress. The exterior walls were built entirely of split logs. The steel roof was steeply pitched so that snow would melt quickly and slide off. There were dormers over the second-story windows and a fieldstone chimney from which smoke was rising. A roofed porch wrapped around three sides, with broad steps descending toward the water. Someday, a path would cut across a green lawn to the dock where Josie would moor her de Havilland floatplane. But for the moment, there was only puddled mud in every direction.

"My God, Jo!" said Charley. "That may be the most beautiful cabin I've ever seen. The pictures you posted didn't do it justice."

"And you haven't seen the ones I didn't post."

"I never saw the photos," I said. "Did you take them all down?"

"When I told Mark people were complimenting his work, he said I shouldn't advertise my camp to every potential burglar with a Facebook account. Jackman doesn't have more petty criminals than other small towns, but it sure as shit doesn't have less of them, either."

"The cabin looks plenty sturdy," Charley said. "All this bad weather we've had hasn't left a mark."

"Wait till you see the craftsmanship up close, Chuck. The joinery is so precise you won't believe it. I don't know what I did to deserve that man appearing in my life."

The rectangular outfitter's tent in which the Redmonds had endured the winter sat at the edge of the clearing. No smoke was rising from its stovepipe. I spotted the hulking yellow skidder behind it, as well as two shapes beneath weather-resistant tarps: undoubtedly the snowmobile and all-terrain vehicle Josie had mentioned. There was no sign of the monster Unimog, though.

I wondered where the Redmonds might have gone. By now, they would have heard the engine roar of the chopper. Was there another way out that Josie had failed to mention? In my experience, every bolt-hole has at least one secret exit.

Then a solitary figure appeared at the tent entrance.

Cady Redmond stepped through the door flaps and stood barefoot in what must have been toe-numbing mud.

Josie had described the girl in glowing terms: almost as a surrogate granddaughter. But the small, bespectacled face staring up at us didn't display happiness or expectation. It looked as tight as a fist.

8

The cabin rose from a sodden, multicolored field. There were irregular mounds of wood shavings like islands amid the puddles. Flakes of bark, as red as scabs, lay in rows where the builder had skinned his cedar logs.

Josie set us down between the pond and the small rise on which Mark Redmond was constructing his masterpiece. The rotors whipped gobs of mud hundreds of feet in all directions. The surface of the little lake rippled away from the shore in ever-expanding half circles to trouble the calm blue waters beyond.

"Tell me that wasn't a textbook landing, Chuck."

"Smooth as a smelt, Jo."

The girl must have learned to keep her distance from the chopper when its rotors were flinging projectiles. But no sooner did Josie kill the engine than Cady appeared on the rise.

She was wearing what looked like one of her dad's waffle T-shirts that hung to her knees and revealed two skinny legs clad in denim. But it was her bare feet that continued to amaze me. The thermometer on Josie's tablet computer—the device that augmented her dashboard displays—showed the temperature to be a balmy forty-three degrees.

The glance at the tablet made me think to check my cell phone, and as I'd expected, there was no service. We were close enough to Canada that I'd hoped we might get a signal from across the border, but the cliffs made the valley a dead zone.

As soon as Josie popped her door, Cady Redmond rushed toward us through the muck.

"Josie, Josie! Wait till you see what I found. A moose antler right outside the tent. He must have shed it passing through camp. I never found an antler on my own before."

"That's awesome, Cady!"

Josie had said the girl was twelve, but she seemed younger. Cady Redmond was small for her age, four-and-a-half feet on tiptoes. She was wearing dark-rimmed glasses made for an adult face. Even from a distance, I could tell the lenses were both crooked and greasy. I wondered how she could possibly see through them.

She was a cute kid, though, with a triangular face, a snub nose, and a little cleft in her chin. She wore her brown hair in neat french braids. You could tell she'd worked hard to get her hair right.

"The antler is a gift for you. I want you to have it. You're always bringing me stuff." The joy in her voice made me wonder if I'd mistaken the tight expression I thought I'd glimpsed. "Did you bring any . . . ?"

"Yes, I brought you your candy. And pork rinds for your dad. God save his arteries. And flour and butter and some other staples to keep you well fed in your labors."

I swung down from the chopper. The sweetness of newly sawed lumber hung on the freshening breeze.

The air stung my nose and cheeks. I was wearing my own Gore-Tex jacket and KUIU hunting pants, as well as the all-weather boots L.L.Bean makes for wardens. Even through the Vibram soles, I imagined I could feel the coldness of the mud in which Cady was so placidly standing.

"Did you bring the book I asked for, too?" Cady said.

"Personally, I think you're a little young for *Animal Farm*, but if your dad thinks you're ready for George Orwell—"

"He already told me the pigs are people."

I understood that Cady was thrilled to see her friend, but her refusal to acknowledge Charley and me went beyond shyness. Even for a preteen, she seemed skittish, awkward, and a little alien. I found her speech hard to understand. Some sentences she spit out in rapid-fire bursts. Other times she mumbled words through clenched lips.

Josie finally acknowledged us.

"Where are my manners? Cady Redmond, I want you to meet my friend, Chuck Stevens. He's a bush pilot, too, almost as good as your great-auntie Jo. He used to be the chief pilot for the Maine Warden Service. One of his jobs was to find little kids who got lost in the woods. Wasn't it you who found Hansel and Gretel, Chuck?"

"Hansel and Gretel weren't real," Cady said, sounding as insulted as only a child can when facing a condescending adult.

Charley bent over and extended a gnarled hand for her to shake. "It's a pleasure to meet you, Miss Redmond."

The girl glanced at Josie, then giggled, "Nobody calls me that." When Cady smiled again, this time wider, she revealed that she was missing two teeth: a lateral incisor and its formerly adjacent cuspid.

"Cady Redmond, what happened to your teeth?"

The girl clamped a hand over her mouth and spoke through her fingers. "I was helping my papa move a log and tripped."

"And he didn't take you to a dentist?" I asked, feeling my anxiety grow again at the thought of Redmond's seeming negligence.

"He said there was nothing to be done about it."

"But when you have an accident, you need to see a dentist."

Josie snapped her gum and nodded in my direction. "And that's Mike. He doesn't have kids of his own."

The girl regarded me warily. She tugged at her sleeves until the hems hung over her fingers. It wasn't the introduction I'd been hoping for.

"I told you that you didn't need to come, Josie," Cady said after a long pause. "Papa says he doesn't know that Pratt man. Why did you fly all the way out here with . . . ?"

I didn't know if she'd forgotten our names already or was having trouble putting a label on the two uninvited strangers.

"Mike wanted to talk with your dad in person."

"But why?"

"That's what I have been asking," Josie breathed.

The girl pressed her lips tight—she was self-conscious about her mouth now—and looked at her muddy white feet.

I tried reassuring the fearful, awkward child. "Your dad's not in any trouble, Cady."

"So why are you carrying that gun?"

She pointed a thin finger at the holstered P226 on my belt. It was my service weapon: a heavy semiautomatic pistol that fired .357 SIG cartridges out of fifteen-round magazines. I'd preferred my old P239, smaller and easier to conceal, before the manufacturer had discontinued the model.

"Game wardens are police officers," I explained. "We're required to carry firearms when we're on duty. Here's my badge. And here are my . . ."

I reached behind me to the holster at the small of the back and removed the handcuffs.

The reaction wasn't what I'd expected. Kids usually found the steel bracelets cool. But the sight of them filled Cady's eyes with terror. I didn't even finish my sentence before hurriedly tucking the cuffs out of sight again.

"Mike's not here to arrest anyone, Miss Redmond," said Charley in his most grandfatherly voice. "Where is your dad, by the way? Josie's been telling us about this big monster truck of his. What did you call it, Jo?"

"A Unimog."

My father-in-law pulled a face. "A Unifrog?"

"A Unimog!" The girl half smiled at him; almost but didn't quite giggle. "It stands for something in German. I only speak French, and I'm learning to read Spanish." Now she let the giggle out. "And English, of course!"

"Where is your dad, Cady?" I asked, repeating Charley's earlier question.

She pursed her lips before she answered.

"He took the 'Mog over to Dubois Pond. He was going to bush-whack up the hill. Sometimes he can get a signal up top. It comes out of Québec, he says. He didn't expect you to fly up here, Josie."

She pronounced the name of the province in the French fashion, like a native speaker. *Kay-beck*.

Josie's description of Mark Redmond hadn't led me to think he owned a cell phone. My image of him was of a mountain man—a bearded and brawny giant with a sun- and windburned face—who'd turned his back on the modern world. But all the machines in the dooryard proclaimed that, whatever else he might be, Redmond was no Luddite.

Who did he need to call, I wondered, *and why this morning?*

But no sooner had I asked myself the question than Officer Na-deau's gin-blossomed face appeared in my imagination.

"Well, I'm here in any case." Josie brushed my shoulder as she returned to the chopper. "We're going to grab the supplies, Cady, and then I want to see that moose antler. I can't take it as a gift, because it's the first shed you found on your own."

"But I really want you to have it, Josie!"

"You'll find another."

"I really want you to have it," Cady insisted with unexpected gravity.

"In that case, I can't say no. I will always treasure it as a reminder of you. Now let's get the Raven unloaded. Hopefully, we won't have to go hunting for your dad."

"He didn't expect you to fly up here," the girl said again, this time under her breath.

9

As we drew near the cabin, the totes heavy on our shoulders, it became increasingly apparent that every claim Josie had made about her builder's genius was true.

Mark Redmond was more than a craftsman; he was an artist who worked in cedar, pine, and fieldstone. From the perfectly smoothed and mitered logs to the meticulous masonry of the foundation and chimney, every detail grew more impressive the closer you studied it. In this way, the cabin was the opposite of most modern buildings, which reveal their flaws and compromises only on closer examination.

Cady left muddy prints on the stairs as she pushed past a curtain of opaque plastic that covered what would become the front door. We followed, parting the heavy sheet to enter the surprisingly warm chamber beyond. The resinous aroma of all those new logs was almost intoxicating.

"You didn't tell me the stove had arrived!" Josie said from beyond the next curtain.

"Papa put it in last week—before the weather got bad."

The kitchen, from which the considerable heat was emanating, was dominated by an antique Glenwood cooking stove. It was a cast-iron behemoth with six burners on the top and an oven next to the firebox. The woodstove easily weighed half a ton.

"How did your dad manage to put this in on his own?" I couldn't conceive of an installation that didn't require multiple strong men.

Charley pointed toward the ceiling.

"I see he used a block and tackle." And indeed, the rough timbers showed signs of smoothing where the ropes had worn grooves in the pine. "The pharaohs of Egypt could've used your dad when they were building their pyramids."

Still, even with ropes and pulleys, I couldn't conceive of one man getting the massive stove off a truck bed and into the kitchen, not unless he was Hercules. My understanding was that Mark Redmond was challenging himself to build the cabin on his own. Josie had never mentioned him having helpers, beyond his daughter.

"Would you like me to make coffee?" Cady asked, revealing her crooked smile. "I'm really good at it. Papa said I could be a barrister."

"You mean *barista*," said Josie. "But you'd make a good barrister, too, I'm sure."

I moved toward the dusty curtain that hung before the door. "Can we have a look around the house?"

"I'd prefer to wait for Mark to get back," said Josie none too warmly. "This is his creation, and he should be the one to show it off."

As the girl scooped the coffee, Josie asked about her studies. Cady said that her papa was teaching her algebra "because I need to know how to solve problems" and "he says math is a tool just like a hammer—only it's a mental tool."

"And what else is he teaching you, Miss Redmond?" asked Charley, warming his big hands at the stove.

"First aid."

"Do you mean bandages and splints?" I asked.

"And stitches."

"Stitches!" Charley and I exclaimed at the same time.

"I am supposed to call them *sutures*. That's the medical term. I've been practicing on beavers Papa trapped. They're already dead, so I can't hurt them. Papa has me shave the fur down, and then I have to suture the cuts in the skin with monofilament because you're not going to have thread in the wilderness, he says."

The North Woods was home to its share of hermits and

screwballs—preppers, too, who believed the apocalypse was only five minutes off. And while I could justify Redmond teaching his girl emergency medicine, given how far they were from a hospital, the means he'd chosen disturbed me. I was the son of a trapper and was an occasional trapper myself, but operating on dead rodents struck me as grotesque, if not ghoulish, for a twelve-year-old.

"Your father sounds like a true pedagogue," said Charley.

Suddenly, blood surged into her triangular face. Her mouth twisted again.

"What did you call him?"

She had mistaken the word for a similar-sounding noun.

I tried to be helpful. "A pedagogue is a teacher."

But she had already decided that I was not her friend. "No, it's not. It's a—it's a—"

"Why don't you go fetch your dictionary?" Josie offered. "You told me your father was teaching you a new word every day. You'll see *pedagogue* doesn't mean what you think it does."

"When in doubt, find a reference you can trust," said Charley.

Cady appeared aggrieved and unconvinced, but she pushed aside the curtain to return to her tent. "I'll be right back. Don't let the coffee boil over or you'll have to clean it up!"

In her absence, Josie and Charley and I regarded each other with expressions ranging from bewildered to sheepish.

For all Cady's esoteric knowledge and surface politeness, I was beginning to pick up on her almost utter lack of social skills. She'd failed to detect cues other children would easily have read. The possibility of her having some form of autism occurred to me, but likely, the rugged conditions under which she was growing up were to blame.

The girl returned with a tattered *Merriam-Webster's* that looked like it had been salvaged from a box in a church basement. She'd clearly already read the definition of *pedagogue*, but learning her mistake hadn't softened her mood. Every muscle in her small body seemed tense.

"Would you like maple syrup pie with your coffee?" she demanded of me and me alone.

"That would be delightful, dear," Josie answered on my behalf.

During my police training, I'd been taught not to accept food or drink from anyone I met on a call. Primarily this was for hygienic reasons. You never know when a poorly washed glass might be carrying some nasty germs, or a fork might have drug residue between its tines. But Josie had eaten and drunk many times at this table; she trusted Cady Redmond, and so I was inclined to as well.

The girl vanished again through the plastic curtain and returned with a pie tin from which two slices had already been removed. The gooey pieces dripped as she lifted them onto aluminum plates. The pie had a silky, almost custard-like texture and a caramel flavor that was less sweet than the name of the dessert promised. And she hadn't been lying about the deliciousness of her coffee.

"This is amazing, Cady," I said, trying to win her trust, knowing I never would. "I haven't had this kind of pie before. I've never even heard of it."

"The Québécois call this *tarte au sirop d'érable*," said Charley between bites. "When I was a lad, washing plates and pans in the lumber camp up near Daaquam, the cookee used to make a version of this pie. But it wasn't as good as yours, Miss Redmond."

"Where'd you learn the recipe, dear?" Josie asked.

"I don't remember."

This seemed odd to me. The kid had a memory like a steel bear trap. Spotting evasions was what I did for a living, and I found myself, perhaps inappropriately, unable to let this one pass.

"Did someone teach you?" I asked.

"I said I don't remember."

The missing mother?

My mind was prone to these sorts of unforced conjectures. I had learned not to trust them. But my gut told me I had hit upon the truth this time.

Charley put down his coffee mug. "How long should we wait for Mr. Redmond before you start the house tour, Jo?"

"I would have expected him by now. He'd have heard the Raven's engine if he didn't catch sight of us coming in. But we can't wait all morning. If the winds kick up, we could be stranded here for days." Josie rose from the table and fiddled with the zipper of her jacket, trying to get the teeth lined up, without success. "I'm going to go check on the current conditions, as the TV weatherman likes to say."

"Do you mind if I join you?" I asked.

"Be my guest."

It hardly sounded like a welcome, but the time had come for me to have a frank talk with Josie Jonson.

While we'd been inside, the yard had been invaded by robins. The flock numbered into the hundreds. The birds were of different shades and sizes; some had breasts as red as rubies; others were worn and faded, almost rusty beneath and pale gray across the back. They didn't take off en masse as we clattered onto the porch. The bigger, bolder ones held their ground, while the others sounded their high-pitched alarms. But eventually, the last birds took to the air, whinnying and chortling to signal their displeasure.

"They must have been finding a smorgasbord of worms in all this mud," I said.

Josie grunted as she studied the darkening skies above the western escarpments. Scree trailed down a few of the ravines like the aftermath of fatal landslides. The breeze had picked up and ruffled her short hair. I could feel the approaching rain in the heaviness of the air.

Her refusal to engage made me prattle on to fill the silence. "Even having been a warden for a decade, it still surprises me to see robins—or phoebes—in the North Woods. I can't help but think of them as suburban species."

"Is that why you followed me?" she asked. "To discuss orni-thology?"

"No. I want to ask you about the Redmonds. I know you've spent a lot of time with them over the past nine months. But how much do you really know about these people—as opposed to what they've told you about themselves?"

She reached into her pocket for a fresh piece of Dubble Bubble. She took a while unwrapping the gum before popping it into her mouth. She worked her jaw while she considered what she should and shouldn't tell me.

"I know that Mark's a good father."

His refusal to bring his daughter to the dentist loomed in my thoughts. "How?"

"Because I've seen him with Cady. You must have noticed she's an unusual child. Challenging, even. But the man is devoted to her. She is his whole world."

"I'm more interested in—"

"You don't think that's enough? Being a good parent? Well, I failed that test not once but twice. So, I'm telling you it's pretty fucking important."

The low-pressure system was keeping the smoke from the wood-stove from rising. The gray cloud spread from the chimney across the muddy clearing, making it appear as ominous as a Civil War battlefield. And there was a foretaste of rain.

"Charley told me about your sons. I'm sorry."

"Me, too. My boys were always headstrong like their mom. But because I turned out OK, I never worried about them. What's that term for people who are overprotective of their kids?"

"Helicopter parents."

"Seriously? That's ironic, considering what I do for a living. Well, it's the opposite of what I was. I let my boys run wild because I thought it was naive to try to protect them from life's hard knocks. I'm more sympathetic to those helicopter parents now that my sons are gone. I should've been more afraid of losing them."

"I can't even imagine," I said honestly, remembering what was waiting for me that evening when I got home: Stacey's pregnancy test.

"No, you can't."

Some of the boldest robins had returned to the far side of the clearing and were pulling comically long earthworms from the muck.

"He never takes Cady to town," I said. "He made her help him with construction and then wouldn't even bring her to a dentist when she had an accident that made her lose two teeth."

"How he parents his daughter is none of our business."

Josie Jonson was not the first person who'd found my persistence exasperating,

"Let me put it differently. If I told you that an armed man was in the area, asking questions about you, wouldn't you be concerned? Or at least curious? Cady claims she told her father about Pratt, and yet Mark left her here alone, unprotected. Would you have done that with a child?"

Josie spit her pink wad of gum onto the torn ground and looked at it in silence. She seemed to be considering whether to pick it up.

"When I say there's something strange about Redmond," I continued, "that's what I mean."

Just then, the robins took wing again.

Birds are easily spooked. And they are far more alert and sensitive to potential threats than humans.

"There's a truck coming," I said.

Josie cupped a hand around one ear. "I don't hear anything."

We waited and listened, and then we waited half a minute longer.

Eventually, she heard it, too—the low rumble of a diesel engine laboring off in the woods.

10

The top-heavy machine that rumbled down the hill was like nothing I had seen before. The Unimog made me think of those Greek monsters that are half lion and half eagle, except this was a hybridization of a Humvee and the world's largest pickup truck.

Painted slate gray but heavily scratched from driving through dense foliage, it rode high on off-road tires that were easily three feet in diameter. The ground clearance was such that Redmond could have driven the vehicle over a fire hydrant without grazing the undercarriage. I estimated the Unimog as being close to nine feet high but only twelve feet long. The unbalanced, foreshortened dimensions only added to the oddness of the design.

Also surprising was the Mercedes-Benz logo on its grille. I knew the German carmaker manufactured more than luxury passenger vehicles. But even by commercial truck standards, this was a bizarre-looking beast.

"Unimogs aren't legal in the U.S.!" Josie shouted. "Or they're not *illegal* exactly. You can't buy one here because most don't meet federal safety standards or something."

Redmond killed the engine. The noise had been like a deep bass line at a heavy metal concert; it left my ears pounding and the nerves in my extremities tingling.

"Did he bring it across from Canada?"

"Well, it's here, isn't it?"

The driver's door opened, and Redmond jumped down, using the wide front fender as a step. He landed with a splash in a puddle covered with a light scum of sawdust.

He wasn't the mountain man I had expected. Instead, he was short in stature, as compact and muscular as a college wrestler who'd kept in fighting trim well into middle age. His recently cut hair and clean-shaven jaw were far from my idea of a North Woods recluse, too. He looked less like Grizzly Adams and more like some dude you might bump into pushing a cart down the lawn-care aisle of a Home Depot.

Only his hands and arms gave away his vocation as a master woodcutter. Thick wrists are often the best predictors of a person's raw strength, and Redmond's were as wide around as baseball bats. He also had the calloused palms and dirty nails of a man who hefted a lot of logs.

"This is a surprise, Josie," he said with a smooth white smile. "Didn't Cady tell you we were doing fine?"

"She did, Mark—and I apologize for intruding—but my guests wanted to check on you themselves."

"No need to apologize. But you said 'guests,' and I see only one."

He spoke like an educated person, or at least someone who'd grown up in a household that valued elocution. He also had a faint accent that I couldn't place. The rumor was that the Redmonds hailed from Alaska. Maybe that explained it. I had no personal experience with Alaskans or their manner of speaking.

He extended a hand to me. His expression had become an easygoing squint. His facial bones were even more pronounced than Cady's, the angles sharper, the chin pointed.

"I'm Mark Redmond."

"Mike Bowditch. Pleased to meet you."

His skin felt like sandpaper, his grip like a vise.

"Mike's an investigator with the Maine Warden Service," Josie said, speaking a little too quickly. "He's here with retired chief warden pilot Chuck Stevens."

"That would be me," said a gruff voice over my shoulder.

"That would be *I*," added Cady, who'd followed Charley outside without my hearing.

"You shouldn't correct people's grammar, chickpea," said Mark Redmond in his unplaceable accent. "It can come across as rude, unless you know them very well."

Charley advanced to shake Redmond's rough hand himself. "I hope you'll forgive us, Mr. Redmond, for dropping in unannounced. Mike and I aren't looking to take more of your time than necessary, and as Jo reminds us, we need to get airborne before that rain arrives."

I was certain that everyone expected me to announce my intentions. But I preferred to begin my interviews with small talk. I let my gaze drift to the Unimog behind Redmond.

"I've got to say—that's quite an impressive vehicle you're driving. It looks like it could beat a Humvee, or a tank, for traversing rugged country. I've never seen anything like it."

"That's no surprise. The United States government doesn't make it easy to import one. The man who sold it to me purchased it in Canada, and he said Customs made him run a gauntlet before he could bring it across the border. But you didn't come here to see my truck."

"No, *he* didn't," sighed Josie.

"I'm investigating a case, and I am hoping you might have information that will help me understand what I might be dealing with."

Again, he offered a glossy smile. His perfectly straight teeth were not those of a person who'd grown up in poverty. "What kind of information?"

"I wonder if you might show us around the cabin first. What you've done here is amazing. It's beyond belief, really."

"All right," said Redmond, who seemed increasingly hard-pressed to maintain his air of nonchalance. "All I ask is that you don't take pictures. Not of the construction, nor of my daughter. I suppose that strikes you as an unusual request. But I have a philosophical objection to my life being tracked by algorithms belonging to corporations and governments."

"It's not a problem," I said. "We won't take any pictures."

"In that case, you won't mind my taking a peek at your phones before we go inside."

"Our phones?"

"Just the photos. I need to confirm that you haven't already taken some. Please don't take this request personally."

I kept my thoughts to myself as I pulled up my photo app and handed my phone to him.

I doubted he knew that wardens often carry two phones: one issued by the department for official business, and a personal cell for texts, emails, and family photographs. I had left my other phone in an inner pocket in my rucksack in the helicopter. Not that I'd taken any pictures with it.

"Yours, too, Jo."

Now it was her turn to be aggrieved. "Seriously, Mark? I know I shouldn't have posted those pictures—but fine. Here you go."

When Charley presented Redmond with an ancient flip phone that lacked the capacity to do anything more than make a call, the builder smiled.

"I think you're good to go, Warden Stevens."

"My friends call me Charley."

"I like to set a good example for my daughter about respecting her elders. If we end up becoming friends, we can use first names with each other."

Josie ran a hand through the hair at the back of her scalp as if assessing whether she needed to get out the scissors later. "Can we hurry this up, please? Can we get to Mike's questions? I mean, Jesus Christ."

Redmond spun on her, but his tone remained calm. "You know how I feel about profanity, Josie."

"Seriously?" she said, releasing the word on an exhaled breath.

"I've told you before not to use profanity in front of Cady or myself."

"Is the name of the son of God profane?" I asked, curious how he'd respond to the question.

"It is in the context she used it. I also insist upon a certain amount of respect from the people I meet. It shouldn't be a hardship not to use foul language in the presence of a child. Or do you disagree?"

"You have a lot of terms you ask people to accept, Mr. Redmond," I said.

His gray eyes revealed, for the first time, a hint of amusement bordering on arrogance. "That's because I've put myself in a position in life to insist upon them. If you can't adhere to my simple requests, then we have nothing to say to each other."

"I was merely making an observation. I wouldn't mind a tour of the cabin if the offer remains open."

Redmond was trying his best to read me. His eyes probed mine. But I was giving him less to work with than he was giving me.

"In that case, we can proceed to the tour," he said. "And then you can ask your questions. Chickpea, would you mind brewing a pot of coffee for your father and our guests while I show them around the place? Use the dark roast we've been saving."

Redmond displayed little enthusiasm in showing off his work or in explaining his methods. He provided the bare minimum of commentary as he hurried us through the tour. He seemed to recognize this was all a prologue to the real conversation; a performance he had to endure before we moved to the business at hand.

Yes, he and Cady had harvested the fieldstones themselves from the cleared lot; his daughter had an uncanny ability to see in three dimensions and select the stones that would make for the best foundation and those that would make the best chimney.

"She's an unusual girl." I chose the adjective for its vagueness.

"If you mean she is altogether exceptional, then yes, that is correct."

"It must be a challenge parenting her on your own."

It was a graceless question, aimed at eliciting information about the missing mother, and it received the nonresponse it deserved.

Redmond regarded me silently with eyes as hard and flat as worn nickels.

Charley asked him about the process of finding and laying the sill logs: the skinned lengths of cedar that formed the frame atop the foundation. Redmond's only response was that it was just a matter of scouting the best cedars with the fewest knots, and once you'd found them, skidding them out of the woods.

"Did you ever work as a timber cruiser in Alaska?" I asked, trying to keep my tone casual.

Again, he showed me the nickels; again, he offered no reply.

When Josie nervously remarked that Redmond had fitted the log walls so perfectly that he hadn't required mortar or even oakum, he corrected her, saying that he'd used elastomeric material to fill the gaps in a few spots.

"I'm not a purist," he said. "I take as much from the old ways as I can, but ultimately, I want the best result. It's not compromising to use modern materials. It's being smart and adaptable."

"The outcome is all that matters," I said.

"Sometimes, yes."

Josie was growing increasingly antsy, casting glances at the clouds massing above the walled hills.

"Before we go inside," I said, "I have a question for Mr. Redmond. It's a simple yes or no."

"Go ahead."

"Did it surprise you to hear that a man from Idaho had come to Maine looking for you?"

He smiled again, but this time genuinely, with his whole face, not just the bottom half. "No."

Redmond had successfully called my bluff.

I needed to gather myself for the rematch. Time was running out.

II

Cady had arranged four seats around the plywood table. Two were folding chairs she'd brought in from their tent. The others were an overturned barrel—a cast-off cask from Moose River Maple Works—and a short stepladder, drip-stained with varnish. The improvised setup attested to Josie's claim that the Redmonds were not in the habit of entertaining visitors.

The girl had given her father one of the chairs, marking his place at the head of the table with a plate of maple syrup pie, a cup of coffee, and a glass of spring water. Charley pulled out the other folding chair for Josie, who rolled her eyes at the chivalric gesture. He took the stepladder for a perch, leaving me the barrel. I could smell the residual sweetness of the syrup coming through the staves.

While we'd been outdoors, Cady had refilled our mismatched mugs. She'd remembered how each of us had taken our coffee. This brew wasn't as good as her first; she seemed to have scorched it on the too-hot stovetop. But I was glad to cup my cold hands around the warm mug.

I glanced at the girl with the missing teeth, noticing a slight swelling on her lip where she'd injured it. I wondered again why her father had made the choice not to bring her in for an examination. Maybe he couldn't justify installing expensive implants while she was young and growing. But not having a dentist look at her mouth struck me as a parental misdemeanor at best.

"Would you mind if I eat while we do this?" he said, tucking his napkin into his shirtfront like a cowboy in an old western.

"Not at all."

The room had grown even warmer from the heat of the wood-stove. Cady must have opened the firebox and tossed in a few more chunks of maple, because there was smoke drifting above us in the rafters, unable to escape.

I set down my mug. "I'm hoping you can solve a mystery for me, Mr. Redmond."

"About this man from Idaho? I don't see how. But fire away."

"It would help if I knew a little bit more about you first. Where are you from originally?"

Redmond let his fork hover above his plate before using it to scoop another bite of pie. "Meadow Lakes, Alaska. Born and raised."

"Meadow Lakes is east of Wasilla, isn't it?" said Charley, removing his rain jacket and tossing it onto a pile of logs.

"West of Wasilla." He grinned, knowing that my father-in-law had tried to trip him up.

"What did you do in Meadow Lakes?" I asked.

"Built cabins. I also worked as a bush pilot and outfitter at a hunting lodge. Moose, caribou. Bears and wolves were my specialty."

This last remark didn't endear him to me, I had to admit. In Alaska, wolves were legally shot from helicopters (which explained Josie's comment about his abilities as a pilot). In my imagination, I pictured a black wolf racing across a tundra while a larger shadow pursued him.

"What brought you east?"

"My wife died, if you must know."

"I'm sorry to hear that."

"And before you ask how—because I know you want to—I'll save you the time. She suffered an injury and developed an addiction to opioids and accidentally overdosed on fentanyl."

He didn't want another expression of polite sympathy, I could tell.

"When was this?"

He brought the coffee mug to his lips. Then he put it down.

"Two years and three months ago. I thought a change of scene would do Cady some good. We spent time outside Whitehorse. That's in the Yukon. Then I was commissioned to build a high-end cabin in Banff, Alberta. My daughter and I don't have a lot of material needs, and that job kept us going until we reached Ontario. A couple who knew my Alberta client reached out to have me build something for them on Lake Nipissing. From there, we moved on to New Brunswick. That is where I met Josie, as I assume you know."

"No stops in Idaho?"

"No," he said with one of his sly grins. "In fact, this is our first time in the States since we left Alaska."

I rubbed the back of my hand across my damp forehead. "How did you handle the issue of your visas? Canada doesn't permit Americans to live and work in their country indefinitely."

Again with the Cheshire cat smile. "I suspect you know the answer already—I made sure not to draw the attention of the Canadian government. I didn't file tax returns there. Nor have I sent a dime to the IRS since I left Alaska. Are you planning on reporting me for tax evasion?"

"No."

"How about we get down to brass tacks then?" he said.

"Do you know a man named Hammond Pratt?"

A hint of a grin pulled at the edges of his mouth. "It's an unusual name. I would remember it. This is the man from Idaho, I presume."

"Two nights ago, a man calling himself by that name and saying he was from Idaho rented an all-terrain vehicle from the owner of Seboomook Farm in Rockwood, and he hasn't been seen since."

"Why aren't you searching for him, then? The fool might have injured himself on that four-wheeler and need rescuing."

Josie let out a giggle. Her reaction puzzled me. Her own son had died in an ATV crash. She motioned to Cady for more coffee.

"Who says I'm not searching for him?" I was finding it harder to concentrate in the infernal heat of the cabin. "You see, before he left Seboomook Farm, he was asking the staff if they knew of a father and daughter hiding in the woods between Moosehead Lake and the Canadian border. You said it didn't surprise you that a man from Idaho was searching for you."

"My late wife's parents believe they have rights concerning Cady. But they don't. It wouldn't surprise me at all if they hired someone to find us."

"So you suspect he's a private investigator?"

"I don't know what else he would be. And before you ask, I have full custody of Cady, which means I am under no obligation to report to anyone or seek their approval on how I choose to raise her."

"That's not true in Maine," I corrected him. "The state requires a parent to file a Notice of Intent to Provide Home Instruction if you're going to homeschool your child."

The room was much hotter than before—sweltering, in fact. I didn't want to remove my jacket, didn't want to appear casual now that the interview had begun, but I could feel my underarms growing wet in this saunalike space.

"Thank you for the heads-up," Redmond said ironically. "I'll file the papers as soon as the roads are passable. It's been hard work clearing them, and I haven't reached the bridge."

Beside me, Charley let out a series of yawns that some part of my brain must have registered as strange, given how intent I knew he must have been on the interview. He was an old man, yes, and he had arisen before dawn, but he was also a combat veteran and career law enforcement officer. When other people tended to feel exhaustion, his energies gathered for the fight ahead. It was the survival instinct in him; his brain only permitted his body to experience fatigue after the threat had passed.

Cady, standing ready with the coffeepot, saw that Charley's mug was empty and refilled it before he could ask. He stared with a questioning expression at the steaming brew but did not sip.

"You said you never reentered the United States after you left Alaska?" I asked Redmond.

He had already finished his pie and his glass of water. He carefully folded his napkin and placed it beside the cleaned plate. He closed his hand around the handle of his coffee mug but didn't raise it to his mouth.

"We had no reason to return to the U.S. Cady and I were hardly *hiding*, by the way."

The comment I'd made earlier must have been working its way like a splinter deeper beneath his skin.

"No?"

"Call me a misanthrope if you want, but I prefer to live my life away from people."

"And why is that?"

"Because I find human beings shallow, self-centered, and pathologically dishonest. I believe this world will be better off after our species inevitably goes extinct."

Now it was my turn to laugh, a little too giddily. "That sounds to me like the definition of a misanthrope, Mr. Redmond."

"That's your opinion. And I'm sure you're sitting there, judging me, thinking, *This guy is the next Unabomber.* But I can raise my hand and swear to God that I have never deliberately harmed another human being in my thirty-eight years on this planet. Can you say as much?"

Not even remotely.

But despite my heavy-headedness, I caught the word he'd slipped into his declaration of innocence.

"Have you ever harmed another human being *accidentally*?" I said.

His mouth tightened, and he did not speak.

It occurred to me that I hadn't seen him take a drink of coffee. Then again, the heat of the room was growing unbearable. I found myself craving a glass of cold water but didn't want to interrupt the interview and give him time to think.

I was beginning to feel feverish from the trapped, hot air.

Jo, yawning now, leaned an elbow against the plywood table, nearly upsetting it.

Redmond didn't seem to notice or care that the dishes clattered. He clutched his coffee mug.

I stared into his metallic eyes.

It was as if he and I were alone in the room.

"I wonder what crime you think I committed," he said, no longer bothering to hide his disdain. "No, I don't have to wonder. Obviously, you believe that I might have had something to do with this man's disappearance."

"I didn't say that, Mr. Redmond."

"I've dealt with enough cops to know that you presume everyone you meet is guilty of something. Maybe it's because you can't face your own troubled consciences. You project your own venality onto the citizens you swear to protect, and it gives you license to . . ."

Those insulting words constitute my last memory of what happened inside the kitchen.

Staring across the table into the hardening gaze of Mark Redmond, like two poker players left in the biggest hand of the night, with all our chips piled between us, we had come to the moment of truth, and that was when I lost the rest of the conversation.

I suspect we continued talking. Or rather he continued to talk while I became groggier, sluggish, and incoherent. Was I aware of us having been drugged? Did I ever try to fight back? I am inclined to think I did resist eventually, because later, I found a fist-shaped bruise above my solar plexus. The mark couldn't be explained by the process of being dragged from the cabin.

12

When I regained consciousness, I found myself seated on the forest floor with vomit on my chest and my arms tied to a tree.

The girl was rifling through my pockets.

I had no clue what drugs they'd slipped us. My experience with narcotics was limited to the prescription painkillers I had received for injuries I'd sustained in the line of duty. If you had told me that the sedatives coursing through my blood were used to tranquilize wild elephants, I would have believed you without question.

Nausea stirred in my gut. I dry heaved a couple of times, but there was nothing left to bring up but saliva. The aftertaste was bitter with coffee and sour with bile.

The drugs must have been in the second pot of coffee Cady had made.

"Use the dark roast we've been saving."

The girl, curling her lip in disgust, reflexively withdrew her hands now as I convulsed. As she did, my unfocused eyes glimpsed the unhealed razor cuts above her wrists. She'd concealed her forearms beneath long sleeves since we'd arrived at Prentiss Pond. These wounds were pink, parallel, and surely self-inflicted.

"You cut yourself," I murmured, still not remotely coherent.

It was bizarre that Cady's incisions were what preoccupied me.

I should have been focused on why she and her father had drugged my two companions and me, on why they'd lashed us to these scaly hemlocks at the edge of the clearing, on what more harm they intended to inflict on us.

My friends were propped against nearby trees. I could glimpse them when I turned my head. They were still out cold. Charley had been sick, too, but I saw no sign that Josie had vomited.

Mark and Cady must have dragged us from the cabin after we fell from our seats. Maybe they didn't want to stumble over our bodies as they evacuated the place. Maybe they had other reasons. I could see the drag marks leading from the cabin porch, past the outfitter's tent, to this tree line. The ground was so sodden from a week of torrential rain that their footprints had already filled with water.

The girl yanked down her sleeves to hide her secret scars. Then she returned to ransacking my pockets.

"Where *are* they?" she said in frustration, sounding even younger than her twelve years.

"Where're what?"

She paused in her pickpocketing to study me. It was as if she were seeing me for the first time.

And in a way, I was seeing her for the first time as well.

Previously, she'd resisted making eye contact and had hidden her gaze behind comically oversize glasses. But now the glasses were gone, like a stage prop that had served its purpose and been discarded.

But there was something else about her face that those phony glasses had concealed. Although she was only in the first flush of puberty, Cady Redmond seemed to possess the eyes of an old woman: the sclera were the ivory of old piano keys, the gray irises were even more faded than Josie's, and the surfaces shone with rheum.

"Don't talk," she told me, not unkindly. "Just try to be still."

She had changed clothes while we were asleep and was dressed now for the coming rain. She wore a Gore-Tex anorak and waterproof pants. The bottoms were tucked into Renegade hiking boots. She had no hips to support the belt around her waist, so she'd cinched it as tight as it would go. I saw that she had stolen my

SIG and holster and had also appropriated Josie's sheathed hunting knife.

They hadn't removed my gun belt, but they'd robbed me of the loaded magazines, as well as my multitool. Curiously, Cady hadn't bothered with my handcuffs in their sheath. Perhaps she saw no use for them when she was so expert in tying knots.

How long had I been out?

The sky, so bright and clear that early-May morning, had grown prematurely dark. When we'd flown up from Jackman in the helicopter, the summit of Boundary Bald Mountain had sparkled with snow. Now the mountain, viewed from across the swollen pond, looked as flat as a mesa: cut off on the bias by the lowering ceiling.

I pulled against my bonds and felt the knots grow tighter as I struggled. Mark Redmond had taught his daughter constrictor knots.

What kind of father teaches his kid how to tie Guantanamo-level restraints?

"If your dad is forcing you to do this, Cady . . ." I began.

"Please be quiet."

She renewed her desperate search of my pockets with fingers as quick and light as a pianist's.

She already had my gun. I had no doubt that she and her father had confiscated every weapon in our possession. Surely they'd confiscated and destroyed our cell phones. The radio in the chopper, too. So what else could she be looking for?

I cast another glance at Charley. My father-in-law had drunk more of the poisoned coffee than I had, but he possessed the constitution of a mule.

Josie was the one who concerned me. The way her silver-haired head was lolling back, unsupported; how her formerly ruddy complexion had drained of blood. She looked like a reject from a wax museum. Her own grotesque simulacrum.

What poison did they use on us?

A haze lay over my memories of the last minutes in the kitchen.

The full-body hangover I was suffering matched the description I'd gotten from women who'd been slipped roofies.

So GHB, maybe? With a dash of Rohypnol?

"Can you check on Jo?" I sounded like I'd bitten my tongue. Maybe I had.

"She'll be OK. The drugs are temporary."

"She's having a reaction, Cady."

"They're temporary," she repeated, her voice rising, as if this detail—the fleeting quality of the effect—excused the assault on us.

"Untie her, at least. She's too sick to fight you."

Busy with her task, the girl pretended not to hear me. She pulled my pockets inside out, scattering coins, a couple of cheap lighters, everything down to the lint.

She leaned back and rested on her haunches. Her mouth bunched up on one side of her face.

"Where are the keys?"

My misfiring neurons finally made the connection.

Josie mentioned that Mark Redmond was a bush pilot himself. He'd hunted wolves from helicopters. Maybe he was hoping to use Josie's Robinson to escape from this wet valley to freedom.

Cady rose and spun in the direction of the unfinished cabin. Her synthetic pants rustled as she turned. Her knees were stained with mud.

She shouted toward the pond, "Papa, I can't find them!"

"Keep looking," came the response.

"I've looked everywhere."

"They've got to be someplace!"

The gusting wind couldn't seem to make up its mind from which direction it wanted to approach, but oak leaves that had remained attached to their branches all winter now downdrafted into the clearing.

After a while, Redmond came striding into view. He moved everywhere quickly and with purpose. I'd noticed that about him from the start: his distinctively determined gait. He was a man whose internal dynamo seemed to always operate at peak efficiency.

While I had been sleeping the sleep of the almost dead, Redmond had changed his clothes as well. He'd put on a camouflage parka over his canvas Carhartt bibs. Steel-toed logging boots peeked out from beneath the frayed hems.

The firearms he was toting were menacing new additions to his ensemble. He carried a serious revolver on his hand-tooled leather belt: a Colt King Cobra. A short-barreled, bolt-action rifle hung on a sling over his shoulder. It was a Ruger Gunsite Scout with a Leupold scope and a suppressor screwed onto the threaded barrel. Both guns were expensive, reliable shooting irons.

He leaned over me, pressing his free hand against the scabrous trunk of the hemlock, forcing me into an even more awkward posture to make eye contact. "Tell me where the keys to the helicopter are, Mike."

"Why would I have them? Those two are the pilots."

"But you know where she hid them."

"No, I don't. If you hadn't poisoned her, asshole—"

With a speed that made me gasp, Redmond brought the barrel of the Ruger up, fed a round into the action, and pressed the silencer between my eyebrows.

The façade of agreeableness had dropped from his expression. The carefully calculated anonymity was gone, too. He no longer felt a need to hide his essential, predatory self behind the bland face of a laborer.

Later, I would realize where I'd seen a stare that fierce before. It was in a daguerreotype of the radical abolitionist John Brown before he'd turned the plains of Kansas red. I was at the mercy of a zealot.

"If the keys aren't in her pockets," I said carefully, "I don't know where they are."

"I don't believe you, Mike. I think you know exactly where they are."

There was no disdain in his casual use of my first name. He was merely done with pretenses. What was the point of formality when death was so near?

"I'm not trying to stall you. I'm worried about Josie overdosing. You need to get her up on her feet and moving around."

"It's a side effect of the gamma-hydroxybutyrate," he said. "Josie will have the worst hangover of her life, but she'll get over it."

"Please have a look at her."

He ran his tongue across his lower lip and then, to my shock, obliged me. He crossed to Josie and tilted her face up for a look. Felt her forehead with the back of his hand.

"She's going to be fine," he said, but for the first time since we'd met, his voice lacked conviction.

"Just untie her and roll her onto her—"

Hemlock needles danced in the air.

"Tell me where the keys are," he said.

"I don't know where the goddamn keys are."

"What did I tell you about swearing?"

That aspect of his character hadn't been part of the act, evidently. Violence didn't bother him, but profanity troubled his sensibilities.

Be smart, Bowditch, I told myself. *Don't push this psychopath over the edge.*

"Whatever you're running from, Redmond, you're making it worse."

He smiled, or at least his lips turned upward at the corners, but his eyes remained cold. "I doubt that would be possible."

"You still have a chance here. You're in control of what happens next."

"Please stop playing negotiator with me and tell me where the keys are."

"I honestly don't know."

He sighed and turned to his daughter. "Grab the last of your things, Cady, and get in the truck."

"Papa?"

"Go!"

I watched the girl as she made her way around the big puddles. She avoided the last blue patches of snow, too. It was amazing there was any snow left after the inches of hard rain that fell.

Redmond listened for the sound of the passenger door slamming shut. Then he brought the business end of the .308-caliber rifle up to my face again. Maybe he'd been waiting for his daughter to exit the scene before he executed us. Maybe he hoped to spare her that gruesome sight at least.

My heart was pounding, but I did my best to keep my composure.

Waiting for the gunshot I would never actually hear, I became aware of the sighing of the wind in the hemlock boughs. I heard the sore-throat singing of a boreal chickadee. I smelled the smoke from the maple fire burning inside the cabin stove.

Finally, he lowered the gun.

"I'm sorry," he said. "Let Josie know how sorry I am. And your father-in-law, too. I never wanted this."

I didn't breathe a sigh of relief—not yet. The situation felt too provisional.

"People know where we are, Redmond. When they don't hear from us, they're going to send a plane. You'll be spotted easily from the air—if you don't bog down in the woods first."

"They won't be able to fly," he said matter-of-factly. "That second round of rain will be here soon, and it's going to ground whatever aircraft the Warden Service or Border Patrol might send for a search."

"Then why do you want the keys?"

"Because it would've been easier taking the chopper to my evac route."

It was almost as if we were having a regular conversation—as if he hadn't contemplated shooting me dead a minute earlier.

I tried one last time. "It's not too late to turn this situation around."

He gazed at me with real amazement. "You genuinely don't know who I am, do you?"

He was right about that. I came to this remote pond with suspicions that he might be trouble. Insufficient suspicions, as it turned out.

The wound to my pride would heal. But I had no idea how we would escape our bonds before the rain came, let alone before help arrived. And I feared for Josie.

Redmond hooked his thumb under his gun sling. He took a backward step. Then he turned away, revealing a bald spot I hadn't noticed before.

I called after his retreating back, "Think of your daughter, Redmond."

He paused as if jerked by a rope. "It's all I've ever done, you idiot. Isn't it obvious by now?"

Two minutes later, I heard a muffled gunshot, unmistakably from his Ruger. He'd fired a round into a metal object, most likely the helicopter controls. Two more shots followed. Even if we escaped the ropes, we wouldn't be going anywhere in Josie's Raven.

At last, the diesel engine of his Unimog sputtered and coughed until its cylinders found their rhythm. Redmond's plan, presumably, was to bull his way through the blowdowns that blocked the skidder road. Undoubtedly, he would have to stop to cut passages through the biggest deadfalls with his chain saw. But he was right about being hours ahead of any pursuers, who would be slowed by the rain. Once he escaped the valley and met up with the interlinked logging roads, he could make his way northwest to the lightly maintained crossing into Québec at Saint-Zacharie.

Even before the rumble of the monster truck faded, I began calling to my unconscious father-in-law.

"Charley! Charley!"

He'd lost his green ball cap when the Redmonds had dragged him out of the cabin. His grizzled head was tilted forward; his big chin rested atop his breastbone. They hadn't seen a need to put his rain jacket back on him; he was wearing only his flight suit. The olive nylon gave the old man a military affect, and I was reminded, without needing to be reminded, that he had been an actual prisoner of war in Vietnam.

With my boot, I tried kicking some twigs and clumped needles toward him—but with no effect.

Cady had used paracord to bind us to the trees. The rope, invented for parachutes, has a breaking strength of 550 pounds, and it is designed not to fray, meaning I could rub it for hours against the bark with no chance of wearing through.

"Come on, old man! Snap out of it."

I was so focused on my father-in-law that I missed the first groans from Josie.

She had her head tilted back against the trunk of the hemlock. Her bloodless face seemed to be taking in the nonexistent sun. As I watched, her lips parted, and at first, I thought she might be drawing a waking breath.

Instead, one of her legs gave a twitch, followed by the other.

Suddenly, she began to convulse. Soon her unconscious body was spasming as her digestive system desperately sought to expel the poison she'd consumed.

"Josie! Wake up!"

But she was as insensible as a blacked-out drunk. Her esophagus was bringing up the dregs of her stomach in a series of wet, strangled coughs. Dark liquid overflowed her mouth: coffee reddened with blood. Her convulsions were severe enough to have ruptured the vessels in her throat.

Pushing against the tree, I managed to bend my knees. Then I got my feet under me. Pushing and pushing—the knots tightening around my wrist—I rose to a standing position, ripping a hole in the back of my Gore-Tex jacket in the process.

I had a prime view of Josie as she began choking on her own vomit.

She and I had never met before that morning. But I felt a powerful connection to her that defied the briefness of our acquaintance.

I rubbed my wrists raw trying to escape. I shouted myself hoarse trying to wake the suffocating woman.

But there was nothing I could do.

Helpless, I watched Josie Jonson convulse. When her boots finally stopped kicking, I knew she had passed beyond a place of all earthly rescue.

Part II

Leave Remorse to warm his hands
Outside in the rain.
As for Death, he understands,
And he will come again.

—Edwin Arlington Robinson, "Bokardo"

13

It was the rain, not my shouting, that finally woke Charley.

"What? What happened?" He tried to blink away the water streaming down his face as if the rain were tears.

By now, the ropes around my wrists had become tourniquets, stopping the flow of blood to my hands. I could no longer feel my fingers at all. The sluggish minutes I had endured waiting for my father-in-law to revive had been almost more painful.

"Charley?"

He examined his legs stretched out before him, the thighs and calves already soaked through, as if they belonged to a stranger. He only seemed to understand that his hands were bound as he leaned forward, away from the tree. "Mike?"

I had chips of bark in my hair from rubbing against the hemlock. "Redmond drugged us. You've been out for, I don't know, two hours maybe. I can't see my watch, so I'm guessing based on the sky."

"Drugged?"

"Charley, you need to listen to me." I gulped down a breath, then let it go. "Josie is dead."

The import of the words took a moment to register. Then, seemingly through force of will, he focused himself, swiveling his head in my direction, and then in Josie's. Still bound, she lay slumped on the fallen needles. The rain had cleaned her chin. Her posture might have been of someone sleeping, but her face revealed the grim reality; her skin had turned as white as the skull beneath it.

"Oh no," was all my father-in-law said. "Oh, hell."

His wet white hair clung to his head, making him appear to be someone I'd never met: a frail old man. His soaked nylon jumpsuit was rapidly turning a darker shade of olive.

"She choked on her own vomit. I watched it happen, Charley. I told Redmond she was in distress, but he shrugged it off. They've gone in that Unimog thing. They left twenty minutes, maybe half an hour ago now."

"Did she . . . ?"

"She never woke up. There was nothing I could do." When I saw him leaning away from the hemlock, I said, "They've used constrictor knots on us, Charley. They'll only get tighter if you pull. My ropes are cutting off my circulation. I can't feel my hands."

He nodded, seeming to listen to me, but his gaze remained fixed on his dead friend.

"I'm such a damn fool," he said. "I knew there was something off about that coffee, the second pot Cady made. My instinct told me it was wrong. But I didn't listen because I couldn't bring myself to refuse that little girl."

"Redmond conned us both, Charley. I was too focused on interrogating him and . . ."

The rain was coming sideways in hard gusts. It was very loud. The drops smacked against the steel roof of the cabin. I saw rain falling on the pond, stippling the surface. Windblown hemlock needles showered down upon us and stuck like adhesive to our clothes and faces.

"You spoke with him, you said?"

I was surprised and not surprised to witness Charley's calmness. Not that he wasn't angry, not that he wasn't grieving. But my friend, a combat vet and lifetime first responder, had seen more death than even an unfortunate person might witness in many lifetimes. Whatever emotions he was experiencing, he was setting them aside, putting them on a mental shelf until he had time and space to process them.

"I came to when Cady was searching my pockets," I said. "She was looking for the helicopter keys. She searched all three of us, but she couldn't find them."

"Because I hid them," he said thickly.

Both of us were dehydrated from the sedatives, an ironic condition for two men in a downpour. I'd been tilting my head back and opening my mouth to catch the precipitation on my tongue. Despite my best efforts, most of it ran down my chin.

"*You* hid them?"

"I swiped the keys from Jo and dropped them in a posthole outside the cabin. Redmond wanting to check our phones for photos gave me a bad feeling. He said it was about privacy, but I was a lawman for three decades, and it reminded me too much of someone looking to destroy evidence. I didn't expect this scenario. But I should have. I should have."

"We don't have time to beat ourselves up. We need to get loose."

"Let me try to wriggle some."

"Careful!"

I blinked rain out of my eyes. Somehow even this subtle movement of my eyelids seemed to increase the hold on my wrists.

"They used constrictor knots on you, you said?"

"Yeah. Why?"

"I'm getting some play in mine. Guess they were only afraid of the strapping young warden investigator. They took pity on me because I'm a geezer. Feels like a couple of half hitches around each wrist."

"That makes sense. I think it was Cady who tied us. That poor kid—"

"Stop talking a minute, son. I'm trying to get free of these restraints, and I need to concentrate."

In three minutes, he had liberated his right hand. I couldn't believe he'd managed such an easy escape and said so.

"I've been tied up once or twice in my life," explained the former POW.

But he was wobblier on his feet than he'd expected. Trailing a length of paracord from one raw, red wrist, he lurched against the trunk to keep from falling. He managed a shaky smile, however, when we made eye contact.

"I feel like I drank a jug of Alcohol Mary's famous 'shine."

The rain had washed away the vomit from my chest, although the smell remained to remind me of my carelessness and stupidity.

Charley staggered to Josie and dropped to his knees in the rain-pool that had formed around her lifeless body. He wiped the backs of his hands across his reddened eyes.

"I'm sorry, Jo." He reached for her cheek with a touch as light as a lover's. "I'm sorry I failed you when you needed me."

I gave him as many seconds to grieve as my sore back and numb hands could withstand. "You're going to need a knife for my ropes. The knots are so tight, I think they're past the point of being un-tied."

He swung his big head my way and nodded. "I'll check the kitchen. See what they might have left behind. Hang tight, young feller."

"That is literally what I am doing."

Somehow, he summoned the faintest of smiles at my dumb joke.

He was gone a long time, or what felt like a long time. I spent those eternal minutes perversely contemplating what my future life would be like as a handless man. Bathrooms would be a problem.

Meanwhile, I was starting to shiver as the rain penetrated the weather-resistant fabrics of my hunting garb. Even state-of-the-art Gore-Tex had its limits, it seemed.

Charley returned from the cabin with a serrated bread knife and a milk jug filled with spring water. He seemed steadier on his feet. He set the jug down and disappeared from my view behind the back of the hemlock. Soon I heard the sound of sawing.

"I feel like Alexander confronting the Gordian Knot with a nail file," he said.

"Just get me free!"

It took a while, but he managed to saw through the paracord, revealing the silky strands inside. He was careful removing the constrictor knots, which had bitten so deeply into my skin that they had opened bloody wounds. I wondered if my wrists would be scarred for life.

"Try bending your fingers. There you go. I don't think the muscles or ligaments are damaged. But be gentle; don't rub them too hard to start the blood flowing. When you're ready, I need you to help me untie Jo and carry her inside, out of this damned weather."

Between us, we polished off the gallon jug of water.

My watch gave the time as nearly 4:35 p.m., earlier than I had thought. The rain made the sky gloomier than it would have been on a clear May afternoon. But despite the darkness, the day wasn't over yet.

Normally, I would have been reluctant to disturb a crime scene, but I wasn't going to fight Charley about moving his friend's body. There was no need for evidence collection. I had witnessed her death. The attorney general had more than enough to charge Redmond with felony murder; the AG would understand the imperative Charley and I felt to cover Josie's body. The brave woman deserved to lie in a sheltered, dignified place.

I grasped her beneath the arms while he took her by the ankles.

"What do you remember?" I asked him.

"It's a fog, mostly. The drug was in the coffee, I expect. I thought it tasted off, but it was a different brew from before, and I figured she'd burned it." Strong as the old man was, he had to pause to get a better grip. "They used some sort of animal sedative, wouldn't you say?"

"Redmond told me it was a drug called GHB. People use it recreationally. In small doses, it produces euphoria."

He laughed through his nose. "Can't say I am feeling euphoria. More like I took a bite of Snow White's poisoned apple and swallowed it, core and all."

My hands were beginning to throb as the blood pumped into my fingertips. Josie was tall and, by my imprecise reckoning, weighed something like 150 pounds in life. But as wobbly and weak as I was, she seemed no burden at all.

We walked parallel, carrying her, until I had to mount the cabin steps backward. As I turned toward the pond, I got another face full of rain. Mist hid the steep hills beyond the valley.

"The last thing I remember," Charley was saying, "is your telling him, 'I know you're lying. You know damn well who this Hammond Pratt is, you son of a bitch.' And him snapping at your use of profanity in front of his daughter."

I had no recollection of having spoken those words.

We laid Josie down on the plywood table in the dark. The thin plank bowed between the sawhorses but supported her weight. Water from her clothes dribbled over the edges and made a spreading pattern on the floor.

The blaze was dying in the stove. One of the Redmonds must have closed the flue. But when I opened the cast-iron door, I saw a log turned mostly to charcoal. The in-rushing air caused the charred wood to grow orange as the fire inside regained its strength. The warmth felt bracing and restorative.

Charley lit a kerosene lamp, then went searching for a drop cloth that he converted into a shroud. Strange to say, but the anonymous shape of Josie's body, showing through the draped fabric, disturbed me more than the sight of her actual corpse. Death robs each of us of our individuality. Josie Jonson was gone, and what remained was a carcass.

I returned to the stove and warmed my aching hands before the firebox. I would need to bind my wrists if I didn't want to keep reopening the wounds. There was a med kit in my rucksack in the helicopter, if the fugitives hadn't swiped it before they'd fled.

"Redmond said something curious," I said. "He told me I had no idea who he was."

"That's true enough."

"I think he meant something different—like he's a notorious figure whom I should have recognized. So who the hell is he? One of those domestic terrorists who plants bombs at county fairs or sends ricin to politicians?"

Stooping, Charley retrieved his ball cap from where it had fallen onto the floor during the scuffle. He beat it against his thigh, raising a cloud of sawdust. He pulled it onto his head and looked like himself again, staring out from under the brim with those hawk eyes of his.

"At the moment, I don't think what he did before matters. What matters is he killed a good woman and is hoping to slip back into Canada, I expect. Odds are he'll do it, too, with no one to stop him. That's where they're from originally, he and his girl. I knew from the get-go they weren't Alaskans."

"How?"

"Little pebbles add up to a big pile. But the giveaway to me was his accent. Alberta or Saskatchewan, if I had to guess. But he didn't head east across Canada for the hell of it. He had a reason for making for Québec and the Maritimes. I couldn't tell you what it was, but I have some guesses."

"Tell me anyway."

"Later. But I'm certain it was Josie's call this morning that sent them into action."

"And I'm sure they had go bags packed for this eventuality," I said. "I bet they sabotaged their radio and threw our phones into Prentiss Pond. I heard him fire shots into what must have been the Raven's controls and radio."

"All the blowdowns and washouts in the woods will slow him, but they won't stop him from reaching Canada. Dollars to doughnuts, he knows a place—or probably places—where he can cross. He'll be gone in the night before the Services frontaliers can catch him."

Rain drummed steadily on the metal roof. The noise echoed

through the wooden rooms with nothing to soften it. The emptiness of the sound made me despair.

"There's no way we can bushwhack twenty miles in the dark with all those blowdowns. We're basically trapped with no way to escape or contact the outside world."

Charley stroked his chin. My father-in-law had more than his share of mannerisms, some of them affected because he enjoyed playing with people's prejudices, but pensively rubbing that big jaw of his was something he did without thinking.

"The Warden Service will come looking for us after the rain clears in the morning. I don't see any alternative to spending the night."

"I can't wait that long," I said. "I'm going after the son of a bitch."

"On foot, in this storm?"

I'd never catch them, of course. But as I gazed at Josie's shrouded corpse, whatever sadness I'd been feeling was being transmuted into white-hot rage. It almost didn't matter to me whether my effort would be in vain. I needed to take action because that was who I was.

"I can't just sit here and wait," I said. "There's always a chance his escape won't go as planned, and I need to be there if it happens."

Charley grinned at me with affection. "Son, you really do have the heart of a bloodhound. And the lack of sense of one, too. They took the vehicle, you said?"

"The Unimog, yes."

He cast a glance toward the nearest window frame. Waves rippled the plastic curtain with each fresh gust.

"He would have been better taking the skidder to clear the road."

"I'm surprised he didn't—unless he thought it would be too slow."

Charley smacked his forehead so hard I was surprised it didn't hurt. "It's because he doesn't know how many trees are down between here and the bridge. He never saw that mess from above like we did. I expect he has a chain saw in the truck bed, and there's a winch mounted on the front. But he's going to have a devil of a time clearing all those blowdowns."

"And when he does," I added hopefully, "there's no guarantee the bridge won't collapse beneath the weight of his vehicle."

I had been pacing without realizing it and had arrived now beside a tarp-covered window.

"Do you think if we dug enough holes out there we'd find Hammond Pratt buried somewhere?" I said.

"Wouldn't surprise me if we did."

"For his sake, I hope he really did get lost on a logging road. Based on how he handled us, Redmond would have made short work of the guy. I'm not sure whether to believe anything he told us about his dead wife or about her family hiring a private investigator."

"You think Mark's wife got custody in a divorce and he decided to grab the girl and run?"

"It's what usually happens. And it would explain why he's worked so hard to stay off the grid. The Canadians probably have a BOLO out for him for kidnapping his daughter."

The acronym stood for *be on the lookout*.

A big gust pushed the curtain inward, then sucked it back into place. I was not actively listening, and yet I found myself perceiving the faintest of sounds: a high-pitched whine coming from a distance.

"Do you hear that?"

The old man shook his head. He had better hearing than most of his peers, considering his life history as a soldier and a pilot. But his ears couldn't pick out the noise that had caught my attention.

"It's a saw!" I exclaimed. "They're still cutting their way out! I might be able to catch them, after all."

"How far off would you say they are?"

"A mile, maybe."

"Meaning they're almost to the bridge. Even if you run as fast as Jim Thorpe, they'll be gone before you get close. And it's unlikely you're going to find any firearms here to stop them. I'm sure they've taken every potential weapon short of a hatchet."

"And disposed of the keys to the vehicles they left behind. I might've had a chance if I could have taken that ATV Josie was telling us they had."

His reaction to this statement was the last thing I expected. He looked at me, his sky-blue eyes alive with hope, and let out a laugh that reached all the way to the rafters.

14

Charley Stevens, you buffle-brain!" he exclaimed. "You really are growing senile."

"What's going on?"

"Go rummage around their tent and see if they left anything useful behind—headlamps, rain gear, a compass. And a hatchet! You'll need one of those. I'll meet you outside, where they parked the four-wheeler and the sled under those blue tarps."

I didn't know what he had in mind, but I grinned at him before I ducked back into the dying day.

The outfitter's tent in which father and daughter had spent the winter was unlike any shelter I had visited. Sixteen feet wide and twenty feet long, it had been erected atop a platform to keep the heat from dissipating into the frozen earth. The walls were of undyed canvas and were staked so resolutely into the ground that the sides looked as tight as drumheads. The Redmonds had left no lantern burning, but the remaining daylight seeped through the fabric, and the rivulets of rain running down the exterior looked like the map of a trackless swamp in a wilderness of entwining estuaries.

They'd bashed their radio to bits, of course. I wasn't sure if Redmond had expected us to get loose of our bonds in time, but he had wanted to be certain that if we did, we'd have no means of alerting the authorities or calling for help. It was a shame. The radio was

Midland's premier Base Camp model. When you were a fugitive, it made sense that you would choose the best.

The top of their four-legged box stove was cold to the touch. Both beds—cots, really—had been made. But the lids of two heavy-duty hunting totes had been thrown open.

One tote clearly belonged to Cady, and I left it alone, at first.

Instead, I crouched over her dad's tote, pulling out everything—folded shirts, pants, underwear, socks—and scattering it across the freshly swept floor. I located a hooded rain poncho that would provide additional defense against the weather and a pair of neoprene gloves that were too small for my aching hands but not so tight that I couldn't bend my fingers.

In a jeans pocket, I found an old trapper's jackknife.

But no compass and certainly no firearms.

I was about to leave when curiosity prompted me to investigate the girl's bin.

There were more clothes—flannel pajamas, wool socks, tees—as well as the dog-eared books her dad made her read: *Lord of the Flies* and *Frankenstein*. At the bottom was a cotton sheet, neatly folded, and under it was a spread of magazines, *Marie Claire* and *Cosmopolitan*, hidden like a man might conceal his pornographic reading material from his wife. The sight of these publications, which brought news from a world Cady would never visit, intensified the anger I felt toward her authoritarian father.

I found no diary, but there were charcoal sketches—some quite well done—of a woman who must have been her absent mother. She had raven-black hair, worn loose, carelessly loose, and multiple-pierced ears and a delicateness in her bones that reminded me of Cady. The girl had used a lot of charcoal, pressing hard into the paper, to render the blackness of the woman's deeply set eyes. The portraits told me little about the subject but a lot about the young artist. Cady Redmond had intense feelings about this person, but whether they were feelings of love, hate, or a combination of both, I couldn't guess.

There was one last treasure hidden among the magazines and sketches: a folded topographic map of the surrounding quadrangle of forest. The chart was marked with permanent marker to show the girl's favorite trails, including the path along Wounded Deer Pond that led to Moose River Maple Works. I snatched it up and pressed it to my chest. Having a map in the wilderness almost made up for not having a compass.

When I emerged through the tent flap, wearing my waterproof gloves and the poncho over my Gore-Tex jacket, I caught sight of the shadowy helicopter down the hill. In the gloom, it looked like a piece of public art designed by one of those sculptors who wants everyone who sees it to be disturbed by modern life.

I doubted the fugitives had left anything of use inside the flightless chopper, but I trotted across the field to be certain.

I had been right about Redmond having shot up the controls and the radio. He had also had the foresight to steal the survival bag. But there was a Pelican box under the seat with a Nitecore flashlight and spare batteries.

The bonanza, however, was the flare gun.

Mark Redmond, it seemed, did make mistakes. While he knew enough to take the pack containing Josie's pistol and emergency gear, he'd forgotten the cheap flare gun duct-taped under the dash along with a sealed package of extra projectiles. A flare pistol didn't qualify in my mind as a weapon, not unless my target had recently bathed in gasoline, but it had a range of uses, not the least of which were its intended ones: illuminating a night scene and signaling for help.

This one was the Orion "twelve-gauge" model, with flares the size of shotgun shells. But woe to the fool who loaded the chamber with real ammunition. The pistol would explode in the hand of anyone who tried to fire buckshot through its cheap plastic barrel.

I found my rucksack under Josie's seat where I had left it. Another mistake by Redmond. I hadn't packed a spare weapon, but inside I found my trauma kit, as well as a tin in which I kept materials for starting a fire, a box of protein bars, and a space blanket.

I realized that the last of the nausea had passed. I would feel the strain in my muscles again when the adrenaline left my bloodstream, but for the moment, I was bursting with energy and eager to begin my pursuit of the man who'd killed Josie.

I found Charley where he'd said he would be. He had brought the kerosene lamp with him and had ripped off the blue tarps from Redmond's recreational vehicles. I noticed he was holding a pair of haircutting scissors, and I couldn't imagine what he had in mind for them.

Without snow, the snowmobile was clearly useless even if we could get it started. But the four-wheeler was no good, either, without its ignition key. It was a pity, too, since the ATV was an old but well-maintained Can-Am Outlander designed for rugged terrain. It had a polymer "scabbard" attached to the chassis for carrying a hunting rifle into the backcountry, but there was no gun inside the case, needless to say.

"I bet the keys to that ATV are in the pond," I said.

"I expect you're right."

"I almost want to plunge in and have a look."

"You wouldn't find them. And I would think you've suffered enough from hypothermia in your life that you wouldn't want to risk another case."

I couldn't argue with the truth of that statement. "I don't suppose you've ever hot-wired one of these puppies?"

In response to what I'd meant as a joke, Charley gave me a slack-jawed look. "Hot-wire it? Why would I go through the rigamarole of hot-wiring it? Don't they teach young wardens engine mechanics anymore?"

"What do you mean?"

In the dancing lamplight, I watched him lean over the wet handlebars with the scissors. With a flick of the wrist, he opened the shears and drove the point of one into the ignition and gave it a hard twist. Then he flipped the shifter into neutral. The engine started in seconds.

"How did I not know this was possible?"

"Beats the hell out of me. I'll give you the shears for the trip, but I wouldn't turn off the engine if I were you. Sometimes you wreck the ignition when you use scissors, and since I don't have the time or inclination to give you a class in remedial mechanics—"

"I get it, I get it," I said. "I need to leave the engine running."

My embarrassment was passing quickly as I realized I might have an actual chance of catching up with the murderous fugitive.

Charley rested a hand on a vibrating handlebar. "Fortunately, Redmond knew to store the machine with a full tank of gas. He didn't want condensation getting into the lines and freezing."

I showed my father-in-law my haul from the tents and from Josie's helicopter.

"I don't suppose you stumbled across a firearm in your search of the cabin?"

"No, but I found a few things that might prove handy." He produced an old duffel and unzipped it, tilting the opening toward the light of the windblown lamp.

Inside the bag was another flashlight, a coil of orange paracord, and an actual, honest-to-goodness hatchet. The blade was notched and duller than I would have liked. But there was no time to sharpen it now, and it remained keen enough to split a man's skull.

As Charley helped me pack the hatchet into the ATV's empty scabbard and secure my rucksack to the front rack and the duffel bag to the one behind the seat, he fell uncharacteristically silent. He kept his eyes on his quick-tying fingers.

"I'm going to get this son of a bitch, Charley. You know I will."

The tarps that had covered the ATV and snowmobile, now unsecured except at a few corners, flapped loudly as the wind shook them. Drops of water flew everywhere, adding to the rain.

"You do believe I'll get him," I said, my voice sounding a little plaintive in my ears. "Don't you?"

He released a drawn breath and looked me hard in the eyes. "Not if you're overconfident. Redmond knows his bushcraft. He's been preparing to run as long as he and his daughter have been holed up here. My point is that he is an old-time woodsman. If you think you're going to outsmart him—"

"I get it, Charley. He's the real deal."

To my surprise, he grabbed hold of my shoulder and gripped it with fingers as tight as talons. "You need to hear this, Mike. You need to listen to me. This man is better than you are in the woods, and if you forget that for a minute, he's going to kill you."

I was prideful enough to be stung by these words. "Thanks for the vote of confidence."

Charley only shook his head and squeezed harder. "The lesson of this cabin isn't that Mark Redmond is a master craftsman. The lesson is that he's a master *planner* who thinks through the smallest of details. Don't presume you ever have the drop on him. Don't presume he's not thinking three moves ahead of your next gambit, however brilliant you think it is."

The old man was genuinely scared for me. More than that, he was concerned that he wasn't communicating the extent of the danger I faced. The possibility was real in my father-in-law's mind that this would be the last time he would see me alive.

And so I tried not to sound offended. "I understand what you're telling me. Redmond's a dangerous man. I swear I won't underestimate him."

The set of his mouth told me he didn't believe me. In all the years we had known each other and all the scrapes we'd been through, I couldn't remember Charley Stevens ever looking so afraid.

"Be careful, son," were his last words to me.

15

The Can-Am had a dying headlight. It took me less than a min-ute to realize I couldn't see as well as I should have, that the illuminated picture rushing toward me as I left the valley was diffuse and off-kilter. But the cause of this lopsidedness eluded me until I had lost sight of Charley's lamp in the side mirror, and I understood at last that I was seeing one side of the road better than the other.

The engine noise also made it impossible to hear the whining grind of Redmond's chain saw. It raised the critical question of how close I could get before he heard me coming. And because I couldn't risk turning off the ignition, on Charley's orders, I was going to have to stop periodically and, staying ahead of the noise, explore on foot.

Fortunately, the ATV's suspension was in good shape. And Red-mond had kept the tires well inflated. The treads gripped the mud satisfactorily.

I decided to make my first stop where the road reentered the woods encircling the valley. Whoever had sold Josie the land had followed the usual practice of first harvesting all the marketable timber, cutting most of the taller trees down to the nubs, leaving only the deformed and twisted ones standing. But poplars, willows, and birches grow fast, and these saplings had already reached ten feet in height. So while the tree line felt less like true forest than scrub-land, there was good cover here. It might come in handy if I hoped to ambush Redmond while he was clearing brush.

I extinguished the headlights and turned the engine to idle, hoping it wouldn't die in the rain, and swung my leg over the seat. It was after six now, the cloud-covered sun had set behind the mountains, and absolute darkness was closing in. I tried to follow the road with my naked eye, but it was no use.

Usually as you travel along a jeep trail at night, you can make out the saw-toothed treetops against the sky, but there was only blackness above me. I had to risk using my second-best flashlight (I needed to save the better of the two for a critical moment), directing the beam in front of my boots.

When I had traveled a hundred feet or so, I could no longer perceive the low growl of the ATV behind me. But I could easily discern the sound of the chain saw ahead. Despite my having closed the distance, the sound seemed farther away, meaning Redmond was making quick work of the deadfalls. He'd nearly reached the bridge.

What to do?

I decided to return to the Can-Am and mount up again. If Redmond made it to the bridge and by some miracle managed to cross those submerged timbers without breaking through, then I would need the four-wheeler to keep pace. The risk remained that he would pause in his cutting and catch the sound of my engine above the windstorm and ready himself to ambush me as I plunged down the hill.

"This man is better than you are in the woods, and if you forget that for a minute, he's going to kill you."

Charley's words stung. He'd seen so little of Mark Redmond's bushcraft, and yet he'd judged the man to be superior to me. I felt an adolescent desire to prove him wrong.

Between the speed of the four-wheeler and the diagonal rain, I couldn't keep the water from blurring my eyes. My vision wasn't much better than that of a swimmer at the bottom of a pool.

I passed a turnoff to the east. It headed uphill through ragged timber, and I decided it must have been the ATV trail Josie had mentioned, the one Cady had marked on her map. The girl had used this path to visit the Stombaughs, who owned the maple sugaring business on the South Branch Road. The passage was too narrow for the Unimog, which was why Redmond had made for the bridge instead.

In the brief glimpse I got of the trail in the unequal high beams, I could tell it had been partly cut—the entrance, at least. The flesh-colored chips and shavings left by a saw became nearly luminescent when touched by light. I wondered who'd cleared the path and if it might be passable.

The thought occurred to me to break off my pursuit and make a beeline for the sugarhouse where, with luck, the owners would have a working radio or satellite phone I could use to call for help. But my heart was as hot as a furnace over Josie's senseless death. I wanted to catch Redmond. I wanted to make him pay.

Because I had promised Charley that I would be cautious, I stopped a hundred yards down the main road.

I repeated my actions of a few minutes earlier, creeping forward on foot. I was relieved to hear the buzz of the saw again. Redmond didn't seem to have detected me.

I was also hearing the stream now, I realized. The road drew near its banks, and the runoff had amplified its usual murmur into something louder, less distinct, and more menacing. The bridge couldn't be far, and past the bridge lay escape and the open road.

I stuck to the edge of the road, with my flashlight trained on the ground immediately ahead. Most of the trees that had fallen were evergreens. The new buds of the firs, strewn across the mud, appeared chartreuse, nearly fluorescent.

Where Redmond hadn't driven over the fallen trees, he'd pushed many of them aside. But the spiked blowdowns presented obstacles to me, a man on foot. I could easily twist an ankle leaping over one, if not impale myself on a spiked branch.

The noise of the chain saw wasn't continuous. Instead, it came in a series of snarls and purrs as the multitoothed blade cut through each tree. Redmond was distracted; he hadn't heard me.

"Don't presume you ever have the drop on him. Don't presume he's not thinking three moves ahead of your next gambit."

Go to hell, Charley.

Now I saw the taillights of the truck ahead, like two dragon eyes glowing in a cave beneath a mountain. And beyond the massive shadow of the Unimog, a fuzzy white nimbus where the murderer was busy at work clearing his escape route.

He doesn't know I'm here.

I have a chance to get close.

What I didn't have was a plan. I had a hatchet to use against a heavily armed man currently wielding a limb-severing chain saw. Even if I could sneak within feet of him, I would still be outmatched.

And given all her other skills, it occurred to me that Cady was probably an expert shot, as well.

Would she really fire upon me, though?

Probably she would if I were attacking her father with a hatchet. But if I managed somehow to subdue him first? I wished I had been able to read the girl better. I'd seen the scars where she'd cut her own arms. Self-harm always indicates deep emotional pain. Was she suffering from the knowledge of her father's evil, or had he brainwashed her? I'd read enough about Stockholm syndrome to know—

The bullet missed the hand holding the flashlight. I felt the nearby leaves disintegrate into shreds. But it wasn't until the gunshot reached my ears that I dove for cover.

I sprawled face down in the mud as bullets ripped apart the bushes above me. Rain splashed from the ground as high as my ears.

My years as a game warden told me, without having to listen or make a mental connection, that the projectiles were coming from a high-caliber rifle. Likely Redmond's Ruger.

He must have set Cady cutting blowdowns while he waited.

Charley had warned me to expect an ambush. I had told myself I was being careful to avoid one. But here I was, lying prone in the road, with nothing to hide behind: the softest target imaginable.

I had one hope: Redmond didn't know if I was armed.

He had to reckon with the possibility that he'd failed to find and dispose of every gun we'd brought with us. The man was arrogant. But he wasn't infallible.

If he'd managed to forget Josie's flare gun, for example—

Bowditch, you idiot.

The bullets were pulverizing the young leaves, turning them into wet confetti.

I pulled the plastic "gun" from my pocket, trailing its attached bandolier of flares and the package of spares. I was glad for the extras. I was glad I'd thought to chamber a flare beforehand.

I extended my arm in the direction of the taillights and pulled the trigger.

The projectile—powered by perchlorate and other compounds—made a red streak as it sparked across the distance. The flare struck the truck bed and dropped, sizzling, to the ground.

The devil-light rising from the spitting chemicals revealed my first surprise.

It was Cady, not her father, whose armed silhouette appeared in the radiant glow. It was she who was firing at me.

Now I understood why I wasn't dead. The girl had never intended to hit me.

If it had been Redmond staring through the scope, he would have punched a .308-caliber hole through my skull.

The rain extinguished the flare even more quickly than normal— three seconds instead of seven—soaking up its light into sudden and absolute blackness. But not before Redmond dropped the chain saw and came rushing around the truck. He started blasting with his Colt revolver, shouting, "Take cover! Get behind the vehicle!"

By this time, I'd had the good sense to roll off the road into something like a ditch full of rushing water.

On my side, I pumped another flare into the action of the toylike launcher.

In this downpour, there was almost no chance of anything— clothes, canvas—catching fire. But I could keep up the barrage until my supply ran out, using each shot to illuminate the scene and temporarily blind Redmond. I needed time to take cover behind something solid—a hemlock stump, some glacial erratic—before he came to deliver the coup de grâce.

My aim was already getting better. The next flare grazed his shoulder before lofting into the bed of the Unimog. As with my first shot, it seemed to land harmlessly. Sputtering and sparking, it created a brief crimson incandescence.

But then something shocking happened—a fire managed to start and take hold in the back of the vehicle.

I couldn't understand or explain it, let alone believe what I was seeing.

Holstering his revolver, Redmond spun around to extinguish the unaccountable blaze, removing his coat to beat at the young flames before they could grow.

He's carrying extra fuel.

Of course. We were miles from a gas station here. And it was my good fortune that one of the jerricans in the truck bed was leaking fumes, if not actual gasoline.

"Get clear, Chloé! One of the cans is leaking."

Even with my head buzzing from adrenaline and excited to have started a fire, I registered the name he used for her.

Chloé?

Not Cady.

I had my hands full with Redmond, but the name had attached itself to my mind like a burr.

While he was putting out the fire, I discharged another flare, this time directly at him. This one bounced off the side of his face. At least he reacted like a man who had been burned. He let the coat fall and slapped at his cheek and hairline as if it might be aflame.

The lapse in concentration was momentary. It took him mere seconds to realize that he wasn't personally combusting. He returned almost without a pause to beating the blaze.

That was the end of my luck, I thought.

I could keep firing flares at Redmond until I was out, but I was only delaying the inevitable. The worst I could do was singe him. And when he failed to hear gunfire coming from my direction, he would know that I was unarmed and helpless. He would come for me, and there would be nothing I could do to stop him.

I opted to fire the next flare into the sky. At least I could see what Redmond was planning.

Dying even before it reached the top of its arc, the projectile revealed the bridge beyond the headlights.

When I had caught up with them, father and daughter had been sawing through the last trees blocking their escape. Now the way was clear to cross. I possessed no means of stopping them.

Fortunately, Redmond was in a rush and chose not to waste ammunition. Because he couldn't tell where I was hiding or what trap I might have set (maybe I'd merely been pretending not to have a pistol), he refused to fire random shots. Whatever minor burn he might've sustained from the flare, he was already thinking clearly again.

He spun around and yelled to Chloé to get inside the vehicle.

And then he darted around to the driver's side, moving with that characteristic speed and sure-footedness with which he performed every action.

I stood up, my face cold and dripping, every part of me cold and dripping, and trotted toward the Unimog as he floored the clutch and the diesel transmission crunched into first gear. The monstrous machine rolled over the last fallen birch, snapping it like a bird bone, and then advanced cautiously onto the bridge.

The stream was so high, it was flowing over the top planks. Only the frothy waves breaking over the structure gave away its position. Otherwise, I might have thought the Redmonds were planning to drive straight into the water to their deaths: father taking daughter with him in a suicide pact she had never chosen.

The huge wheels turned ever so slowly as Redmond edged the heavy machine onto the flooded crossbeams. The supports were holding.

Did he build this bridge? I wondered.

Then I realized that of course he had.

But did he know how much weight it could and couldn't support?

The high water had changed the calculus. And hydrodynamic force is already among the most difficult numbers to estimate, especially when your life is on the line. He could only guess at what would happen. He could only pray the timbers didn't give way as he inched across the planks to the far bank.

Above the rain and the rushing stream and the chugging engine of the Unimog, I listened for the straining of the timbers. I prayed for a sudden crack and crash. But the bridge seemed determined to hold.

I was standing and watching as the truck reached the middle.

The son of a bitch is going to make it.

I needed the ATV, I realized. I would have to cross that same half-drowned bridge on the four-wheeler. Unless I gunned the engine, I wasn't confident the water flowing across the planks wouldn't sweep my lighter vehicle away.

I began sprinting back up the hill in the rain-soaked darkness.

Just before I reached the Can-Am at the top, I heard a crash that was loud enough to be detected a mile away, storm or no storm.

The bridge had collapsed.

16

In the dark, running toward the stream, I stumbled over a rock exposed by the melting mud and nearly fell. I regained my footing but barked my shin on a log left behind by the chain saw.

I could probably chance a light now, I belatedly realized. If the vehicle had gone into the water, my fugitives would be distracted trying to escape. But after having nearly received a frontal lobotomy via a high-caliber bullet, I decided to play it safe.

The hazy headlights of the Unimog came into view through the skinny trees even before I rounded the last turn, and I could tell from their crazy vector—shining downward and also downstream—that the machine had broken through at the far side of the bridge.

The Redmonds had almost made it across before the sodden timbers gave way beneath the weight of the truck. And now its ponderous engine was angled into the water, its rear wheels raised into the air and still spinning for the moment, even as the current pushed the vehicle steadily south. The raw power of that moving water was all the proof I needed that trying to swim Prentiss Stream would be an act of suicide.

With my view mostly obscured by the rear of the Unimog, I heard Redmond shout to his daughter. Objects from the bed of the truck, totes carrying food perhaps, fell over the side and were swept away by the current. The driver's door was open. I wondered if I might see Redmond climb out, pulling Chloé after him before the machine slid entirely off the supports.

Then I glimpsed movement at the edge of the light. Two silhouettes scrambled up the far bank, mere seconds ahead of calamity. The
Unimog was once again in motion—pulled down by gravity, pushed
forward by the flood. The diesel engine didn't sputter; it died with a
hiss like an extinguished campfire, and then the headlights went out
and all was darkness on the far side of the stream. There was one last
groan as the vehicle rolled onto its side, and nearly everything the
Redmonds had packed for their escape to Canada was carried toward
the Penobscot River, a mile to the south.

In the quiet—not silence, because the rain was loud and the stream
even louder—I could make out their raised voices.

"Chloé, are you all right? Are you sure you're all right?"

"I lost your Ruger, Papa. The sling got caught, and I—"

"Forget the rifle. As long as you're all right. Come on. Come on
now. We have to go."

They'd had a fright, but he was already collecting himself—I
could hear his decisiveness—and so I risked popping another flare
into the pistol and fired it upward. The burning red projectile arced
over the stream, and I saw them clearly. Redmond had managed to
hang on to his pack—he was holding it by one strap—but Chloé
had nothing in her hands.

Faster than I imagined possible, Redmond had his revolver out
and pointed at me. It was like a magic trick. One second the gun was
in its holster, the next it was in his hand. He fired two shots, and one
tore my sleeve. I felt the near miss before I heard the report of the
Colt. And once again I found myself face down in the mud.

But we were separated by an unbridged and unbridgeable torrent
now, and my first thought, lying there, was that they were on the right
side and I was on the wrong. They might be on foot, but they'd gotten across a barrier. The muddy road continued below. In less than a
mile, it joined the access road. Nothing stood between them and the
logging highway that entered Québec at the Saint-Zacharie crossing.

Meanwhile, I was cut off and unable to pursue them. Not unless
I could find a way through the woods.

Was the ATV trail to the Stombaughs' sugarhouse passable? Someone had begun clearing it. There was no way for me to know how far it was open without trying it. But if I got halfway and found the path blocked by deadfalls, I would have no choice but to return to Charley in defeat.

Moose River Maple Works was the nearest structure I knew of, and hopefully it was occupied if the owners had stayed to finish cleaning their evaporator and tanks, as Josie had said they were doing.

I could no longer see or hear the Redmonds on the opposite bank, but I was gun-shy enough at this stage to crawl away on hands and knees until I was out of range of the Colt. And then, to be extra safe, because Charley had been right about how lethal Redmond was, I crawled a little farther.

I'd seen expert snipers make shots everyone deemed impossible until the target was examined and there were holes in the bull's-eye. Mark Redmond possessed that level of marksmanship. I would never underestimate his proficiency with a firearm again.

On the rainy trail, I pulled out the topo map and unfolded it and turned on my flashlight.

Chloé's ATV path, I saw, climbed steeply out of the valley and over an unmarked hill or series of hills before it skirted Wounded Deer Pond. Then it looped south to pick up the access road near the Stombaughs' sugar shack. It was hardly a shortcut, in other words, and the only reason I could think that the girl had gone that way was because all-terrain vehicles were prohibited on private roads in these townships.

Redmond had designed their lives to avoid any public attention. *Why?*

In my head, I heard him asking me, "You genuinely don't know who I am, do you?"

As if I should have known. As if he had done something that would have gotten his photo on wanted posters and into the database the FBI maintains of its most dangerous fugitives. As if he were a figure of legitimate notoriety instead of an internet ghost.

At the same time, he had somehow passed back and forth across the border at official checkpoints. If Cady was really Chloé, was Mark Redmond using an alias, too? Did he have a passport under his assumed name? And how would a builder of log cabins have obtained such an unforgeable document?

For the moment, I needed to shove these mysteries aside. It was enough that I knew the man to be a murderer. The one question that mattered was where he was headed next.

Moose River Maple Works was the obvious guess. Perhaps too obvious. But what other choice remained to him if he'd lost his transportation and the supplies he would need to reach the crossing?

Redmond was calculating and unpredictable. He might be headed in the opposite direction from the sugarhouse because he could anticipate which way I would choose to go.

He might, he might, he might.

I was in danger of outsmarting myself, I realized.

Most of the people I investigated had the brainpower of an opossum. It had been ages since I was confronted by a criminal whose practical intelligence scared me.

Mark Redmond scared me.

It might have meant losing them, but my only choice was to follow the ATV trail to the sugarhouse. I needed to make contact with the outside world. The Stombaughs' sugar shack offered my best chance at calling down the wrath of Maine law enforcement on the head of Josie's murderer.

And so I returned to the Can-Am. Thankfully, the four-wheeler was still idling away, scissors in the ignition, hood steaming, engulfed in a miasma of exhaust. I flicked on the mismatched headlights and pulled a U-turn, heading back toward Prentiss Pond.

When I relocated the entrance to the ATV trail, I revved the throttle and shot forward beneath the arching branches. The path was so narrow that my arms and shoulders were brushed by wet bushes and I needed to duck at times to keep from getting face-slapped by spruce and fir boughs.

And yet the way was mostly clear. Someone had labored hard with a chain saw and an axe to open up this trail. They must have worked during last week's storm, because the cuts were all new; the severed ends of the branches were still pink.

Had this been another of Redmond's escape routes? I wondered.

If taken by surprise, would he have gathered up "Chloé" and snuck out this way on the Can-Am while the wardens and state police and, hell, border agents, too, wasted time searching the gravel roads?

Or maybe Redmond had cut this path not for himself but as a trap for anyone who might follow him. Stringing piano wire at neck height to behead a pursuer seemed very much the kind of homicidal scheme he would implement.

The danger of getting ahead of my headlights, literally and figuratively, was real.

And yet I found the speed bracing. It sharpened the sting of raindrops against my face. But the sensation energized me, too. I would need to stay alert for whatever the night had in store for me.

"Never mistake motion for action," Hemingway had also written.

Maybe not, but I was glad to be moving again. I was no longer trapped. And action, in this case, was enough.

17

Before I reached Wounded Deer Pond, I encountered my first blowdown. The spruce must have fallen in the present storm. I could see there was no going around it—the understory was too tangled, too dense—except on foot.

Fortunately, the tree was a "little twig of a thing," as Charley might have said: only six inches in diameter. But chopping through the springy trunk with a notched hatchet delayed me a good fifteen minutes. I was glad to have Redmond's neoprene gloves to protect and warm my hands. Even gladder to be moving again.

The rain was slackening from a steady downpour to a fine drizzle. I knew I was getting close to the pond when I saw mist in my head-lights. The night air was warmer than the spring-fed lake, creating fog that filled the bowl of the valley and sent exploratory tentacles up the trails and ravines.

I paused when I reached the flooded shoreline because the path was now submerged by an outlet stream. I idled forward, feeling the mud beneath the surface sucking at my tires. Then the water was over my boots and halfway up my shins, and I was beginning to wonder if I would make it across before the engine conked out. But soon I was climbing again.

Feeling like time was slipping away, I didn't stop until I had crested the last wooded rise above the access road.

The Stombaugh place must be near now. On the flight into Prentiss, we'd seen the smoke from its chimney pipe.

I had an unwarranted sense that I was in the home stretch, that I had won my cross-country race against the footbound Redmonds, when I rounded a turn too fast and nearly collided with a wall of windblown trees. The storm had pushed over the largest of them, a dying fir, which had brought down its smaller neighbors, creating a green barricade.

This time, there was no chopping my way through. The forest was choked with deadfalls, as if giants had played a game of pick-up sticks. And where there weren't fallen trees, there were huge boulders lurking. Carpets of moss concealed ankle-breaking holes between the logs and stones.

I had no option but to abandon the sturdy Can-Am. It had proved a faithful steed.

Circumventing this second blowdown was even more of an ordeal than I'd first imagined. As so often happens in the woods at night, it felt like the trees were malign beings intent on tripping me with their roots and grabbing me with their branches. But eventually, I emerged back onto the path with no more than a dozen new cuts and bruises.

My second-best flashlight had been failing for a while, but it chose the moment I finally stepped onto the trail to give up the ghost. I was left with the brighter Nitecore, an improvement in every way, except that I no longer had a spare.

Soon I detected the odor of burning hardwood on the wind. The low-pressure system that had brought all this new rain was pushing the smoke down as firmly as a hand held flat above a candle.

When I glimpsed the first exterior light, a halogen bulb mounted above a loading dock, I extinguished the Nitecore, not wanting to reveal my presence too soon. I didn't think it was likely that Mark and Chloé had arrived before I had, despite their having the shorter route. But again, I couldn't make assumptions where Redmond was concerned.

Moose River Maple Works looked out of place in this setting: a mostly windowless structure with red clapboards and a steel roof that was steeply pitched on one side. I heard the chugging of its industrial generator and something that sounded like a blower drawing air from inside. The smell of woodsmoke was very strong.

Sugar shacks in Maine range from literal sheds, barely large enough to contain a vat to boil sap, to massive factories that gleam with stainless steel evaporators and air-sucking vents. This modest building fell somewhere in between.

On the side of the building facing the South Branch Road were two entrances: a large rolling gate atop the loading dock and a human-sized door to its left. It occurred to me that the factory's lack of windows might be based on a need for security: no doubt this building stood empty much of the year, and opportunistic break-ins were so frequent in the North Woods that many owners didn't even bother locking their doors.

A single pickup was parked outside: a late-model GMC with a crew cab and an eight-foot bed. Its tires were still wearing their winter chains. And its rear bumper was plastered with stickers displaying a political sensibility that leaned decidedly leftward: the famous COEXIST logo made up of peace signs and ecumenical religious symbols. But also LOVE YOUR MOTHER with an illustration of the earth. And DON'T WORRY BE HIPPIE. I found it hard to square these environmentalist sentiments with the gas guzzler advertising them.

But we live in an age of contradictions.

I devoted a few minutes to scanning the mud around the pickup and the doors for fresh footprints: anything to indicate that the Redmonds had arrived ahead of me. When I found none, I released a long-held breath. I set the hatchet against a wall, not wanting to scare the Stombaughs.

Then I removed my clipped badge from my belt and knocked hard at the side door.

"Game warden," I nearly shouted. I needed to be heard both

above the generator and whatever other industrial machines were whirring and churning inside. "Mr. and Mrs. Stombaugh? Hello?"

There was no answer.

I knocked again and repeated myself word for word, only louder now, and deepening my voice to project what cops call "command presence."

Eventually, the door opened, spilling light as gold as syrup into the darkness.

A man stood firmly in the doorway, showing no signs of fear or caution. I recognized I was dealing with someone truly brave—considering that even I would have been careful, answering a knock at the door on a stormy night, miles from civilization.

From the hippie-dippie bumper stickers, I wouldn't have been surprised if Bob Stombaugh was bearded, with long thinning hair and possibly even a ponytail. But he was, if anything, the opposite of my stereotyped preconception: a ruggedly built man of late middle age, with white hair cropped close to his head, pink complexion, and steel-rimmed glasses. His nose was crooked and flattened as if he might have been a boxer in his youth. If he had been, he'd probably fought as a heavyweight.

He wore a plaid shirt over a white tee tucked into relaxed-fit jeans that were held in place by a two-pronged belt. His boots were low-end Timberlands. At first glance, he didn't appear to be armed.

His gaze ignored the badge I was holding as if he didn't need to verify my identity, as if the only person who might appear at his door on a night this dreary had to be a game warden.

"You're far from home," was all he said.

My throat was raw from vomiting up Redmond's poison. "Farther than you know."

"I am guessing you wouldn't mind getting out of the wet. Come on in and get warm. We've got hot coffee and a few things to eat if you're hungry."

The reason for my visit didn't seem to interest him.

The thought of coffee turned my stomach, but I realized that I was, in fact, famished.

As Stombaugh turned, I saw that I'd been wrong about his not being armed. He had a pistol tucked into his jeans at the six o'clock position—or directly between his ass cheeks.

In my job, you learn to recognize a firearm's make and model from the grip and the hammer (if it has one). Bob's was a Browning Hi-Power: now discontinued but once the favored service weapon of militaries and police forces around the world. This one had walnut grips and a blued frame that, no surprise, looked flawlessly maintained.

The floor that I tracked water and mud across was made of concrete, easy to sweep and mop. The air smelled of a powerful industrial cleaner, some chemical potion heavy with chlorine bleach.

This part of the building was one massive room that contained most of the equipment the Stombaughs needed to reduce raw sap down to grade A maple syrup. There were flue pans and pipes and, of course, the evaporator: a state-of-the art Steam-Away the size of a Toyota hatchback. Fluorescent lights mounted to the beams overhead gave no warmth to the space.

I knew the basics of sugaring—Charley and Ora had always tapped trees—and I'd visited many sugar shacks on my winter and spring patrols. Moose River Maple Works was by far the cleanest and most professional operation I had seen.

We exited the shop floor and entered a break room with a coffee maker, a hot plate on a counter, and a refrigerator humming beside a commercial sink. Bob Stombaugh still hadn't asked my name or why I was there.

"Do you take anything in your coffee?"

"Actually, I'm fine."

"You sure about that? No offense, Warden, but you look wet as a dog."

He poured himself a cup, black. The mug was a blaze orange and emblazoned with the logo of his business.

"Are you alone tonight, Mr. Stombaugh?"

"No, my wife is here. She's using the facilities. You're welcome to clean up when she's done in there. We've got a shower. And soap that will peel off the top layer of your skin. Sugaring is sticky work. I guess you're expecting me to ask what you're doing here, but I already know."

"You do?" I had been running both hands through my wet hair, trying to dry it a little.

"You need to use our radio because there's no reception tonight. You've got to let someone know where you are and that you're safe. You can call me Bob, by the way."

As he sipped from his mug, I noticed that his ears were scarred and a little misshapen.

Definitely a former boxer.

"Is a stranger showing up at your door a regular occurrence?"

"Not regular. But not irregular, either. If you're wondering why haven't I asked your name, it's because I already know who you are, Warden Bowditch."

"Have we met before, sir?"

"I heard Josie on the radio talking with Cady last night. Then we saw the chopper flying in this morning. I expect you all got stranded at the pond and are having trouble calling out. It happens a lot up in that valley. And because you have a wife at home worried about you, Mark loaned you his Can-Am."

He'd spotted my wedding ring when I'd removed the neoprene glove. It was a simple silver band. I still wasn't used to wearing it.

One of the fluorescent bulbs was flickering. It only added to the sense of surreality I was experiencing.

I had a decision to make. Most Mainers are salt-of-the-earth people. Stombaugh had given me no reason to doubt his integrity. And yet he was a self-proclaimed friend of the Redmonds.

"Josie's dead, Bob," I said at last. "That's why I need to use your radio."

He was lifting the mug to his lips as I spoke these words. He kept the cup suspended for a long time. Then he returned it slowly to the stainless steel counter.

"How?"

"Your neighbor, Mark Redmond, poisoned her. Poisoned *us*, I should say—not just Josie but my father-in-law, Warden Charley Stevens, and myself, too. He used a powerful sedative called GHB. Josie Jonson choked to death on her own vomit."

He paused, then shook his square head. "I find what you're telling me hard to believe."

"I saw her die in front of me, sir. I need to report what happened to the state police."

A line appeared in the center of his forehead running down between his eyebrows. "What you're saying makes no sense. Mark and Jo are friends. She's like a grandmother to Cady."

"I don't think he meant for it to happen. He just needed time to make an escape. Call it a terrible accident if you want. The charges will be for the police to decide. You don't strike me as a callous man, Bob. You must understand why it's necessary for me to contact the authorities. I desperately need your help."

His pink complexion was deepening in color. The transformation reminded me of a shellfish boiling in a pot.

"No," he said.

"No what?"

"No, I don't believe you. Let's see that badge of yours again."

As I moved to unclip it from my belt, he reached around his back for the Browning.

Keeping the pistol at waist level, he pulled back the hammer and aimed the barrel dead center at my stomach.

18

I 'm telling the truth, Mr. Stombaugh."

"Like hell he is," came a female voice from the noisy shop floor behind me.

In spite of the gun pointed at my midsection, I turned toward the woman I presumed to be Rose Stombaugh.

"Eyes on me, please," said her husband. "No sudden movements."

It was the first time I'd heard those words uttered outside of a movie or television show. But when it came to extreme situations like this one, people often resorted to expressions they remembered from Hitchcock movies or episodes of *Miami Vice*. We Americans are a people programmed by popular culture.

When Rose Stombaugh finally showed herself in my peripheral vision, I saw that she, too, was toting a firearm. It was also aimed at me.

Not being at liberty to move, I couldn't have told you the make and model of the shotgun, but the thinness of the barrel announced it as a .410 bore, one of the smallest calibers you encounter in the North Woods. The pellets packed into its shells are no bigger than BBs, too light to take down anything but a grouse or a woodcock. Even a snowshoe hare is questionable.

Not that I relished being shot by a .410. A single pellet, no matter its size, is capable of piercing the flesh above the carotid artery. Sever that blood vessel and a minute later, you're dead from exsanguination.

Given rural Maine's general whiteness and her husband's corn-fed complexion, I hadn't expected that Rose Stombaugh might be black. Her hair, held back from her forehead by a bandanna, was reddish and curly, and she had a spray of freckles across her nose that were paler than the rest of her face. There was a gauntness to her features that suggested some recent or chronic illness.

She looked to be a good ten years younger than her husband. And her clothes, while appropriate for work, appeared downright fashionable: her sweater might have been merino, her pants bamboo. Her boots, I saw now, were Blundstones: brown leather Chelseas spotted with sap and scuffed from hard use.

"Your neighbor isn't who you think he is."

"That's what he told us you'd say." She spoke with the charming remnant of a French accent. "Not *you* specifically, but the game warden or police officer who eventually knocked at our door asking about him."

"He killed Josie, Mrs. Stombaugh. I swear I saw it happen."

"Why should we believe you?" Rose said. "You're making this up as an excuse."

"An excuse for what?"

"Paul Renaud is a good man," Bob stated. "I've seen how gentle he is with his daughter. I've seen him tear up after shooting a deer. And you're telling me this kind and sensitive soul is a murderer?"

So he was Paul Renaud now. No longer Mark Redmond.

If he'd shared his real name with the Stombaughs, it meant that he had trusted them to protect a valuable secret. I would have my job cut out for me persuading them that I wasn't their enemy as well as his.

"Call him whatever you want," I said. "But Josie is dead because of what he and Chloé did to us."

The barrel of Rose's shotgun drooped until it was aimed at the floor. "How do you know her name is Chloé?"

They waited for me to answer. But I didn't.

Their not knowing what information I possessed about the Redmonds—or the Renauds, as I needed to think of them—was the only leverage I had.

I heard the big generator growling. Rain beating on the roof. Spilled coffee sizzling on the burner.

"I'm sorry, Warden," Bob said. "But we're going to need to hold you awhile."

"So the Renauds have time to escape to Canada?"

"It's not personal. We understand there will be consequences. We've talked a lot about what would happen if this moment came, Rose and me. Find some rope to tie him up, *ma chère*."

"I have handcuffs on my belt," I said a little too quickly. "You can use them."

"You also have a key to use to escape," added Rose. "Nice try."

"The key is on the key ring in my pocket. I've already been tied up once today and nearly lost the use of my hands." I raised a wrist so they could see the rope burns, bruises, and scabbed skin. "Cops aren't taught some secret way to escape our own cuffs. I'm not Houdini. Don't make them too tight, please."

They seated me on one of the break room chairs, and Bob cuffed my hands behind my back while Rose covered me with the .410. She wasn't afraid of getting the barrel close to my nose.

When it was clear that I was sufficiently restrained, Rose returned to her interrogation.

"How do you know her real name is Chloé?"

One thing I'd learned about lying is you need to commit fully to the falsehood. "Because I know what happened in Canada."

"That's bullshit," said Rose. She looked so frail. Her expensive clothes hung off her as they might a gangly teen. "If they'd been identified, they would have the entire state police after them."

"We weren't positive the Redmonds were Paul and Chloé Renaud. I was working off gossip that's going around Rockwood. It doesn't even qualify as a tip. But I thought I should check it out."

Bob tucked the Browning into his belt again, this time at his side, where he could get at it more easily. He pulled a metal chair across the concrete, took a seat opposite me, and rested his boxer's fists on his knees. The knuckles were bulbous and grotesque with old scars.

"Paul Renaud did what any good father would have done," he said. "He rescued that girl from an unstable, abusive mother. But the law never takes the man's side, not even in Canada. Especially when the mother has someone in her family with money and clout."

Rose Stombaugh jarred me with her next move. She lifted her right hand from the butt of the shotgun and swatted her husband, firmly but lovingly, on the back of his head.

"He's bluffing about what he knows and doesn't know, Robert. And now you've gone and—"

He flushed a coral red. "We're holding him at gunpoint, Rose. We've handcuffed him to a chair. Do you think it matters what he does and doesn't know about Paul and Chloé? What matters is that he sees we're willing to break the law to protect them. I want to explain why. Even if he doesn't have the whole story, he's going to get it as soon as this storm clears and we let him go. I want Warden Bowditch to hear from our lips why we've made the decision to help those poor people."

She clutched her veined hand to her sallow face. "Oh, Robert, my love. You can be such a noble idiot."

"Because I won't apologize for protecting a good man from an unfair accusation?"

"This so-called good man killed your neighbor," I snapped. "Josie told me that you weren't on the best of terms. But I'd think the part about her dying would trouble your consciences a little."

Rose set the shotgun on a side table. The firearm didn't weigh more than a few pounds, but she was clearly exhausted from the burden. "You yourself said it was an accident."

"It doesn't matter, Mrs. Stombaugh. When a person is killed in the commission of another crime, the attorney general brings a charge of felony murder. And by holding me here and keeping me from pursuing them, you will be prosecuted as accomplices to that murder. If you release me and let me use your radio, I'll explain the circumstances to the AG. It would be up to him to bring lesser charges."

"Did Jo suffer?" Bob asked, and there was the faintest tremor in his voice.

"Very much so, yes."

His eyes pleaded with me. "I don't believe Paul would've stood by and watched it happen."

"They were gone by then. He and Chloé had already taken off in the Unimog, leaving us tied to trees in the rain."

"So he didn't realize she was dying," Rose insisted.

After what I'd witnessed and endured, I had no patience with the Stombaughs or with their self-justifying excuses.

"You can't slip someone a dangerous drug and expect they'll just wake up."

Despite my rage, I was inclined to think that the husband at least was a man with a moral compass. As long as there was a chance of talking sense into him, I had decided not to feel for the handcuff key hidden in my belt. I'd need a diversion in any case before I tried picking the lock. Hurrying and dropping the spare key on the floor would be the perfect ending to this day of blunders.

"You have a chance to make this right," I said with all the patience I could muster, "or at least to stop things from getting worse for yourselves and your friends. Because I guarantee you, when the police hear about Josie's murder, both Paul and that little girl will be in danger."

"In danger from the cops, you mean?"

Those bumper stickers on the truck should have warned me how she viewed law enforcement.

Now it was Bob I had offended through my careless words. "If you hurt that little girl . . ."

"Her father is the one putting her in this position."

Rose's mouth tightened into a sneer. "I never used to think the police were fascists. But that love of violence is always just beneath the surface with you cops, isn't it? Have you ever shot anyone, Warden? Have you ever killed a person?"

I could have lied again. But on this subject, I always told the truth because I never wanted to foster denial in myself. "As a matter of fact, I have."

"Then you're a hypocrite."

"The people I killed were trying to kill me."

"People? You admit to killing multiple people? And you think you're in a position to judge Paul Renaud?"

"No, ma'am, I don't. It's not my job to judge anyone. But it *is* my job to apprehend a man I saw kill another human being. The judging will be up to a jury, provided I can bring him—and Chloé—in alive."

Rose spit out her next words: "You disgust me. You hypocritical—"

Before she could finish the sentence, her sunken eyes widened suddenly, her face became shockingly gray. She rushed from the room. A moment later, I heard the bathroom door slam.

Bob rose from his chair as if to go after her, but paused on the threshold.

I perceived a new opening to try. My prior approaches hadn't persuaded them. That much was clear.

"What kind of cancer does Rose have?" I asked.

His dry lips parted. "How did you know she has cancer?"

"She's obviously ill. The weight loss . . ."

"Lymphoma."

"Bob, you need to hear me out. Do you honestly want Rose to spend the time she has left awaiting trial or in prison after being sentenced? I appreciate your defending your friend. But you should think of your wife. What are you willing to do to protect *her*?"

His expression didn't change, but I saw his shoulders sag. He returned to the chair opposite me, removed his glasses, rubbed his eyes, and returned his glasses to the bridge of his crooked nose.

"I know apologies don't mean anything," he said. "I wish we

didn't have to do this to you. I truly do, but maybe when you've heard the truth—instead of the story you might've gotten from the Canada Border Services or the RCMP—you'll understand why my wife and I agreed to help the Paul and Chloé Renaud. All I'm asking is that you hear me out. Are you willing to hear me out?"

What choice did I have?

19

This was the story Bob Stombaugh told me.

He and Rose were from Canada originally, although he'd always had dual citizenship because his mother was from Buffalo. He'd grown up on a farm outside Toronto; his wife was a child of the Montreal suburbs. He'd never attended college or university, but Rose was an honors graduate of McGill. They'd met when she was hiking the Bruce Trail with a former roommate and happened to stop at the farm stand of the dairy he had inherited from his parents and was struggling to keep afloat.

It was important, he stressed, that I understand their history together, his and Rose's.

"I was a man who could only focus on the day's chores and the season ahead. She was already an up-and-coming music journalist, publishing in all the magazines. Rose was the door through which I walked into the wider world. Before she entered my life, I was just a shell of a man, although I didn't know it. How could I, being so ignorant of everything that lay beyond my farm, my church, my village?"

She'd never asked him to sell the farm, but he had. For a while, having married, they had traveled in Europe and the U.S. until Rose had become pregnant. They agreed that they wanted to raise their daughter on a farm since Rose could write anywhere, and Bob, despite all the eye-opening discoveries he'd made in their explorations, had begun to miss the routine that came from living in sync with nature's clock and calendar.

Bob's family had always tapped trees so they'd purchased a sugar bush in the Eastern Townships of Québec. Seven months into her pregnancy, Rose had miscarried. She suffered damage to her uterus that made it impossible to get pregnant again.

"And we'd both wanted children so much," he said. "That was our dream. To have a house full of children."

Rose had suffered from postpartum depression, which ruined their chances to adopt a child when the agencies learned of her multiple hospitalizations. Eventually they saw a syruping business listed for sale in Maine. Hoping for a fresh start, they decided to take advantage of Bob's dual citizenship and move to Jackman.

"It wasn't so much that we wanted a new life," he said, "as Rose wanted our old life back. Those days on the maple farm in Knowlton, you see, were the happiest she'd ever been. You can't recapture joy that way. Life doesn't work like that. We've been content enough here in Jackman the past twelve years. But I think we both knew we were living the shadow of the life we'd wanted and lost."

And then, one day, "Cady Redmond" had driven up to their door on her father's snowmobile.

"That little girl was everything Rose had hoped our daughter would have been if she'd lived—curious, brilliant, tough as a nut. And 'Mark' reminded me of myself when I was a young man, although I could see he had suffered—suffered horribly—and become harder as a result. He and I were both country boys and good with our hands. He helped me repair some storm damage to my sap lines, and I helped him with the cabin when I could. We put in a big cookstove last week."

One mystery explained, I thought.

"When we'd met, Mark had told me they were from Alaska, but being Canadians ourselves, we knew this was a fib. I recognized his accent from when I'd competed out west in the Golden Gloves. But they were such kind people, they must have had a good reason for lying, Rose and I decided."

Then one snowy evening, Mark Redmond—or rather Paul Renaud, as he reintroduced himself—had opened his heart to them.

He and his daughter, Chloé, were from Alberta, although he'd grown up in Chichester, Québec, before his father had moved the whole clan west to live in the Rockies. It was there, working as a cabin builder and outfitter, that he'd met Chloé's mother, Selene. She was the daughter of one of the wealthy families that had made Banff unaffordable, and her parents had been vehemently opposed to her marrying Paul, who would never be able to provide the financial security they thought she deserved.

"Maybe her family's opposition made their romance feel forbidden and exciting. But Paul described their first years together, living in a place he'd built himself outside the national park, as being out of a storybook. Selene gave birth to Chloé a year after they'd eloped, and she'd done most of the girl's homeschooling—Paul never had much use for governments after he completed his military service—until she got pregnant again a few years ago. Their second child was a stillbirth. And Selene began to suffer serious psychiatric problems from the trauma."

She began using, then abusing, antianxiety medications, Paul had told them, and she experienced mood swings that became violent, until one day she pushed Chloé down a staircase in a rage. The girl broke her wrist, but Selene's family persuaded the police that she had tripped and fallen.

Disgusted with his wife's family and determined to protect his daughter, Paul had filed for divorce. But distrust in the system proved prescient. Bankrolled by her parents, Selene fought for and won full custody of Chloé.

"'They arranged it so I couldn't even see her on my own,' Paul told me. 'My visits had to be supervised by a social worker. It was as if I, who'd never put a hand on my daughter, were the dangerous one.'"

When he showed up for one of his scheduled appointments and saw that Chloé, in distress, had begun cutting herself, he realized he had to take drastic action. He abducted his daughter from her grandparents' house and spirited her away east. He had no plan except to stay ahead of the authorities and hide from anyone who might report them to the RCMP. They'd lived in the woods in Ontario and then New Brunswick before a chance meeting with Josie Jonson had brought them to Maine.

I'd wanted to interrupt him half a dozen times as he'd recounted Renaud's tale of woe. But somehow I held my tongue.

"And you believed this fantasy?" I said at last.

Bob Stombaugh reacted as if he'd been punched. I had been so quiet and attentive. He interpreted my silence as meaning that he was convincing me of the righteousness of Renaud's cause.

"Of course we believed it," Bob sputtered. "We saw what a caring father he was. Their relationship wasn't an act! Any person with open eyes could see Paul would give his life for that girl."

I let my head drop and gave it a weary shake. "You two are so gullible."

"What? How?"

"She's still cutting herself, Bob. I saw the wounds on her arm, and they were fresh. If she feels safe living this fairy-tale existence with her woodcutter father, why is she still injuring herself?"

He brought one of his big hands up to his mouth and clutched at his lips and jaw. When he took it took it away, his palm shined with saliva. "I haven't seen any cuts."

"When they arrive, ask her to roll up her sleeves."

"Bob?" came Rose's quavery voice. She'd left the bathroom and crept up behind me without my hearing her above the industrial racket. "What have you told him, Bob?"

Blinking, he looked past me to the door where his wife leaned unsteadily against the frame. "The truth."

"But why?"

"I thought if he knew all the facts—"

"The facts." I tried not to let my disdain for these credulous people get the better of me. "Do you mean the fact that Selene allegedly suffered a stillbirth that mirrors what happened to you, Rose?"

She staggered into my peripheral vision again, looking as wan and shaky as she had when she'd gone running for the toilet.

Bob rose so fast from his chair that it tipped over. "How dare you insult my wife!"

Rose held up a trembling hand. "I want to hear what he has to say, Robert."

For the first time since Bob Stombaugh had pulled a pistol on me, I sensed I might have a chance to get through to them.

"You said Paul Renaud told you this story after you'd known him a while. He didn't come out with it right away."

"He didn't trust us yet. You can hardly blame him for being careful. For all he knew, we might—"

"Be quiet, Robert," said his wife, leaning against the counter as if remaining upright in this moment might be a problem. "Let him speak."

"Before he told you how and why he became a fugitive, did he ever ask you about your own lives?"

"He didn't grill us if that's what you're suggesting," said Bob.

"That's because he didn't need to. I've known you for less than an hour, and you thought it necessary to give me your life story. You had to preface your defense of Renaud with how you and Rose fell in love. You felt compelled to share the tragedy you suffered and how you came to buy this maple business in the Maine woods."

"What are you getting at?" Rose asked. "What are you implying?"

"Paul Renaud paid close attention to your emotions as you told him about yourselves. Then he tailored his story so that you would be receptive to it. He fed you the tale you wanted to hear. But because you were blind to your own weak spots, you accepted his bullshit without question."

Bob Stombaugh cleared his throat once, then twice. "That's not true. Rose is an intelligent woman. She wouldn't accept . . ."

His eyes sought out his wife's face, but she looked dazed, stricken. I knew she was finally hearing me. But she was struggling to accept the importance of what I was trying to tell her.

"What are you saying, Warden?"

"What I'm saying is, why did he tell you his story at all?"

"Because he trusted us," Bob blurted out.

"Because he knew he might need allies in Maine he could depend upon if the shit hit the fan. He realized there was a chance he would be recognized by a Canadian passing through Jackman or Greenville. Or that some local busybody would get suspicious and decide to spend hours poring over the internet. Or that Josie herself might begin to wonder why he was so determined to remain anonymous."

Now they both looked shocked and wounded.

Even having been held at gunpoint, even having been handcuffed, I felt bad for them. The Stombaughs struck me as decent people, mostly. And I had just inflicted horrible pain on them.

"I'm sorry, but Paul Renaud has been playing you for suckers. You two have never been his friends. You were always a couple of dupes he might need on a night like this."

My timing has never been great. It was especially bad now. No sooner had I spoken these words than there was a banging at the door.

"You can't let him in," I said from the chair. "He killed Josie. He tried to kill me. If you don't uncuff me, there's going to be another murder."

A small voice called through the rain-smeared window of the break room. "Bob? Rose? It's Chloé. Can you hear me?"

I had run out of time. I began fiddling with my fingers for the handcuff key hidden in my belt.

Bob appealed to his wife. "What should we do, Rose? What should we do?"

Her answer didn't matter because the banging stopped.

136

In that same instant, my fingertips touched the handcuff key hidden in its leather seam.

Then, above the din of the machines, we heard Paul Renaud's raised voice call from the factory floor. "Hello? Is everyone all right in here?"

20

Rose whispered to her husband: "You *gave* him a key?"

"Maybe. I might have given him one in case they needed something while we were in Jackman."

"Oh, *cher*," she said softly. "*Espèce de noble idiot.*"

"Bob? Rose? Anyone home?"

This was the first time, in our brief acquaintance, when I would have described Renaud's voice as sounding friendly.

Drenched and muddy with bits of vegetation clinging to his clothes, he appeared on the threshold just as I managed to pinch the handcuff key with the tips of my fingers. He'd thrown back his hood, and his face shone with rain but showed no signs of exertion. He and his daughter had covered something like three miles in a storm to reach this place, but he wasn't even winded.

"I saw you had a visitor," he said, locking gazes with mine. "His tracks were all over the yard."

There was a minor burn along his jawline from that flare I'd shot at him. It gave me some small satisfaction.

"Fuck you," I said.

"Thank you for restraining him," he said, then turned a concerned yet benign face to the Stombaughs, taking in Rose first, then Bob. "How long has he been here?"

I clutched the handcuff key in my fist as if my life depended on it because I was certain it did.

Rose's voice came out as an uncharacteristic warble. "Not long."

Renaud appraised her with calculating eyes. He'd heard how she'd forced the words out.

"I'm so sorry it came to this. What has he been telling you?"

I needed time, I realized. Ten seconds to get free of the cuffs. Another ten seconds to grab one of the Stombaughs' firearms.

I needed more than time. I also needed a distraction.

Chloé's voice echoed from the other room. "Papa, I need to use the washroom."

"You go ahead, chickpea."

Bob Stombaugh wasn't going to make my life easier. He lowered his tone as if to protect the girl even though she was no longer in danger of overhearing. "He said Josie is dead, Paul."

Renaud reacted with an expression of pain. I couldn't tell if the response was genuine or another mask he kept in his bag of faces.

"What? How?"

"He says you poisoned her."

"We didn't poison them, we *sedated* them. It was our only chance of getting away, Bob. I can assure you that Josie was fine—she was asleep—when we left."

Did I detect an undertone of uncertainty? He must have remembered my pleading with him to check on his unconscious client. He must have recalled his own readiness to shrug off my warnings about her condition.

"You missed her choking to death on her own vomit, *Renaud*."

"You're lying."

"Why would I lie about that?"

"To get Bob and Rose on your side." He turned with a grin to the wife. "*Did* he get you on his side?"

She managed to put some heat in her reply. "If he did, he wouldn't be handcuffed."

"And yet you told him our story. You gave him our names. Why would you have done that?"

I followed Renaud with my eyes only, not wanting to draw his attention.

"He already knows who you are," Bob Stombaugh said, cementing his place as the worst liar I had ever met.

"He *doesn't* know who we are, though." Renaud reached slowly across his midsection as if to draw his revolver. Instead, he pretended to scratch at an itch to the left of his belly button. But the gesture sufficed to make the threat. "When they showed up at the cabin, all he had were vague suspicions. He tried to interrogate me, but the more questions he asked, the clearer it became that he was grasping for information he didn't possess. So why did you tell him about us, Bob?"

"Well, I guess . . ." Stombaugh indicated the carafe on the machine across the room. "Can I get you some coffee, Paul? I just made that pot."

"Why did you tell him?"

I would need to keep Renaud's focus off me, which meant sitting quietly. When he glanced at me, I tried to appear helpless and frustrated. I couldn't give him a reason to suspect I might have a plan.

"It wasn't Rose—she was in the other room," Bob said. "I thought that if the warden only understood the truth, he might let you go. You told us how Selene and her family fooled the authorities. Maybe I was naive—"

Try as he might, Renaud couldn't suppress his disdain. He usually possessed too much self-control for such displays of emotion.

"I made a mistake, OK?" Bob sounded frightened now, and that wasn't a good thing. Despite having forty pounds on his "friend" and scars on his nose and hands indicating he knew how to hold his own in a fight, he was rattled by the younger man.

Rose broke in: "It doesn't matter, Paul. He's handcuffed. He's not going anywhere."

"He was tied up when I left him," said Renaud wryly. "I didn't think he was going anywhere then, either. Less than an hour later, he was firing flares at us while we tried to cross Prentiss Stream. He forced us into the water. We lost the Unimog and all our supplies."

"You know you're welcome to anything…" Rose said, her voice as unsteady as her husband's.

"Papa? What's that man doing here?"

Chloé Renaud circled behind her father, keeping his body between hers and mine like a protective barrier.

"Warden Bowditch escaped, chickpea. I guess you need to keep practicing your knots."

"He couldn't have," she said, her mouth tightening. "I double-checked them. I *triple*-checked them."

"Well, somehow, the warden got free, Chloé. How he did it doesn't matter right now. What matters is he's been telling lies about us to Bob and Rose. He's been trying to turn our friends against us."

"What lies?"

I saw the opening I had been waiting for.

I practically barked the words. "Josie is dead, Chloé."

A tremor ran through her from head to toe. "No."

Renaud took a threatening step toward me, but he stopped lest he give himself away, once and for all, in front of the Stombaughs.

"I saw her choke to death," I said. "When I got loose, I felt for a pulse, but she was dead. Charley and I had to carry her body into the cabin to get it out of the rain."

It tortured me to be so cruel to a little girl. But it was the only way to get free. I needed to provoke her father.

"No."

"Those drugs your papa put in the coffee killed her."

"No," she said, the vowel rising to a scream.

Without a word, Paul Renaud slapped me hard in the side of the neck.

People who haven't been in fights think punches must hurt the most. Bone on bone, bone on cartilage, bone on muscle—those impacts can be agonizing if you're on the receiving end. But an open-handed blow delivered by someone trained in combat can be much more painful. And if the attacker also happens to know the location of pressure points, he can inflict more damage than a ring-trained pugilist like Bob Stombaugh.

Renaud missed the nerve bundle beneath my jawline, but the force of his blow knocked the metal chair over on its side, taking me along with it. My head struck the concrete, just above the temple. How I managed to hang on to the key I will never understand. But within seconds of finding myself on the floor, I knew I had the advantage.

Chloé, meanwhile, was melting down. She was hugging herself so hard it looked like she was trying to squeeze the life from her small body.

"She's not dead, she's not dead, she's not dead."

Her father dropped to one knee, his back to me, to embrace his daughter.

"No, she's not," Renaud was saying soothingly. "The man is lying. The police always lie. How many times have I told you that?"

No one—not the Renauds, not the Stombaughs—was watching me now. The spectacle Chloé was making had consumed everyone's attention the same way fire sucks oxygen from a room.

I fitted the key into the handcuff and heard it click.

In spite of everything, Renaud somehow did, too.

He began turning his head in my direction, but not before I'd kicked my chair toward his calves. The blow caused him to stumble into his daughter. As he tripped, I lunged for the pistol in Bob's belt before falling back to the floor.

Trailing the handcuffs from my left wrist, I chambered a round in the Browning and brought the sites up as Paul Renaud yanked his own weapon from its holster.

"Drop it! Drop it, Renaud, or I swear I will kill you!"

I lay on my back on the concrete with my knees bent and my back arched. I aimed between my legs at the fugitive. He froze when he realized I was in position for a clean head shot.

In the meantime, the Stombaughs had shrunk away from us, husband pulling wife aside with a strong arm around her shoulders.

I was aware of Rose losing her balance. But with all his farmer's strength, Bob kept his sick and suffering wife from falling.

My hands were as steady as could be. "Drop the gun, Renaud, or so help me—"

"What?" he said sharply. "What will you do?"

Even as he asked the question, he moved the barrel of the Colt. He turned it ever so slightly—but not in my direction. Instead, the desperate man aimed at his daughter's neck, just below her chin.

21

It was Bob, of all of us, who found his words first. "What—what are you doing, Paul?"

Chloé had gone rigid: stiff as a board, as the saying goes. She looked terrified. This, I was certain, was not one of their rehearsed stunts.

Watching me for any hint of movement, Renaud pressed the revolver into the V of the girl's jaw. Not hard, not painfully. He only wanted to demonstrate that he would not hesitate. "I think it's clear what I'm doing."

The threat he was making against his own daughter had startled me, but it hadn't caused me to lose my aim. I had his head squarely in view. But my thoughts and emotions were all ajumble.

"Drop it," I said again.

"No, I won't."

"If you don't drop the weapon . . ."

"I'll kill her, Mike. So help me God, I will. You might think that if you hit me in the medulla oblongata, I'll be dead before I can squeeze the trigger, but are you sure you can hit me there? Are you sure, if you do, that I wouldn't get off a round on my way to the floor?"

"You wouldn't kill her." My mouth had gone suddenly cottony. "You love her. You said protecting her is all you've ever done."

Now his voice rose to a shout. It was the first time I'd heard him at this register. "What do you think I am doing?"

I wanted to get to my feet but was afraid if I budged, I would either spook Renaud into firing or provide him with an opening to turn the Colt on me.

"Papa?"

"Be still, chickpea. The warden isn't going to shoot me."

"But, Papa . . ."

A urine stain appeared as a creeping line in the fabric of her pants before it dripped around her boots in a spreading puddle. She definitely wasn't acting. She couldn't possibly be acting.

"It's all right," he said in a kindly whisper. "I know, I know. You don't have to apologize for losing control. It's natural when you're afraid. But your papa is here to protect you from this evil man. Neither of us is going to die."

Keeping the revolver pointed at his child, he maneuvered himself to her side.

The index finger of my right hand applied steady pressure to the trigger. What was the pull of the Browning Hi-Power out of the box? I didn't have the slightest idea, but an ounce more might have caused the gun to fire. And I had to take seriously what he'd said: no matter what damage my bullet did to his brain, a reflex might cause his finger to jerk and send a .357 Magnum round through his little girl's head.

"You're not going to murder your own daughter," I said, trying my best to sound certain on this point.

"I won't let her be handed over to a system designed to destroy her. I will absolutely take her life. It would be an act of mercy."

Rose found her voice, however quavery. "Please, Paul. You have to surrender."

"It's not about me," he said. "It's never been about me."

Now it was Bob's turn. "I know you, Paul, and you're not a murderer."

"Not yet. Not unless the warden forces me to become one."

It was a wildly insane claim. He'd killed Josie Jonson mere hours before. He was the very definition of a murderer.

"Don't put this on me, Renaud. You're the one with the choice to make. And you know in your heart what the right one is."

He smiled again, that knowing, slightly rueful smile that was part of his practiced repertoire of expressions. "Yes, I do know what the right choice is, but it's not the one you think."

The coffee maker had begun to scorch the bottom of the near-empty carafe, filling the room with an acrid smell that overwhelmed even the powerful chemicals the Stombaughs had been using to clean their machines.

"Put the gun down. I won't ask again."

"So shoot me, then." Now he dug the barrel into Chloé's neck. She squeezed her eyes shut. Tears gushed down her angular face. She had never looked smaller or more vulnerable than at that moment. "I dare you. Get it over with. I'd welcome an end to our suffering."

He really is a zealot.

Game wardens, even game warden investigators, receive very little training in dealing with hostage takers. Call the state police if possible is what we're taught. Don't take on a responsibility for which you are unprepared, intellectually or emotionally.

But sooner or later, every cop finds themselves in a situation where an individual is making threats, against themselves or others. And often there is no time to call for backup. So you try to defuse the situation as best you can. You use the subject's first name to establish a rapport; you speak calmly but firmly as you might with a child having a tantrum. But by no means must you sound condescending. You give up meaningless things as part of the negotiation to create a feeling of obligation to reciprocate on the part of the hostage taker. You ask questions to find out what the person really wants in order to make a deal.

But what do you do when the hostage taker has gone all in and pushed his chips again to the center of the table?

I had no idea.

Renaud, in his swing from wild shouting to scary calm, had

convinced me he was ready to die. He had convinced me, too, he would take Chloé with him into the dark beyond.

Fuck.

He had begun shuffling sideways, edging around the room. In doing so, he compelled me to my feet. I watched him through the rear sights of the Browning.

"Please, please, please," Rose was mumbling under her breath, the way an old parishioner might recite her rosary.

"You're not leaving," I said. "This is the end of the line."

"That's up to you, Mike. But what are you really willing to risk here? Keep in mind Bob and Rose are witnesses. They'll testify to your negligence: how you failed to save Chloé."

I would have grinned if I had it in me. "If you knew me at all, you'd understand that threatening my career is no way to persuade me. I'd throw my job away without hesitation for your daughter. I'd throw away my life, too. You're not the only one here who's prepared to die."

Renaud paused.

He'd thought he was dealing with another easy-to-manipulate cop. He'd managed to drug me once, but I had proven more resilient and persistent than he'd anticipated. I'd shown ingenuity in commandeering his ATV and ambushing him at the bridge. Because of me, his Unimog had been swept away by the flood. I had even managed to reach the sugarhouse before he had.

He extended an open palm toward the Stombaughs, huddled in the corner. "Toss me your keys, Bob."

"No," I said sharply. "Don't do it, Stombaugh."

"But if he hurts her . . ."

"He won't."

"But he will!" said Rose, on the verge of tears. "Can't you see he's serious? We don't have any choice."

Bob Stombaugh dug a big hand into his pocket and came up with the key fob and ring. I barked at him to stop, but he swung his arm underhanded, and the keys arced across the room. Paul caught them with ease. The man was a natural athlete, at home in his own body.

"I'm going to take your satellite phone, too," he said.

I should have realized the Stombaughs owned one of those miraculous devices. In such a remote township, they never would have trusted their safety entirely to a two-way radio.

I followed Renaud as he backed his daughter across the gray factory floor. I maintained a distance of ten feet the whole time. No more, no less.

He'd managed, during the millisecond when I'd been watching the keys flying through the air, to move the gun to her temple. The hollow-point bullet would pierce her skull and rip a mushrooming hole through the frontal lobe of her brain before it exited.

I kept looking for an angle, a shot I could take that would safely bring down Paul Renaud before he could terminate his daughter's existence. But after having felt like a gambler all day, I seemed to have reached my risk threshold. I was unprepared to take the big bet.

I'd seen dead children in my job. Too many dead children. Drowned, crushed, strangled, shot, and burned. But I'd never witnessed the murder of one in real time.

Renaud had been ruthless enough to awaken that fear in me, and in doing so, he'd shaken my resolve.

Without turning, I sensed that the Stombaughs had approached the door to the break room. They felt compelled to watch the confrontation. But I couldn't blame them for not wanting a close-up view of what might yet become a bloody slaughter.

Again, Renaud was staring across our metaphorical table into my eyes and, with a seven-deuce hand, had managed to bluff me into folding.

"Put the pistol down on the evaporator." He was testing to see if he could push me further.

"No fucking way."

His eyes wrinkled at the corners, and he gave a nod, as if to indicate, *Hey, it was worth a try.*

Then, having reached the desk where the Stombaughs kept their two-way radio, he stopped.

"Chloé, I want you to pick up the radio and smash it as hard as you can onto the floor. Understand? You need to destroy it, chickpea. If you don't, the warden will call for backup and we won't make it out of the woods alive."

"I understand, Papa." She sounded almost agreeable now, as if her fear was passing.

Young and scared as she was, she was smart enough to recognize that her father was near to getting them out. No doubt she was terrified, but she looked almost smug as she lifted the Midland and swung it overhead as if smashing some living thing, a turtle, to death. The plastic casing shattered across the concrete.

"Good girl. Now take the sat phone. You'll find it in the top drawer of the desk."

When she'd located the handheld device, exactly where her father had said it would be, she pressed it to her chest. I recognized the model, if not the make. It was a top-of-the-line Beam Iridium. The Stombaughs had been willing to pay a premium for a dependable communicator they could trust in bad weather and worse terrain.

Meanwhile, I had only my personal iPhone that Renaud had failed to find in my rucksack and which had failed to find a signal since we'd departed Jackman airspace.

What can I do to stop them? There's got to be something.

Shoot out a tire—hopefully more than one tire—before they could race away? He could travel a good distance on his flats if he were willing to utterly destroy the rims of the Stombaughs' truck.

Renaud reached behind his back for the doorknob, twisted, and pulled. A damp gust of air entered as if it had been waiting miserably on the doorstep to be let in.

Before he stepped outside, Chloé tucked against him, the Colt pressed to her temple, he reached for the wall and hit all the lights.

The room was plunged into sudden if not total darkness. The soulless luminescence from the break room stretched across the factory floor, and I saw my own shadow. Then Chloé pulled the door shut.

Fuck.

I rushed across the cavernous room and caught hold of the doorknob. But as soon as I began to twist it, there was a burst of gunfire. The shots were terrifically loud and created bumps in the door where the bullets almost penetrated the metal. They could have come from Paul's Colt, or they could have come from the SIG P226 semiauto that Chloé had taken from me. Both weapons fired heavy-hitting rounds.

But I'd spent enough time at the range to recognize the report of my service weapon. The recognition left me reeling. A hostage to her insane father moments before, Chloé Renaud was now providing suppressing fire while her dad got the truck started.

He'd been ready to end her life with one shot. Now she was an active and willing participant in their escape. If I lived to be Charley's age, I would never understand the psychodynamics of brainwashing.

Keeping clear of the smaller door, I lunged at the glowing console beside the loading dock and pushed the top yellow button. At once, the overhead winch began to pull the segmented door upward on its rails. A bullet struck the edge of the dock and caromed into the room, hitting nothing of consequence.

Chloé's attention was divided. She had to swing the pistol back and forth between the two doors, unsure of which one I would use. And as good a shot as she might be, she was too young and inexperienced to make snap decisions. There is a vast gulf between shooting at a target and firing hollow points at a human being.

Through the growing gap between the loading dock and the rising door, I heard the truck engine roar to life.

And then Renaud shouted, "Get in the bed, Chloé! Get in and keep shooting. You need to cover us. He won't fire on the truck if he's afraid of hitting you."

For once, Paul Renaud was wrong about me.

He was mistaken about the limits to which I would go to stop him.

I wasn't the best shot in the Maine Warden Service. Not by a mile. But I was above average with handguns, if not rifles, and I had the advantage of having survived real-life firefights.

When the next of Chloé's bullets struck the side door, I threw myself flat on the loading dock, extended my arms, and drew a bead on the left rear tire. I had a vector on the sidewall. My first round pierced the rubber between the tread and the hubcap.

As soon as he realized what was happening, Renaud fishtailed the vehicle. Hitting the tires side-on would render them unfixable. The sudden jerk caused Chloé to tumble in the bed. She would be unable to shoot at me until she regained her balance.

I had one more shot, this time on the right rear tire. I lined up the sights of the Browning on the wheel as it spun mud into the air.

I squeezed the trigger.

I missed.

22

I found the Stombaughs embracing in the anemic glow of the break room. Rose was sobbing on her husband's shoulder while he rubbed his hand up and down her spine mechanically.

"We couldn't have known," he said into her ear. "He seemed like such a good man."

"But Chloé . . ."

"I know, I know."

In the excitement, I had nearly forgotten the handcuff dangling from my left wrist. "You don't have another satellite phone, I'm guessing?"

"Just our personal cells—but you won't get reception until you reach the Golden Road, maybe not even then in this weather."

"I'll take the phones, anyway. What about a spare radio?"

"There's a mobile in the truck!" Rose seemed not to understand that this did me no good at all.

I accepted their phones and did my best to memorize the passcodes.

"I need to get after them," I said. "Do you have another vehicle here? An ATV? A dirt bike? Anything?"

Bob raised his head as if it were as heavy as a bowling ball. He blinked at me through his wire spectacles. "We towed the Polarises into town the last time we were here. That truck was our only way out."

I stooped and picked up the handcuff key where I'd dropped it. I opened the lock and returned the cuffs to the sheath on my belt. Then I slid the key back into its seam in my belt. I'd learned not to toss items willy-nilly into my pockets. Tools needed to be where they belonged, so I could find them without having to test my memory.

My wrists looked like an iguana had been chewing on them. I would definitely be carrying new scars from this night.

"What about a chain saw?" I asked.

Bob seemed under the influence of some pharmacy drug whose side effect was drowsiness. "Well, yes. We have several."

"Then I need you to help me, Bob. We've got to clear a blowdown a hundred feet up the Wounded Deer Trail. I had to leave Renaud's Can-Am there. I might need a pair of scissors, too."

"Scissors?"

"And spare mags for this Browning? I'm taking the pistol—and the shotgun, too. I don't suppose you have other firearms here."

"Just the .22 in the truck."

Gray-faced Rose Stombaugh touched the hollow beneath one of her cheekbones. "You're not going to arrest us, Mike?"

"Me? No. But the state police will eventually. Renaud played you, but you were still accessories. I'm not tying you up, either. I'm not particularly worried about you going anywhere."

"Thank you." Bob smiled and seemed like he might be preparing to embrace me. I dearly hoped he didn't try.

"I'm not finished," I said. "I'm not promising anything. But if you tell the responding officers what happened tonight—and by that, I mean *everything* that happened—I might put in a good word for you with the attorney general's office. It's going to depend on how things play out from here. If this continues to go south, all bets are off—especially if something happens to that kid."

"We understand." Rose dabbed at her eyes with a paper towel.

I meant what I had said, but I couldn't have cared less about the Stombaughs, about their suffering or their guilty consciences. I needed Bob, with his farmer's strength and his boxer's hands, to help me clear a path, and beyond that, these gullible people were of no use to me.

The light rain had become a cold, all-permeating mist. It took nineteen minutes to break down the fir that was blocking the ATV trail and to prune the widowmakers it had created as it had toppled across the path.

I struggled to replicate Charley's feat restarting the Can-Am. He'd warned me that using the scissors blade could wreck the ignition. I was genuinely shocked when the engine finally turned over. I doubted I would be able to pull off this stunt a third time.

My last sight of Bob Stombaugh was of him holding his chain saw carelessly, with the end brushing the ground.

"I want to apologize," he said, extending a hand, which I refused to shake.

"Save it."

"We were such fools to be taken in. Paul might have killed you tonight."

"He still might kill me," I said. "But at least you and your wife won't be there to see it."

And with that, I shifted gears. I felt the Can-Am lurch forward like a racehorse when the gate opens. And once again, I was on the move.

I had forgotten about the trippy effect the mismatched headlights made against the darkness. I had to be careful lest I veer reflexively in the direction of the brighter one.

But at least I had a gravel road beneath my wheels and tracks in the mud to follow. The state of the pickup's deflated left tire soon showed itself: parallel gouges from driving on the rim. Continuing without replacing the tire would destroy the wheel eventually, but the fugitive was in too much of a hurry to take the extra minutes to put on a spare. He wanted to put as much distance between himself and pursuit as possible.

Renaud had to know I would be after him.

Even if he had no idea that I'd found a way through the obstacle that had blocked my way, he could no longer doubt my determination. If I were him, I would be glued to my rearview mirror because I would understand that the man chasing me was relentless.

And armed now, as well.

I liked to think Paul Renaud might be feeling fear, but the part of my brain that wasn't tripping on adrenaline understood that I was merely projecting my own wishes. He hadn't survived this long by letting emotions cloud his thinking. He might be having second thoughts about me as an adversary, but he was as dangerous as ever. He wouldn't make the mistake of underestimating a Maine game warden again.

He also had to know, too, that I would be gaining confidence the longer the chase went. It occurred to me that he might even use my proven boldness against me.

I braked hard and skidded on a slippery carpet of dead leaves.

I had been flying along so fast I might have missed warning signs. He might, for instance, have let his daughter out of the truck. Setting an ambush remained a smart move even if he'd set the same trap before. Who was to say that his daughter wasn't crouched in the puckerbrush, waiting with my own handgun to pot-shoot me as I came screaming along in mad pursuit?

Was Chloé capable of that?

Could her father trust that she would be capable?

I had no insight into that strange, tormented child who had shown flashes of both kindness and rage.

Idling forward, watching the road for a sign to indicate she might have hopped out, I pictured her in the sugarhouse. Shocked, terrified, and confused, she had believed her beloved papa might kill her. Her fear hadn't been an act like the one she'd performed at Josie's cabin. Chloé Renaud had known her dad was deadly serious.

The man was mad. That much I understood. But his insane fears had a peculiar focus.

What was it he'd said to me?

"I won't let her be handed over to a system designed to destroy her. I will absolutely take her life. It would be an act of mercy."
An act of mercy . . .

If there was any truth to the stories he told about his wife, shouldn't he have said something instead about refusing to return his daughter into the custody of a mentally unbalanced woman?

This image he'd presented as a loving, protective father was premised on his being the undeserving victim of a rigged divorce. The corrupt Canadian authorities had placed the girl with a dangerous, unstable addict. What decent man, in the same position, wouldn't risk everything to rescue his daughter from such a hell? But there was something more going on here that I couldn't figure out—assuming I could trust anything he'd said at all about his life.

The rain was picking up again as a fresh phalanx of heavy clouds advanced over the mountains from the west. The mist hardened into a drizzle. Then it began to truly pour.

The bulb in the left headlight was almost dead. I might have been mounted astride a cyclops. Not wearing a helmet, I found myself blinking constantly or peering between clenched lids at the illuminated cone revealed by my monocular headlight.

Between the potholes and washouts, the ungraded road had already been difficult to read, especially at the breakneck speed at which I was traveling. The tire tracks disappeared for stretches where they crossed sandy patches and bare rock. Now they were melting away altogether.

I leaned over the handlebars and considered my options. There was nothing to do but keep going.

23

Skidder trails branched off from the main road, climbing up into the high timber. Some of these narrow cuts led to cul-de-sacs where the loggers dug for gravel to repair their roads or parked their heavy machinery out of sight. I passed turnoff after turnoff. There were too many avenues to explore. The Renauds might have been hiding down any one of those dead ends: engine off, lights extinguished, waiting for me to pass.

Soon I came to Penobscot Brook, the stream that flowed out of the lake of the same name. It, too, was overflowing its banks, carrying flotsam and jetsam along on coffee-colored rapids. I stopped at the bridge to inspect the planks for scattered sand or gouges in the wood: any indication that a partly disabled GMC pickup had passed this way.

But if there had ever been signs to mark the Renauds' passage, the cloudburst had erased them. Pacing along the splintery boards, I began to doubt myself. I worried that I had gone too far.

The time had come for me to refocus. It wasn't enough just to mindlessly follow tire tracks. I needed to take a minute to use the knowledge I'd gained to anticipate where he might be headed.

Putting the ATV into neutral, I engaged the foot-activated parking brake.

I tried Bob's phone first, holding it up to the sky. I got a face full of mist, but no signal.

I tried Rose's next. Hers was just as useless and nearly out of juice. Lastly, I tried my iPhone. Again, nothing.

I pulled out Chloé's topo map and unfolded it.

I hadn't looked at the north side of the chart, but I did notice now where the South Branch Road ultimately intersected with Maine's lumbering highway, the famed Golden Road. The thoroughfare was privately owned and maintained by timber companies and land-owners who leased their woodlots to logging concerns. The historic road stretched nearly a hundred miles westward from the shadow of Mount Katahdin, through nature preserves and industrial forest-land, before it ended at the Canadian checkpoint at Saint-Zacharie.

The Warden Service kept a cabin near the crossing called Bound-ary Cottage. Under normal circumstances, I could have found help there from the resident warden. But my bureau, like most law en-forcement agencies across the nation, was having trouble hiring good people, and the position was currently unfilled.

Why was I even assuming that Renaud would head to an official border checkpoint? How would he explain to the agents of the Ser-vices frontaliers why he and his daughter were trying to cross into Canada in bad weather at an ungodly hour and behind the wheel of another man's truck (which also happened to be lacking a rear tire)?

I already suspected he might have accomplices in the Canada Bor-der Services Agency—and maybe in the U.S. Customs and Border Protection—but he would have needed to have paid off the entire district office to guarantee safe passage. Not only was that impossi-ble, knowing the integrity of those officers, but where would he have come up with the money to bribe even a single agent, let alone many?

There was a brazenness to Paul Renaud's behavior that I couldn't crack. He'd been keeping a low profile at Prentiss Pond, and yet he had traveled widely for supplies, Josie had said. He seemed less like a man hiding than one who believed he would not—or could not—be caught.

I was missing key elements to his story, and without them, there were limits to my ability to predict where he might go.

If only the North Woods weren't so vast. I dragged my gloved finger across the disintegrating topo map. Green contour lines indicated changes in elevation: hills and mountains. Blue blobs marked lakes and ponds.

Again I had to remember Renaud was a man who chose his words carefully. He'd been desperate to find the keys to Josie's Raven so he could fly the helicopter to his "evac route."

His plan hadn't been to fly it across the mountains. He would have known that, whatever his connections, a private aircraft crossing into Canada would have attracted attention from any number of agencies.

Instead his words suggested that he'd hoped to pilot the R44 to the beginning of a path he could follow from one nation to the next.

I moved my light across the top of the map, lingering at the expanse of Penobscot Lake. Seasonal camps and cottages were marked as black squares on the water. Most of them would still be shuttered because of the ferocity of spring storms and the near impassability of the roads. But a few of these cabins might contain provisions, hand tools, perhaps even modes of transport of use to a fleeing criminal.

The international boundary passed near the western shore of Penobscot Lake. By land, the portage into Canada was less than a quarter of a mile. But a small boat could bring you even closer by following a tributary stream to the doorstep of Québec.

A rough road, very nearly a jeep trail, split off the South Branch and darted northwest to the outlet of Penobscot Lake. The map showed a concrete spillway where Penobscot Brook came rushing through and a backcountry campsite above the dam. There was something else as well. Small and faint: a red dot made by the tentative touch of a permanent marker. The same pen Chloé Renaud had used to claim the other landmarks of her woodland domain.

A tiny red dot.

Barely the trace of a dot.

I couldn't know what it indicated. Maybe Chloé and her dad had camped at the spillway in the fall and enjoyed a memorable afternoon of fishing in the splash pools below. Maybe her hand had hesitated over this place on the map because, upon reflection, the fishing hadn't been that good, and the dam was unworthy of being added to her atlas of personally significant places.

But as I scanned the chart for other landmarks, I found nothing else to guide me.

My instinct told me Penobscot Lake was my best bet.

I backtracked past one westward-heading trail, then another—growing increasingly pissed at myself for having been deceived so easily—until I finally saw the sign I was searching for.

Having driven a quarter mile toward the Golden Road, Renaud had stopped on an exposed ledge, not easily marked by tires, and turned west up one of the more obscure skidder trails. The heavy machines had trampled this hillside down to its stony foundation, and the rain had carried away the mud.

If my headlight had been functional, I might have spotted his game. But that was no excuse. He'd outwitted me again and cost me time I didn't have.

I turned up the mostly cleared trail and began creeping forward, aware that he'd already sniped at me once and might try another ambush. Now that he'd lost his Ruger rifle, it wouldn't be as easy a shot, but I had no doubt Paul Renaud was good enough with a revolver to end my life with a bullet.

From the road, the trail had looked passable, but I soon discovered blowdown after blowdown. Renaud had managed to weave his way around these deadfalls and, in one case, driven beneath a leaning widowmaker, undoubtedly gouging the top of Stombaughs' cab. The obstacles were many.

Then, as I rounded a subtle turn, a hundred yards up the cut, I came across a sight I never would have expected.

Somehow Renaud had managed to run the GMC smack into a boulder at the edge of the underbrush. The lichen-crusted rock was the size of a dumpster. It was what geologists term a *glacial erratic*: dropped here by the last receding glacier, ten thousand years ago.

The collision between truck and rock had been brutal, and there were wisps of steam escaping the crumpled hood. All the doors hung open as if father and daughter had grabbed whatever they could and had hightailed it away mere minutes earlier.

How had this meticulous man managed to hit the one boulder guaranteed to total his escape vehicle?

I got out Chloé's topo map again, as thin now as wet tissue, and shone my light on the area, hoping to locate the dotted line that corresponded to this logging trail. I used the tip of my gloved finger to trace several possibilities before realizing why Renaud had been heading this way. What had looked like a road to nowhere was, in fact, a cut-across to the dam below Penobscot Lake.

I had been right. That little red pen mark was their destination all along.

My new predicament was that I couldn't trust that the way ahead would be passable on my four-wheeler. I'd dodged too many blow-downs on the way up. A man and girl on foot could negotiate those hurdles, though not with ease, and they might well know secret shortcuts that I would miss if I wasn't proceeding slowly with the light trained on the needles, leaves, and moss.

No, I decided; it would be a better move for me to return the way I'd come. I now possessed the advantage of having a motorized ve-hicle while they were left to trudge through the woods on foot.

If I returned to the gravel road and then made directly for the out-let of Penobscot Lake, I should reach the dam ahead of them. I could stash the ATV out of sight and set up my own ambush, waiting for the Renauds to emerge, dripping and exhausted, from the forest.

And so I zigzagged back the way I'd come until I found the road. In no time, I reached the fork to Penobscot Lake. I was feeling ex-cited, almost giddy, at having deciphered their escape route. Charley had warned me against overconfidence. But I finally felt like I might have gained the upper hand.

There was only one mystery bothering me, and it wasn't a small one.

Try as I might, I couldn't arrive at a justification for Renaud having deliberately wrecked his vehicle. He didn't seem prone to distraction. I doubted he would have been forced to swerve to avoid a large animal—a moose or deer—given that he had been creeping along.

So what had happened that caused him to crash into the boulder?

My usually overactive imagination couldn't conjure a single scenario that explained the ruined truck.

24

The road to Penobscot Lake was unnamed on the old map. Nor did I find signs directing me to the dam. Occasionally, I glimpsed strips of the tape used by foresters to mark valuable trees for cutting. These were bright pink, tied to branches, and they rippled in the wind. The way they fluttered made me think of a girl running with ribbons in her hair.

I was about to open the throttle wider when a glimmer revealed itself through the trees to my right. The glimmer was coming from the depths of a roadside pit. I might easily have missed it had I been traveling faster.

I slammed on the brakes and felt the rear end of the Can-Am shudder as I slid to a stop over slick stones.

Renaud wouldn't be that dumb.

Even if he had needed to use a light to review a map or to bandage an injury incurred when he'd crashed the GMC, he wouldn't reveal himself so near the road. At the very least, he would shield the glow beneath his coat or a blanket.

So what exactly was I seeing?

I pulled the Can-Am over to the weedy shoulder and engaged the parking brake. The engine seemed loud as I walked away, its pumping cylinders announcing that Mike Bowditch was here. Just wait, Paul, and in a few seconds, he'll step from the shadows into your gunsights.

With that caution in mind, I slipped into the woods to skirt the edge of the pit. I advanced between the mossy trunks of the spruces and the smooth-skinned beeches, lifting my feet high to avoid stumbling over the dropped branches that lurked everywhere underfoot. When I was clear of the idling engine, the sounds of my passage made me wince: the snapping of twigs, the squishing of moss, occasionally even the crunch of old snow. But I was getting closer all the time.

I reached the felled trees at the edge of the pit. All at once, the source of the unexpected light was revealed to me.

It was coming from an old—no, ancient—yellow school bus. Through the broken windows, a greenish glimmer was emanating. It wasn't a fire, that much was obvious. Nor did it seem to be coming from one of those green filters that campers screw onto flashlights to protect their night vision.

It was a cheap glow stick, I realized. One of those plastic tubes containing chemicals that, when the tube was snapped, would produce just enough illumination to warn a motorist that someone had broken down on a benighted highway. As light sources went, a chartreuse glow stick was the gadget of last resort.

My guess was that the bus had been hauled into this pit decades ago and then simply been junked and abandoned to rust away down to its long-deflated tires. Maybe the last leaseholders had used the vintage vehicle to transport workers into this wild country. Or maybe it had served as an improvised camp kitchen during those first land-bound years after the logging drives had ended.

This old Ford had been backed into position against the pit wall. Years of sun had faded the paint to the color of curdled buttermilk. A black line, now charcoal, followed the eight glassless windows down to the back end. I couldn't read the words on the side that designated its original school district, but the number 2 remained, big and bold. The hinged door had been wedged permanently ajar. There was an empty space, like a toothless mouth, where the windshield had been. No one had bothered to remove the license plate.

From the rust-rimmed bullet holes piercing the sides of the bus, I could see that it had become a favorite object for target practice. Men in the woods with guns often feel an overmastering need to use up their ammo, the more so when the deer and partridges have proven elusive.

I listened but didn't hear any sounds, not at first.

The eerie light was issuing from the depths of the vehicle.

Given the brief life span of those cheap sticks—shorter than that of a mayfly—I had to believe that the person who'd lit this one was inside. I didn't believe for a second that it was Paul Renaud. Even as a ruse to draw me in, the fugitive would have been much craftier setting his trap.

Then finally a shadow appeared: someone was moving clumsily about.

The bumping was followed by the last noise I anticipated. A loud, almost interminable fart. Succeeded by a deep-voiced groan that lasted almost as long.

What the hell?

I had more than a few courses of action from which to choose. I could fire a flare through the missing windshield to scare the bejesus out of the flatulent man. I could bark out my status as a police officer and demand he come out with his hands up. Or I could charge into the bus with the Browning drawn, in case he was armed and dangerous.

I chose option three.

25

The bus door was more cracked than fully open. And I doubted that the manual handle that controlled it had worked for many years. So breaching the vehicle was going to require sliding sideways through the gap and then locating the man in back in my gunsights before he could get a drop on me.

Worried that the frayed hem of Renaud's poncho might get caught on something, I chose to remove it. I made sure the magazine of the pistol was fully loaded and that there was a round in the chamber. I gripped the Nitecore in my left hand to illuminate the scene and, hopefully, blind the unknown person into a submissive and cooperative frame of mind.

Then I edged up to the front of the bus, keeping low so that the engine block was between me and the passenger compartment. I slipped around the side so I was facing the gap between the door and the frame. I took a deep breath, and then exhaled halfway.

Timing my actions, I simultaneously turned on the flashlight and squirmed through the doors, shouting, "Police! Don't move!"

As I gained the top step, I had my wrists crossed so that both the Browning and the Nitecore were pointed at the back of the bus. But instead of discovering an enemy preparing a surprise attack, I found a big-bellied man stretched out across the bench seat with one leg propped atop the second-to-last seat.

He lifted his shaved head, revealing a long salt-and-pepper beard.

Then he threw up a big hand to shield his eyes from the glare of the flashlight. "Jesus! What are you doing? Are you trying to blind me?"

"Hammond Pratt?"

"No."

"No?"

"It's *Ammon* Pratt, doofus."

He had a deep bass voice befitting his massive chest. Discomfort and ill temper had made it even deeper.

"Took you long enough to find me. I thought I was going to freeze to death out here. And my ankle's twisted, too. I can barely put weight on it. I hope you guys brought something to eat. And maybe a nip. I could really use a slug of brandy."

The son of a bitch thought I was a Saint Bernard.

I'd moved the flashlight beam out of his face but kept it close enough that I could examine him. Brandon Barstow had given me the idea that Pratt might be armed with multiple handguns. And for all the big man's bluster, I couldn't be sure he didn't pose a threat.

"Sorry, but I gave all my Hennessy to the last person I rescued. Who the hell are you, Pratt, and what are you doing here?"

He was trying to pull himself upright while swinging his propped leg down. These were not easy movements given his general lack of flexibility and the considerable circumference of his belly.

Hunkered down in the drafty bus, he seemed to have pulled on every piece of clothing he'd brought on his ill-conceived expedition. The outermost layer was a hooded parka lined with what appeared to be genuine coyote fur.

"If you know my name, Ivanov must have told you. I was ATVing in the woods when I got caught in the storm."

I stood my ground. "Except it was already raining when you left Seboomook Farm. I know you were riding around, searching for Paul and Chloé Renaud. Don't bother denying it."

He was struggling to reposition his wide bottom on the bench seat. "Do you know where they are?"

I wasn't about to answer his question, let alone recount the sequence of events that had brought me to the bus.

"Hands where I can see them," I commanded.

"What the fuck? I haven't done anything. Aren't you supposed to be rescuing me, bub?"

"Hands where I can see them."

He grumbled into his impressive beard, but complied, showing hands that rivaled a gorilla's in size and were probably as powerful. I could understand why Ivanov had so readily knuckled under to Ammon Pratt. Even seated, the man seemed as formidable as Goliath.

I also understood why Stacey hadn't found any reference to him online. Being Russian by birth, Ivanov had misheard Pratt's first name, turning it into the familiar Maine surname Hammond. Sometimes a mystery isn't a mystery: it's just a mumbled misunderstanding.

Keeping the gun trained on his strongman's chest, I did my best to make my way down the aisle. The bus had become a repository for crap over the years, everything from empty soda bottles to water-stained pillows to the rib bones of covertly butchered deer. The smell was musty and mildewed with a trace of urine.

Pratt had piggish eyes made even smaller by the bushiness of his brows. Like Bob Stombaugh, he had a flattened nose that looked like a memento of a fistfight he'd lost badly. His grizzled beard was so long it merged with his coyote fur collar.

"If you're not searching for me, what are you doing here? And what's with the gun in the face, bub?"

"I'm not aiming at your face."

"Figure of speech. You're police, you said."

"Maine game warden. And yes, I have been actively searching for you in this craptacular weather." He was obnoxious enough I didn't mind stretching the truth in this instance. "When you didn't return to Seboomook Farm, your host began getting nervous."

"Fucking Ivanov," he grumbled, pulling on his beard as if he were trying to yank out any hairs that might be loose. "I knew I couldn't trust that Russki to keep a secret."

"What happened to you, Pratt?"

"I went off the road, dumbass. That four-wheeler Ivanov rented me was defective. Steering didn't work. Lucky I didn't break my skull, crashing into a tree. I haven't decided if I'm going to sue the SOB."

"When was this?"

"Night before last."

The math was plausible—he'd traveled more than ten miles from Seboomook Farm to reach this godforsaken pit. But I wasn't inclined to believe anything he told me after he'd blamed the all-terrain vehicle for his present difficulties.

"And how'd you end up here?"

"Wandered around lost. GPS stopped working the first day. Battery got wet, I figured. Went around in circles, then tried going cross-country and tripped over a downed tree. Lucky I sprained my ankle instead of breaking it. This was the first shelter I found. Can I put my fucking hands down now?"

"Sure," I said, "if you put these on instead."

Taking the light between my teeth, I reached for my handcuffs and tossed them onto the ripped bench seat beside him.

His flat nostrils flared. "What the hell? You want me to cuff myself? What is it you think I've done?"

"Just put them on, Pratt. One on your wrist and attach the other to the metal bar atop the seat in front of you."

"You're fucking whacked, bub. This is bullshit. I'm an injured, innocent man."

"Just do it, Pratt. Once I'm confident you're secure, I'll give you some food and water. And then you and I are going to have a frank conversation."

In truth, I was of two minds.

Part of me wanted to continue my pursuit of the Renauds, knowing that I was losing the initiative with every minute that passed. For my plan to work, I needed to arrive at the Penobscot Lake dam ahead of them. I could always leave Pratt chained here and call in his location when I finally found service.

On the other hand, the big man possessed a trove of information about the father and daughter. He wouldn't have come to Maine otherwise. I had passed the point of mere curiosity long ago. What I needed was to know who Paul and Chloé Renaud really were.

"Put the cuffs on and I'll give you some food," I said.

He was hungry enough to agree to my demand. Even after I heard the ratcheting locks, I double-checked the bracelets to be sure they were fastened. His wrists were so thick the cuffs barely fit him. Only once before had I encountered a man with forearms that stout, and he'd been morbidly obese, which Pratt was not.

I found a couple of protein bars and offered one of my several water bottles, which he wasted no time in draining.

I took a seat several rows ahead of him, gripping the Browning but resting my gun hand on the shredded vinyl where he couldn't see it. I let the beam of the flashlight wander to his left. His puny eyes observed me closely.

"What exactly do you do, Pratt?"

He ate with his mouth open, losing crumbs from the corners. "What do you mean?"

"I mean, what do you do for a living, and why are you doing it here? You told Ivanov you'd come to Maine to do some four-wheeling, which was a lie. I'm guessing you never rode an ATV before two days ago."

He stuck the nail of his little finger between two molars to clear an almond that had gotten stuck. He was in no hurry to answer.

I was getting frustrated. "You told Ivan Ivanov that you came from Idaho."

"Which I do."

The glow stick was dying its slow death. A cross draft made me zip my jacket up to the top. As shelters went, the bus was little better than a lean-to.

"What do you want with the Renauds?"

He began to stroke his neck beneath his beard. The skin of his throat was shadowed with hair in need of trimming. His scarred skull didn't show the same stubble. He must be truly bald, I decided.

"If you're not going to talk, I'm happy to say good night and be on my way. I promise to send a truck for you tomorrow morning after I return to Seboomook Farm. That's provided I don't get delayed."

Even burping oafishly, with his beard full of crumbs, he projected enough menace to keep me on my guard.

"You've seriously never heard the name *Ammon Pratt* before?"

"No."

He stared at me with his mouth open. "How about Pitbull Pratt?"

"Wasn't he the king of the Bulgarians?"

My new friend didn't like that joke at all. "Fuck you. I'm a fucking celebrity. Don't people in Maine use the internet?"

"How are you a celebrity?"

"My YouTube channel! My podcast! I've got more than seventy-three thousand subscribers across six social media platforms, and I haven't even expanded to TikTok yet. My agent in Hollywood is in talks with HBO and Netflix to make a documentary about my cases."

"Do you investigate unsolved crimes or something?"

"Fuck no. I'm a bounty hunter, man. Like a real-deal skip tracer and the bane of wanted men."

"I take it you gave yourself the nickname 'Pitbull Pratt.'"

"Because I never give up. Most of the guys on TV are phonies who are all about the shades, mullets, and tats. They're, like, pretend personalities, not real-life investigators."

"I suppose you must have a PI license, then?"

"Damn right I do."

"Let's see it."

"Did you not hear me say I lost my gear when that defective machine crashed?"

He'd said nothing about losing his gear. I distinctly remembered him claiming to have used a GPS unit before its battery died. Whatever else the man might or might not be, he was definitely a liar.

"Did you lose your firearms, too?"

"What firearms?"

"We found two empty boxes of ammunition in your room back at Seboomook Farm. I'm going to go out on a limb and say that you have at least one gun hidden on your person. More than one, I bet. Maybe a full-size pistol in your waistband and a compact strapped to your ankle. And you've got a couple of knives on you, too. Am I right?"

For the first time since we'd met, Ammon Pratt treated me to a smile. He had a gold tooth. One of his premolars. I wondered if it was real or something he snapped into place before he went on camera.

"No," he said, "you're wrong."

"You're saying you're unarmed. That if I search you now, I am going to come up empty."

"That ain't what I'm saying at all. One, there's no way in hell I'm letting you put hands on me. Cuffs or no cuffs. And two, I never said I was unarmed. I'm saying you got the number wrong. The actual number of pieces I'm carrying is three."

26

Huffing like a bear, Pratt reluctantly revealed his armory. I made him stand up to the extent that was possible in the low-ceilinged bus and asked him where I could find each of his hidden guns. Carefully, I patted him down. In his belt, he was carrying a Glock 21, a true cannon, firing .45 ACP rounds capable of piercing a car door. He was wearing a shoulder holster under his parka with a CZ 75 balanced with two magazines beneath his other armpit. As I'd predicted, he'd also outfitted himself with an ankle holster. It held a Ruger LCR revolver: the model with the concealed hammer.

"And the fourth one," I said, having set the others down on a seat beyond his reach.

He affected a tone of outrage. "I told you I had three guns."

"Which means you're hiding a fourth from me."

He snorted now, almost in appreciation. "Belly band."

I lifted his chamois overshirt, then his pullover, and found a well-concealed neoprene wrap held in place above his undershirt by Velcro patches. It was a cheap contraption, but well hidden by his bulging stomach, and in a small pouch it contained a two-shot Bond Arms Backup. The dual barrels were no longer than my pinkie.

Pratt's eclectic choice of firearms told me a lot about his character, more than he would have wished.

The first was that he valued the cool factor over practicality. The ammo was not interchangeable between his assorted guns. Each took a different caliber cartridge. Stupid, stupid, stupid.

The second clue to his character was that, by any objective measure, he was over-armed. A single well-maintained pistol, with spare mags and maybe a revolver as a reliable backup, was more than sufficient for any fracas this self-proclaimed bounty hunter might encounter here or anywhere.

His thin patience had rubbed entirely away while I'd disarmed him.

"First, you detain and restrain me without cause, and now this. Because if I'm not under arrest, you have no right—"

"You voluntarily agreed to be handcuffed in exchange for my giving you food."

He rattled his cuffs hard enough that the one secured to the bar scraped paint from the metal. "In that case, I want you to let me out of these fucking things right now."

"And then you voluntarily showed me your Glock."

"Voluntarily? That was intimidation. You don't have a right to confiscate my firearms for no reason. I have Second Amendment protections here. I could file a complaint. Fuck, man, I'm going to plaster your face across my platforms as an enemy of 2A." He glowered at me now. "Why are you smiling?"

"Because you didn't let me finish. You voluntarily showed me your Glock, which happens to be outfitted with this little aftermarket part." I raised the pistol for the purposes of demonstration. "As I'm guessing you know, Glock switches convert semiautos into de facto machine guns, making them illegal under federal law."

All the anger and outrage evaporated before my eyes.

"Have a heart, man."

"Ammon Pratt, I am arresting you for possession of a prohibited device under the National Firearms Act of 1934."

"I take back what I said about filing a complaint and everything. I bought that gun at a gun show in Boise. The guy who sold it to me never said I needed a permit."

The idiot kept digging his grave deeper and deeper. The only thing he had going for him was that I was desperate to find the Renauds. I glanced at my watch to signal that my patience was at an end.

"I'm wet as a dog and can't even think straight," he implored. "If you're a forest ranger—"

"Game warden."

"Whatever. Can't you make a fire at least? So we can get warm and talk this out. I can't afford to be arrested. I'll lose my PI license."

"I want you to tell me everything you know about Paul and Chloé Renaud. If you do, I might be willing to cut you some slack."

"Make the fire first," he said.

Normally, I would have refused to negotiate the point. My instinct told me Renaud was getting away, but Pratt and I were both soaked to the skin, and Charley hadn't been wrong about the perils of hypothermia, even when the temperature was edging toward the fifties.

Soon I had a merry blaze going. The gusts blowing through the jagged windows made the smoke restless. It swirled and moved this way and that. I knew we'd both stink of burnt spruce later.

"Who are the Renauds?" I said, wiping my dirty hands on my pants.

"How about you uncuff me first?"

"How about I don't."

"I've been on their trail for a while," he said. "I chased them all across Canada. I thought I'd lost the scent until I happened to hear about a guy in New Brunswick—retired Border Services with a booze problem—who couldn't stop jabbering about this genius who'd built a fishing camp for him. By the end of our friendly conversation, I knew the Renauds had come to Maine."

No doubt Pratt had threatened the man into giving up this information.

"Renaud told his most recent client that they were Alaskans. He told someone else that he and his daughter were actually Canadians from the Banff area."

He showed me his gold tooth again. "You're getting warmer."

"I'm not positive about this, Pratt, but I'm pretty sure Canada doesn't offer bounties on bond jumpers. So someone must be paying you."

"This is a PI job. I'm looking at a one-hundred-K payday. And that's in U.S. dollars."

I glanced at my watch again and saw my advantage ticking away with every second. "How about we cut to the chase."

"And ruin the story? I'm getting there, bub. The first thing you should know is that Renaud comes from a long line of politicians, although he never had much use for the family business, from what I can tell. He's also ex-military. He did five years as a member of the Second Canadian Ranger Patrol Group. He was stationed up around James Bay in the Arctic before he decided to return to 'civilization,' if you can use that word for the Laurentians."

"Do you mean the Laurentian Mountains in Québec?"

"Bingo."

"You're saying that's where they're from?"

"He grew up around Calgary. But his last known address was a village called L'Ascension, near Mont Tremblant."

"That's where all the shit went down," he added. "In the Laurentians."

"By shit, you mean the divorce?"

"Divorce?"

"Paul Renaud didn't abduct his daughter from his ex-wife, Selene?"

"Renaud didn't divorce his wife. He murdered her."

Now it was my turn to reel. "What?"

"The brutal SOB shot her through the heart, and not even cleanly. The Mounties said it took her fifteen minutes to die. The guy really hated her, is all I can think. He wanted that lady to suffer."

"The story he told his Maine neighbors was that she was mentally unstable."

"That part's true. But through the fucking heart, man! That is ice cold, no matter how crazy she was."

"They also said she came from money."

"Who do you think is bankrolling this hunt? Her rich parents. Not that Paul was exactly a redneck. The dude's father is some mucky-muck in Ottawa. Former senior cabinet member, current MP."

"How have I not heard about any of this? It must have been big news in Canada."

"So you're a close follower of Canadian media is what you're telling me?"

"Interpol distributes red notices on fugitives."

"And the last time you reviewed a red notice was when?"

He was right to call me out. Wardens wouldn't have been briefed on Renaud unless there was a credible report saying he might be seeking to cross into the U.S. via the Maine border. And I'd been preoccupied with my own cases.

I slumped against the torn seat and turned my face away so that I was no longer inhaling smoke but breathing the clean, wet air coming through the broken windows.

Why did any of this surprise me?

I had identified the mark of the zealot on Renaud. I'd watched him walk away from Josie when he'd known she was suffering serious effects from the drugs. Hours later, I'd seen him entirely ready to blow his daughter's brains out.

"Was Chloé there when he shot her mother?"

"I don't know. Probably. Father and daughter were gone from the house before the police responded, so it's not like he ever signed a statement saying what happened in the house that night."

"How have you been able to track them?"

"Pitbull Pratt doesn't reveal his methods."

"Clearly, he's had an accomplice. Maybe multiple accomplices. Somehow, he's managed to travel around Canada and cross the border into Maine without being flagged. Does he have known connections with the RCMP or the Services frontaliers? What about U.S. Border Patrol?"

The big man smirked as he caressed his salt-and-pepper beard. "More than you will ever know, Ranger."

"Warden. So tell me about his network."

"If I tell you and you catch the SOB before I do, I ain't getting paid my hundred K."

"You don't care about bringing a murderer to justice?"

"What I care about is my payday, plus what this story will do for my brand. There's no way I don't get a TV series if I catch Paul Renaud. This guy is one of the most elusive fugitives of the century. That asshole is going to make Pitbull Pratt a household name."

I climbed to my feet. My knees were stiff. I hated to be reminded that I was on the cusp of middle age.

"Too bad you won't be the one to catch him."

He squared his wide shoulders. "What do you mean?"

"I mean, I'm leaving you here for the night, Pratt. Sorry if the cuffs make it hard to sleep. But as soon as I connect with the outside world, I promise to send some wardens and state police officers here to escort you back to civilization."

"We made a deal you wouldn't arrest me!"

Now it was my turn to laugh. "Did we?"

What happened next caught me by surprise. Pratt lurched to his feet with more speed than I thought he had in him, being such a large and ungainly man. He swung his free fist at me, missing by a mile, while he jerked hard with his other arm against the cuffs. For a split second, I worried the links might snap. But he'd miscalculated the angle, and instead of breaking, the bracelet scraped harmlessly along the rail.

By then, I had backed down the aisle and had the Browning pointed at his reddening face.

"Now I am definitely arresting you. Attempted assault on a police officer is a Class D crime. I'm only leaving you here because I have no means of bringing you into custody."

"You can't do this to me, bub!"

"Have a good night, Pitbull."

Outside, I paused a minute to gather up Renaud's poncho and

shake off the rain from its exterior. I "borrowed" Pratt's revolver and ankle holster, as well as the CZ pistol, and stashed his other guns under the bus, where I doubted he would think to look for them if, by some miracle, he managed to get free. As I set off down the skidder trail toward the ATV, his shouted obscenities grew fainter and fainter.

27

The rain stopped at last before I reached the outlet of Penobscot Lake.

The cascade below the dam was deafeningly loud and so white with foam it seemed to create its own ghostly illumination. I could make out in the blackness the frothy and roiling water as it plunged down from the ancient embankment.

I parked the Can-Am in a cluster of prematurely leafy alders and took the final chance of killing the engine. The third time starting it would not be the charm, I decided, so I had better be right in my hunch about this being Renaud's evac route.

Above the dam, the lake was gray and misted in the beam of my flashlight. In the shallows, I glimpsed the silver and orange flickers of fish. At first, I assumed they must be rainbow smelt completing their annual spawning run. Then I remembered that Penobscot Lake was one of the few bodies of water in Maine that held endangered blueback trout. These slender forage fish had moved close to shore to feed.

For a moment, the anger and excitement that had driven me all evening subsided. Nature had this effect on me. I felt a childlike wonder that could almost make me forget the atrocities of the day.

I knew I had no time for marveling or introspection. I had wasted too many minutes with Ammon Pratt.

Pacing along the trail that crossed the dam, I tried Bob's phone and was shocked to see the SOS function illuminated at the top of the screen. I must have been getting a signal from across the lake and hills, from somewhere across the border in Canada. I pulled up the keypad and tried 9-1-1, but the call dropped before I heard it ring.

Next I tried a brief text identifying myself and requesting immediate emergency assistance.

After an eternity, the text showed as undelivered.

My own phone, meanwhile, displayed no signal at all. I had to fight the impulse to hurl the useless device into the lake.

I had to remind myself that the Renauds might be arriving at any moment.

I found a hiding place behind some small firs close to the water and checked my supplies. Three flares remained to be fired from my flare gun. I had stupidly left the hatchet behind at the sugarhouse and wished I had a better knife than the blade I'd scavenged from Paul Renaud's footlocker.

But thanks to Pratt, I possessed an arsenal of firearms. This was the first time in my career when I would not have described myself as being outgunned. I readjusted the ankle holster, which had already begun to slip, and checked to see that there was a round ready to go in the action of the Browning. I left the CZ in my rucksack as a weapon of last resort.

Now that I had stopped moving, I felt assailed by exhaustion. Aches appeared in my bones; strains made themselves known in my muscles. The absolute dampness of my clothes—every layer soaked— brought on a bout of sudden shivering. I was, in a word, miserable.

I ate my last protein bar and refilled my water bottle from the lake, figuring that the risk of picking up parasites was minuscule compared with the more dangerous chances I was taking. The odds were against my surviving the night.

I crouched behind those trees, listening, waiting, before the doubts began to descend.

Renaud had an accomplice, likely *more* than one accomplice, on the Canadian side of the border. But he had referred to an "evac route." And if I was right that the outlet to Penobscot Lake was where he'd planned to launch his escape, then I'd missed a key detail. He couldn't have counted on having a cell signal here, any more than I had.

So how would he have summoned help? Even if he had accomplices, Paul Renaud would never have depended for his survival solely on having another person swoop in to rescue him. Charley had emphasized what a careful planner he was. No doubt Renaud had built in redundancies in case one method failed. He would have wanted control of his fate at all stages of his escape.

Using my Nitecore, I began prowling the alder tangles above the high-water level.

In fewer than ten minutes, I found the motorboat under a blind made of camo-colored burlap. It was a Zodiac inflatable, battered and saggy, not worth stealing, because a thief would assume it would probably sink. The outboard was a Mercury two-stroke, one of the old, carbureted models: bombproof and easier to maintain than anything on the water.

Plus a set of oars, of course. Just in case.

Renaud or his helper had chained every last part of the boat and engine to hardwood trees that wouldn't come down without a big-toothed saw. And you would have needed three-foot bolt cutters to sever those zinc-plated links.

Now I've got him, I thought.

I could lie in wait near the boat, with firearms at the ready. When Paul and Chloé arrived—as they surely would—I could spring my trap.

There was one problem.

What would keep him from trying that same stunt where he threatened to shoot his daughter?

If I didn't incapacitate him instantly, I would find myself back on the factory floor of the sugarhouse, held hostage by his merciless will.

Again, I pictured Chloé's face the second she had felt her father's pistol dig into the soft flesh beneath her jaw. She'd been genuinely shocked. As capable an actor as she'd shown herself to be, she couldn't have faked the bewildered terror of that moment.

She'd believed her dad could kill her.

Who was to say he wouldn't yet pull the trigger?

But shooting him preemptively would be cold-blooded murder. I had to be honest about the indelible stain the act would leave on my heart. This entire night had felt like a test of the man I had become. Fallible, certainly, but resourceful as well.

At every decision point, Paul Renaud had chosen expediency over his humanity. I needed to stop him, but not at the expense of my soul.

I could disable the outboard.

I could fire shots through the Zodiac's floats or its rigid bottom until it was no more seaworthy than a sieve.

But every option I considered seemed to lead to the same two choices: a standoff I couldn't win against a father capable of the worst atrocity imaginable, or committing premeditated murder before Paul Renaud could take his daughter's life.

I decided to litter the path with twigs and branches prone to snapping. Spruce cones, too, which would crackle to pieces underfoot. These little traps would be hard for two weary walkers to avoid, even two seasoned outdoorspeople practiced in deer stalking and moving silently in the woods.

Never having explored Penobscot Lake, I knew next to nothing about it. Small squares on the topo map indicated a handful of camps or structures on the western shore where a brook flowed out of Dingley Pond. But the chart was decades old, and who was to say those buildings were still there, let alone occupied?

An hour passed.

Complaints issued from every part of my body: my sore throat, my clammy skin, my overstretched ligaments. The waiting was making me sleepy. I yearned to curl up like a sled dog in a storm.

I forced my mind into action. I wondered what Charley was doing. Had he stayed put, or had he ventured out of the valley to locate a cell signal?

And, of course, I thought of Stacey.

Renaud had made me rethink every conception I had about fatherhood. He was a loving parent devoted to his daughter's education; he was also a vile and worthless human being. He'd pledged his entire existence to protecting his girl from harm. He was ready, maybe even eager, to end her life in a muzzle flash.

Lost in thought, I didn't notice that the wind had died, not until a loud splash startled me alert. I guessed it was a moose, wading across the outlet. Then came a loon, startled into a panic by the moose.

And then another noise: faint, human-made, increasing in volume.

A boat was approaching stealthily down the lake, its outboard engine scarcely more than a purr. It had to be a trolling motor.

For a fleeting second, I thrilled at the boat's arrival. In my excitement, I thought of firing a flare to attract the driver's attention. Then a chilling recognition took hold of my being. No innocent person was out for a midnight cruise on Penobscot Lake.

Renaud always had a backup plan.

I knew he must have accomplices.

The boater was one of them, and I was about to meet him.

28

I finally had an answer—if not *the* answer—to my question about who Paul Renaud had been in such a hurry to call that he'd bushwhacked to the top of Dubois Hill earlier that morning.

The boat had its running lights off and hid in the mist rising from the placid waters of the lake. When it was a hundred yards or so offshore, I heard the telltale splash of an anchor being dropped. In the dark and fog, I couldn't make out even the faintest outline.

The boater was waiting for Renaud's signal before he landed.

Maybe I could attempt to trick him. Fake Paul's voice. Shine my flashlight three times for help.

Good luck with that. Whatever code they had wouldn't be so rudimentary and easy to crack.

I contemplated where the stranger had launched from. Was there a ramp at the top of the lake? I puzzled over where he intended to ferry the Renauds. Mostly I wondered who he was.

Nadeau?

Because of his unannounced visit to Josie's farm, the Canadian border officer had solidified his place at the top of my list of suspects. The irony was this: he was so obviously dodgy that I doubted he could be the man in the boat. Most bad guys, in my experience, weren't eager to announce themselves as being bad.

At the same time, I felt increasingly confident that Renaud possessed not just one accomplice but several, perhaps even a network of collaborators. I couldn't fathom how a builder of log cabins, even luxurious ones, could have assembled a cadre of people willing to assist his lawbreaking. Pratt had claimed the man came from money. And cash has a miraculous ability to sway consciences. He'd also mentioned that Paul's father was a person of some influence, I now recalled.

As the cloud cover had moved off, the temperature had risen, and the air was becoming almost balmy. The wind was blowing now from the southwest, bringing midwestern warmth to New England.

A twig snapped to my left.

"Shhhh," hissed a man.

"I'm sorry, Papa. I'm sorry," Chloé replied in a whisper.

"It's all right, chickpea." Her father kept his tone soft and reassuring. "I know you're exhausted. You've got nothing to apologize for."

I hunched even farther down in the alders. I listened for approaching footsteps, waited for the crunches and snaps from the booby traps I'd laid.

"Hmm," I heard Renaud say after a branch broke. He'd sensed there was something off about this section of the trail.

"What?"

"Keep walking heel to toe, Chloé. As soft as you can."

"Are you in much pain, Papa?"

"No."

But I'd heard the extra force he'd put into the denial.

"I'm sorry I made you crash the truck."

"You were upset. You didn't know what you were doing. I shouldn't have allowed myself to be distracted."

Then the shadowed shapes of Paul and Chloé appeared in silhouettes against the mist. The father, previously ramrod straight, had acquired a stoop. He was injured but doing his best to soldier through the pain. His daughter, meanwhile, was pressed close to his midsection as if to catch him if he stumbled. I doubted she possessed the strength, but she had surprised me all night long.

Chloé, it seemed, had caused the truck to crash into the boulder.

Had Renaud been badly hurt in the collision? It seemed too much to hope for.

Being unable to see his hands also made me cautious; he might have had that massive revolver drawn. If he did, he could get off a shot at Chloé or me before I even broke free of the bushes.

I would wait for him to signal his accomplice.

The three of them would be distracted as the boat crept to shore. Their focus would move to the lake.

Renaud was wary enough to give a thought to the road up which they had come.

But he would have no reason to suspect his adversary was hidden like a panther in the underbrush, mere yards away from their landing place.

I would wait for the boat to bump shore, and then when the Renauds were busy embarking, I would fire a flare to reveal their exact locations. I would capitalize on the sudden illumination and their surprise to get the drop on them.

I'd have to take down Renaud first; throw myself on him and hope my size and rage—and whatever injuries he'd incurred—would be enough to win the wrestling match. I had a gut feeling that even wounded, he would be a fierce fighter. But if I could get his gun away before he acquired a target—

There was one problem, though. Wasn't the man in the boat also likely to be armed?

Then what would I do?

Before I could sort out those questions, Renaud hit the strobe function of his flashlight; a staccato burst of light sprang from the bulb.

No one spoke, but I heard the wet anchor line being pulled up, the rough cordage scraping over a gunwale, and then the big-cat purr of the trolling motor being engaged.

The boat was a broad, square-sterned canoe with the engine mounted at the back. Charley owned one of these Grand Lakers. So did most of the fishing guides I knew in eastern Maine. There was simply no better design for negotiating waterways that might range from white-capped lakes to skinny-water streams.

Paul kept casting glances at the shore around him. The tilt of his head suggested he was alert to any sound. I caught a glimpse of his empty hands; the Colt remained in its holster.

The mystery boat edged into the waterweeds and pipewort that grew in the shallows. I could make out the profile of the hooded driver. Silent and menacing, he might have been the daemon Charon from Greek mythology preparing to ferry the Renauds across the River Styx into Hades.

Paul couldn't seem to hold his head up. The way his left shoulder slumped suggested the arm might be broken. Now was the time for me to spring.

Or it would have been.

Because, all at once, Renaud had the Colt in his hand. He spun and squeezed off a round down the road at some large, loud, crashing shape that was quickly closing the distance between them. I fancied for an instant it was a bear on its hind legs. But the surprise attacker was too small for a bear.

The bullet must have hit Ammon Pratt. It couldn't possibly have missed that big gut of his.

But somehow the impact didn't slow the charging bounty hunter. Nor did it prevent him from swinging the metal bar in his hands. It was the railing I'd cuffed him to in the stupid belief he'd never escape the bus. Pratt hadn't been able to snap his chains, but he'd yanked the pipe loose and was using it now as a club.

Renaud staggered back, lost his footing in the wet sand and the leaves that blanketed the shallows, and fell hard against the hull of the Grand Laker.

From there, it was all chaos. The boat tipped to port from the weight of Chloé crawling over the gunwale. Charon waved his arms as he tried to keep his balance and stop the Grand Laker from capsizing. And Pratt continued his savage attack on his adversary, who was now seated upright in the cold water.

"Fuck you, you murderous fuck!" roared Ammon Pratt.

I chose that moment to fire my signal flare.

The effect was as I'd hoped. The four others were struck dumb and motionless by the sudden red brilliance.

"Police! Drop your weapons!"

I saw Chloé's skinny, booted legs sticking up from inside the boat.

Charon, nearly faceless in his olive-green hood, reached for a pistol concealed at his belt.

Renaud brought up his King Cobra again from his submerged holster.

Pratt swung his metal club at the shining revolver and the outstretched hand that clutched its grip. The railing struck the barrel of Renaud's gun just as he pulled the trigger. This time, the bullet went astray.

Now it was Pratt's turn to lose his footing. The gargantuan man fell hard into the lake, making such a splash that the waves pushed the Grand Laker away from shore.

Charon had a pistol in his hands now. But he had no interest in the thrashing Pratt. Instead, he aimed at my position amid the alders.

From its first report, I knew it was a full-size semiautomatic.

Branches scratched my hands on my way to the muddy ground. I tried to keep the rotting log on which I'd been sitting between me and the shooter. But the heavy-grain bullets shredded the decaying wood.

As wood chips exploded around me, I returned fire with the Browning. I was careful to aim at the man standing in the boat. I feared hitting the little girl with so much as a ricochet.

One of my shots hit Charon in his center-mass. Whatever satisfaction I might have felt lasted less than a second when I perceived the thump of my bullet striking a Kevlar ballistic vest.

"The boat," I heard Renaud gasp. "Shoot the boat."

For a split second, I thought he was addressing me. I was confused. Why would he be giving *me* instructions?

The spitting flare, as it arced toward the lake, was already fading.

Charon had dropped to one knee to lower his profile. I saw the minuscule green glow of his laser sights as he scanned the shore. I fired at him again, and this time heard a howl.

Renaud hadn't continued to fire at Pratt, he was too intent on making his escape. The fugitive swung one leg over the gunwale while his daughter pulled on his unbroken right arm to assist.

Charon, meanwhile, began returning fire again.

Only instead of training his pistol at me, he aimed at the bushes. Three, four, five bullets struck the inflatable Zodiac.

"*Shoot the boat,*" Renaud had commanded.

Even wounded and in desperate pain, Paul had the presence of mind to command his accomplice to do the essential thing. The imperative was to render the potential pursuit boat inoperable.

The Zodiac was semirigid. The inflatable floats were strengthened by fiberglass, and the bottom had a wooden hull. But Charon's bullets sounded as if they were doing real damage to the protective coating. Even if I managed to get the boat loose of its chains and pull-start the engine, it might well sink.

Damn it!

The boatman stopped firing. His passengers were all aboard. He needed to speed away before one of my bullets ended the fight.

It took Charon fifteen seconds to restart the trolling motor. I scrambled on my knees and elbows to the lakeshore while the boat drifted into deeper water. The flare had robbed me of my night vision. But I thought Chloé might be standing in the bow. The Grand Laker vanished into blackness as the hooded man steered toward deeper water.

I fired my second-to-last flare, but all it did was turn the mist red.

Soaking and enraged, Pratt was on his knees in the shallows shouting every obscenity in his vocabulary at his escaping quarry. Those four-letter words were the last weapons he had left in his arsenal.

After several useless seconds, my arcing flare hit the water hundreds of feet distant. There was a puff of crimson smoke. Then came the sputter as the flame was extinguished, and the night again went fully dark.

29

Pratt, you son of a bitch," I said. "I should shoot you for the inconvenience you've caused me."

There were bits of lichen and other plant matter in his beard. And
his shaved skull was dappled with mud. He looked like a troll who
had crawled out from beneath a bridge.

"Inconvenience? I didn't fuck up your plan, bub! You fucked up
my plan! I had the son of a bitch." He squeezed thumb and forefin-
ger together. His right wrist remained handcuffed while the other
manacle hung suspended by the links of chain. "I was this close to
bringing him down."

"I saw him shoot you, asshole."

He glanced down at his belly but waved away my words. "Yeah,
yeah."

"And if I hadn't been here, his accomplice would have put another bullet between your eyebrows."

We were facing each other across the trampled mud where he and
Renaud had conducted their wrestling match.

I had the Browning in my hand but felt no pressing need to keep it
trained on him. But I sure as hell wasn't going to make the mistake I'd
made before of assuming he was incapacitated and posed no further
risk. The Nitecore aimed into his eyes was far more effective at keeping him submissive.

"Hold out your arm," I said.

"Why?"

"Because I want my handcuffs back."

He obliged me, and very carefully, I unlocked him and returned the bracelets to their leather pouch on my belt.

"Now pull up your shirts so I can have a look at that wound."

His answer to this command was a laughing snort. "This ain't the first time Pitbull's been shot, bub. The dude only winged me. I don't plan on meeting my maker tonight."

I dropped the flashlight beam to his broad midsection, where it exposed a spreading red stain.

"Drop the act for a second, Pratt. I'm guessing you know that gunshot wounds to the stomach can be fatal if not treated. You're losing a lot of blood. Even you have to admit that."

Ammon Pratt wasn't a man who sighed, per se. Instead he released air from his diaphragm to express his displeasure. It vibrated on the way up his throat in an ursine way.

He'd lost his parka somewhere between the bus and the lake. His outer layer consisted of a waterlogged sweater with shredded elbows and loose yarn at the ends of the sleeves. He reached his sausage fingers under the bloody hem and carefully peeled it upward.

I was surprised by the item of clothing beneath his belly band. Instead of a bare stomach, he wore a pristine white undershirt that looked unlike anything I had seen for sale at Walmart. I'd missed its significance when I'd taken the derringer from its elastic hiding place.

"I'm a Mormon," he growled. "What about it?"

"No, I just—"

"Never seen 'magic underwear' before? Listen, fuckface, I've been doing this job for twelve years, and these temple garments have always kept me safe."

"Until tonight."

He let the sweater drop.

"You don't think an LDS can be a badass? You should read up on Brigham Young, my friend. He held the U.S. Army at bay for a whole winter during the Utah War. I'm one of his direct descendants on my mother's side. Well, not direct. We're actually descended from his brother Joseph. But I've got the same genes as the Lion of the Lord."

I motioned for him to turn around.

As I'd feared, there was no exit wound. That .357 Magnum bullet was lodged somewhere amid his inner organs and visceral fat. It hadn't severed or grazed his thoracic aorta or he'd already be dead. And given how agonizing I'd heard wounds to the gut were, I couldn't believe he had the energy to give me a lecture on his illustrious ancestors or the indomitability of his faith.

"We need to pack that wound and apply as much pressure to it as possible."

"Yeah, yeah."

"You're going to die if you don't, Pratt."

"Every man dies. Not every man really lives."

"Is that a quote? Are you quoting a movie or something? Because this is serious, Ammon." I looked him hard in the eyes. "You. Are. Dying."

Speaking to him like a child seemed to produce the intended effect. He ran his tongue around the inside of one cheek, then hung his bearded head. "Don't suppose you got a first aid kit with you?"

I made him lie on his back while I fetched my trauma kit from my rucksack. I rubbed my hands with antiseptic. Then I applied a compression dressing to the wound, clipped it into place, and taped over and around his midsection to hold the bandage tight.

"You ever done this before?" he growled.

When I didn't answer, he snarked, "I bet you did, and the poor SOB died of septic shock."

"I need to concentrate here."

"Let me breathe at least," he said through clenched teeth. "Man, that bandage is tighter than a Vietnamese rubber."

"It needs to be secure to staunch the blood flow." I stood above him, inspecting my work. "I think you're supposed to continue lying on your back with your knees bent. My wife is an EMT. I wish she were here."

"Me too! You're going to fucking kill me with your amateur combat medicine."

But instead of obeying me, he used one of his muscular arms to push himself onto his knees. Wincing from his several injuries, he climbed shakily to his feet. I am a tall man, six two, and yet he loomed over me by seven inches.

"What do you think you're doing?" I said.

"Getting in the boat."

"What boat?"

"The one they were shooting in the bushes. They didn't want us using it to chase them. I might have been shot, but I wasn't blind or deaf. I saw and heard what happened."

"You're in no state to go anywhere, Ammon."

"So you're planning on leaving me here and what—returning later for my corpse? No thank you, Ranger."

"*Warden* Bowditch."

"I don't fucking care what your name is, bub. What I care about is using this boat to follow those fucks. Or at least find a spot where we can pick up a signal for you to call 9-1-1. Maybe there's a truck across the way we can drive to a Canuck hospital. Make no mistake, though. You're not fucking leaving me here."

I tried to keep some distance between us as we examined the Zodiac in the alders. Charon had hit the hull in three places, cracking the fiberglass coating. I couldn't hear sighs of air leaking from the interior flotation tubes, but that didn't mean the sponsons were intact. One shot had carved a groove along the hull. Another had skipped off the top of the outboard. The third was harder to assess. Little wrinkles radiated from a worrying hole.

Not that any of it mattered, I realized. Because the chains securing the boat were the definition of unbreakable. The zinc-plated links would have been hard to sever even if I'd had heavy-duty bolt cutters in my pack, which I most certainly did not.

Pratt asked me to shine my light on the heavy padlock. It must have weighed five pounds.

"Easy-peasy," he said.

"You can't shoot a lock off like in the movies," I said. "At least not with the calibers we have."

"I know that, asshole."

He certainly wasn't acting like a man with a bullet lodged in his belly. Ammon Pratt was a physical specimen of a sort I hadn't met before. Maybe he really was half troll.

"An AR-15 might be able to do it, but—"

"Are you really as dumb as you look, Bowditch?" He then knelt awkwardly beside the lock, steadying himself against the boat. With his free hand, he reached for his ass. "Hold the light on the cylinder."

From his back pocket, he produced an overstuffed wallet, and from the wallet, he produced a lock-picking card. It was the size of a driver's license, made of metal, and the individual picks, rakes, and tension bars popped loose as needed.

"I can actually do this blindfolded, but it'll be easier with the light."

My first reaction was that I was about to witness another of Pitbull Pratt's vaudeville acts. He would pretend to nearly pick the lock and then, when he'd failed in the attempt, blame the tools, saying that if he'd had the full set he normally carried on jobs—

Before I could even finish the damning thought, he'd managed to pop the lock open.

"The one holding the motor is even more basic," he said.

And it was.

In a matter of minutes, we'd removed the last of the chains.

Despite my command that he stand clear, lest he loosen his compression bandage, he insisted on helping me lift the Zodiac out of its sunken hiding place. The effort left him puffing, though, which he attempted to conceal behind a series of coughs. We set the boat in the water, where a push from one of the oars would be enough to get us moving—provided we could stay afloat.

I wasn't relishing the prospect of rowing up a lake that looked to be several miles long, but as I was double-checking the oarlocks, Pratt used the tip of a Buck knife I had failed to find to access the outboard's terminal.

I didn't even see where he produced the spare wire from—his wallet, another pocket—but he used it to run voltage from the live wire to the engine wire. The hot-wired Mercury turned over immediately. Vaporized petroleum rose around us, flashing with iridescence and causing me to gag.

I turned to Pratt in actual amazement.

"Easy-peasy," he repeated, although I noticed that his face had grown noticeably pale from his efforts.

"I'm driving the boat," I said. "It's not up for discussion. Move aside."

He snorted another laugh and crawled into the bow, letting out a single groan as he settled his bulk.

I wondered if he knew that the bullet inside him wasn't necessarily going to stay in place. Any small activity, even another cough, could shift the hunk of lead a fraction of an inch. And if the hollow-point already happened to be close to his thoracic aorta, a hundred bandages wouldn't suffice to staunch the blood loss.

There were no life jackets in the boat. If we went into the water, we'd succumb to hypothermia in minutes. It happened every week to boaters who overestimated the temperature of these icy lakes. Then again, we'd survived this long, against odds that defied calculation.

The absurdity of our predicament left me feeling almost lightheaded. It was an emotion I recognized from hard experience. Only someone who has survived a close call with death can feel it.

But my giddiness didn't last long.

Less than a hundred feet from shore, the boat began taking on water.

30

The bullet that had struck the existing crack in the fiberglass was sufficient to start a full-scale breach. Without ever noticeably gushing, water quickly began to fill the bottom, rising fast over our boots.

Pratt, mindful of the pain that twisting could cause, asked, "You wouldn't have anything in that backpack I could use to bail?"

I reached for my rucksack and tossed it to him. "You might try my water bottle."

"Yeah, that ain't gonna do it."

I turned toward the western shore and saw a steep, tree-studded hillside emerge from the fog. With the boat taking on water, I needed to stay in view of land.

"Hang on to the sides," I said. "I'm going to open her up."

"You'll only sink us faster!"

"Not if you lean back. We want as much weight as we can in the stern. If I can keep the bow elevated—"

"You can't. Not enough. The crack is below the waterline."

"Then I'm going to try to get us as far up the lake as possible before we have to start swimming."

I'd warned Pratt I was about to rev the engine, but he managed to topple toward me, anyway. The impact of his fall nearly capsized us. Lying on his back across the middle bench seat like a man sunning himself, he glared at me upside down, with spittle in his beard. The whine of the two-stroke engine sounded like a cicada had crawled into one of my ears and taken up residence inside my skull.

"I'd kill you if I didn't need you to get out of this alive," he growled, trying unsuccessfully to work his arms over the rounded floats and use them to sit upright. At least his awkward position was helping elevate the bow of the Zodiac.

Unfortunately, he was right about the crack letting in water. If anything, our increased speed seemed to be forcing more into the bottom. The heaviness only added to the weight of the overladen Zodiac. After our quick burst of acceleration, the lake began to drag at us like an anchor.

I risked the flashlight with my free hand, knowing any illumination would make us an easy target. But I needed to find a place where I could swamp the boat. The lake was freezing, and I dreaded a long swim.

The pockets of air in my rucksack caused it to float for half a minute before the weight of the gear inside began dragging it underwater.

"My pack!"

Pratt was mostly supine, with his legs submerged. "What?"

"Toss me my backpack!"

But it was too late. The bow, weighted with gallons of icy meltwater, seemed to hit an elastic wall that stretched but failed to give. Suddenly, we were at a full stop and sinking fast.

My rucksack was gone and with it my trauma kit, my tarp, my emergency blanket, spare water bottle, Bob Stombaugh's phone, and Pratt's CZ pistol.

Under normal circumstances, I would have untied my boots to keep them from dragging me down, but I had managed to enter the outlet where Deadwater Brook poured into the lake. The swim to shore would be less than thirty yards. I didn't want to lose my boots and be forced to continue the chase in stocking feet.

The water in the cove was well above my head, though. And it was even colder than I had anticipated, especially beneath the top layer, where the newly fallen rain floated above the thermocline.

As I'd desperately hoped would be the case, Pratt knew how to swim, but the agony of his wound was causing him to panic. I'd seen it happen to accomplished swimmers; in choppy waters—sometimes even in calm conditions—they would panic and forget how to doggy-paddle to safety.

"Help!" Pratt burbled as his bullet head went under.

"Damn it," I said, crawling toward him with steady, measured strokes.

In warden school, I'd received a few hours of instruction in what to do if you capsize: how to rescue any passengers you might have in the boat with you. The tutorial had included far too little on the specific challenges of lifesaving. I was unprepared when Pratt, feeling my hand grapple around his wrist, decided that the best way to keep his nose above water was by pushing down on my shoulders while he kicked violently. As a further insult, he managed to knee me in the sternum.

Now I was the one submerged and fighting for air. I'd clamped my mouth shut before he'd pushed my head under, but some inhaled water was burning my sinuses as if I'd taken a snort of carbolic acid. Pratt was as powerful as a sideshow strongman, and his newfound terror had made his grip unbreakable.

Blind under water, feeling as if I were being deliberately drowned, the only thought that occurred to me was to go on the offense, so to speak. I drove my fist hard against Ammon Pratt's belly, close enough to his gunshot wound that he seemed to lose not just his hold on me but his will to live.

My head popped above the surface, and I drew in enough air that my lungs strained to contain it all.

"Stop it, Pratt! Just stop it. Let me tow you to the shallows."

Wide-eyed and cursing, he tried to climb on top of me again.

This time I dove, escaping his gorilla hands as they sought to grab me.

I submerged myself until I was well beneath the flailing man—the lake was deeper here than I'd imagined—and then came up behind him. Before he could swing around to get at me, I wrapped my arm around his throat, stretched out my body, and began to kick with all my might.

One hand found my biceps. "Choking me!"

If I'd actually been choking him, he wouldn't have been able to sputter at all.

"Stop it," I breathed as he continued to fight me. "Relax."

Eventually, he seemed to get the message.

This low to the surface, where the mist was thickest, I couldn't see a damned thing, but I had a sense we might be getting close to land. I stopped kicking and let my legs fall toward the bottom. But my boots encountered nothing but more water.

Pratt's panic returned as he tried the same maneuver and failed to find support.

"Stop it," I whispered in the same tone I might have used with Shadow—another dangerous, half-wild creature.

The next time I felt for the bottom, I found it.

Pratt managed to get hold of a sapling growing amid the tumbled rocks, but when he tried using it to drag himself ashore, he succeeded only in pulling the young tree up by the roots.

"I think you really hurt me with that punch," he groaned.

Above us, a cliff face plunged almost straight into the lake. Even fresh and uninjured, I would have had trouble pulling myself out here. Pratt had no chance whatsoever.

I dug my gloved fingertips into a gap between two stones while I continued treading water. "You were in the process of drowning me."

"You deserve to be drowned." He tried to cough up the pints he'd swallowed, but the pain tested his endurance. "How do we get out of this fucking lake?"

"We need to cross this outlet. It's where Deadwater Brook flows in."

"I'm done swimming for the night, bub."

"That's what you think."

Uncharacteristically for him, he accepted this grim reality without a fight. "Then what do we do?"

"There's a point due north of us. The topo map showed a path to a little stream called Dingley Brook. I'm almost positive that's where Renaud and his accomplice are headed."

"Why?"

"If they manage to navigate up the brook, they can land almost within sight of the Québec border. Now, can you swim across the outlet, Ammon? Or are you going to panic again and try to drown me?"

"I didn't panic until you fucking punched me."

"Whatever."

31

The last leg seemed to take forever. But eventually, we waded out of the muck, heavy-footed and trailing tendrils of pond vegetation like Creatures from the Black Lagoon. The lake fog seemed to wrap around our torsos and thighs as if unwilling to let us go.

For the first time all night, I heard frogs: thousands of spring peepers making an earsplitting din in the marsh. The individual amphibians were smaller than my thumbnail. But collectively, they had the power to drive a person insane with their ceaseless, high-decibel songs.

"You said there's a path somewhere," Pratt said between labored exhalations.

"It's above us and runs parallel to the shore. Keep in mind the map I have is old."

"Now you tell me."

"We're lucky we got this far. We may be no closer to civilization. But if we can reach the slash ahead of them—"

"The slash?"

"The cleared corridor in the woods between Maine and Québec."

"Is there something magical about this slash?"

"You might say so."

Despite his nearly having drowned me, I was having second thoughts about the bounty hunter. My initial impression of him as a buffoon who lacked all common sense remained. I sure as hell wasn't going to share secrets about how the United States border is surveilled.

But I was beginning to feel a certain grudging respect for his grit. In his less bombastic moments, I almost felt affection toward the ungentle giant. But whatever his rude charms, I knew better than to trust him. When he'd said his only goal was catching Renaud to secure fame and fortune, I had known he was telling the truth.

As we stumbled into the tree line, I tried the Nitecore, fearing the battery might have gotten wet, but the gaskets had held, and a beam shot ahead of us into the thin mist.

"Hang on a sec."

Pratt cast an ill-tempered glance over his shoulder. "Shouldn't we keep going?"

"I need to take inventory."

I had the Browning and its mags, zipped into my Gore-Tex jacket, and the flare gun with its one remaining flare. The Ruger revolver remained hidden at my ankle, but Pratt's CZ pistol had gone down with my rucksack. I also had two Bic lighters. And a pocketknife. As well as the shredded remains of Chloé's topo map. The chart was faded and coming apart at the seams where it had been folded and refolded, but it remained readable.

Perhaps most important, I still had my iPhone. The bright white apple appeared like a hope fulfilled when I powered it up. As long as I had one functional cell, we weren't out of chances.

Then a look at Pratt reminded me of what I had lost. He was leaning an elbow against a platy-barked yellow birch while he breathed through clenched teeth. Without my trauma pack, I had no way to dress his wound again.

I used the flashlight to locate the trail running along the western edge of the lake. I was a little shocked to find it, and within a matter of minutes, too. Nothing had gone easily for me all day. So locating the path seemed less like good luck and more like a potentially bad omen.

Gazing down at the lake, I saw that the mist was dissipating.

Pratt trudged before me now with rounded shoulders. Every few yards, he needed the help of the tree trunks to pull himself along. He seemed to be suffering more than before he'd gone into the water. What if I *had* effectively killed him by punching the gunshot wound and moving the bullet?

"Tell me something," I said, trying to distract him—and my conscience. "How did you really find out that Renaud had crossed into Maine?"

"I ain't sharing my professional secrets with you, bub."

"You beat someone up, I'm guessing."

He halted and gave me a cock-eyed, amused expression, as if I'd happened on the truth.

"You did beat someone up." But before I could ask who, the answer became immediately obvious. "The man whose camp Renaud built on the Cascapédia River! But how did you find him?"

Pratt kept walking, or rather, staggering.

"If you die tonight," I said, trying to make the words sound like a tease instead of a prophecy, "you're going to wish you'd told me your secrets so I could share the details of your final adventures on TV."

"I ain't going to wish anything because I'll be dead."

"I thought Mormons believed in heaven."

"I'm doomed to the telestial—*not* celestial—kingdom. You are, too, Bowditch. Men like us don't live in glory. We don't get to enjoy grace in the heavenly paradise."

I couldn't come close to parsing this statement, nor was I interested in having a theological discussion with Ammon Pratt, PI. I kept quiet, hoping his natural braggadocio would win out.

"The guy in New Brunswick, I had to rough him up a little," he admitted at last. "Like I said before, he was retired from the Canada Border Service. So, as it happens, was the guy whose cabin Renaud built before that, in Ontario."

We were leaving the cacophony of the peepers behind. I found it easier to think without the frogs piercing my eardrums.

"So Paul has been trading carpentry work for favors with influential officials in the Border Service," I said. "It's how he's managed to elude capture. But how did he get through an American checkpoint? They have access to Interpol's database in Jackman. Paul and Chloé had to have fake identities on authentic passports."

Pratt made that disappointed ursine sound that wasn't quite a sigh.

"Unless he has someone working on the U.S. side, too," I said as my mind caught up with the ramifications. "Who the hell *is* Renaud? How has he been able to outwit law enforcement agencies in two countries?"

"I ain't telling you that one."

"Why not?"

"I don't care if I take my biggest secrets to the grave. I ain't going to let you get rich pretending you were the one who figured it all out."

"If getting rich was my goal in life, I never would have joined the Maine Warden Service."

Pratt continued shuffling forward. "Or maybe you're just a fool."

I tried to keep the light trained on the ground ahead of him so he wouldn't stumble over a log or trip on a rock. But he kept moving slower and slower. He was pressing his left hand against the wound, and when we paused and I asked to see his stomach, blood trickled through his fingers.

"I'm sorry for punching you."

"Fuck you, Ranger."

"Warden."

He waved his red hand at me. He had grown tired of our little game. I couldn't blame him.

We'd just started forward again when he collapsed. He used a bendy cedar sapling to steady himself as he took a seat on a boulder. We'd entered one of those dark, wet stretches of woods you find in ravines and other shadowy areas that receive little sun even in summer. Shreds of lichen hung in the trees like torn green rags.

"I'm done," he said.

"No, you're not. You're going to make it."

"I didn't say I was dying, fuckface. I said, 'I'm done.' As in, I'm staying here. I don't care about Renaud. Just call for help, bub. Find a cell signal ASAP and get some EMTs out here with about six pints of O Positive. A hundred grand won't do me any good in a Boise crematorium."

He'd displayed such drive—albeit zero judgment—since he'd arrived in Rockwood. Few people in his place would even have made it to the shelter of that school bus. Ammon Pratt had crossed a lake, swimming half the way, with a high-caliber bullet in his abdomen.

"Leave me one of your lighters, OK?"

"I can make you a fire."

"And waste more time while I bleed out. No thanks. I was a Cub Scout once, hard as it may be for you to believe. I earned the badge for making campfires."

I was deeply uncomfortable with the thought of leaving him behind. The image of returning with help and finding a corpse was vivid enough that it seemed almost a premonition.

But Pratt was slowing me down, and if I shifted my goal from trying to find the fugitives to searching for a cell signal, I might manage to both save the dying man and alert two border services that Paul Renaud was escaping into Québec.

"Don't move from this spot," I said. "If you do, it'll lessen the chances of anyone finding you while you're still breathing."

"I got it, bub, I got it. Don't go nowhere."

My last sight of him was leaning over a curl of birchbark with a flickering Bic. He was trying and failing to get the edge to light. His face was all screwed up with concentration.

I doubted whether I would see Ammon Pratt alive again.

32

The path curved westward, through the marshy gap into Canada, but I chose to bushwhack down to the lake. I wanted a quick look at Dingley Brook before I headed inland. From the shreds of the map, I had no idea whether the stream was navigable. It made a difference which way they'd gone.

I nearly stumbled over the Grand Laker abandoned in some willows at the edge of the outlet. I froze like a deer in case my enemies were waiting in the shadows. Then I realized they would have concluded they'd left Pratt and me well behind. If they'd caught sight of us clowns in our sinking boat, they would have had a good laugh and continued on with confidence. Even I, who had endured the dunking, would've put odds against us having survived. I was certain our deliverance had been blessed by whatever saint looks out for grown men with the terrible judgment of teenage boys.

I understood at once why they'd left the boat behind. Despite the high, burbling water, the stream had proved impassable. A peek up the brook with the flashlight showed logs jammed helter-skelter between boulders.

I next inspected the Grand Laker, removing some of the fern fronds and balsam boughs they'd used to camouflage it. There was blood in the boat, all of it pooled in the stern. I must have hit the man I was calling Charon with my second shot. I'd more than winged him. There was a lot of blood.

I went looking for their trail.

Had the woods-wise Renauds been alone, I might have missed their tracks. Even injured, Paul left only the faintest of traces behind him, and I saw no sign of Chloé's elfin prints in the leaf litter.

Charon's clumsiness was what gave the fugitives away. Between the kicked-up moss, flattened fiddleheads, and spots of blood, he'd left the equivalent of a painted arrow pointing the way toward their destination.

Who is he?

Most likely a corrupt agent in the Services frontaliers. But his firearm hadn't been one of their duty weapons. To my knowledge, the Canada Border Services Agency didn't equip its officers with big, booming .45s.

A stubborn hunch told me he had to be Nadeau.

Sometimes, when I got overconfident in my predictions, Charley would suggest that I practice humility "just for the novelty of the experience."

I could guess what my father-in-law would tell me now. *"What makes you so damned certain your hooded man isn't American?"*

His nationality didn't matter much at the moment. But it might matter a great deal if I had to make a fateful decision—to cross or not to cross—the border.

Climbing over the low rise between the watersheds, I found a stand of cedars so closely packed their boughs might have been artfully braided. Within the cover of these deer-nipped trees, I checked the topo map one last time. The soaked paper dissolved between my fingers.

But by the glow of the Nitecore, I could see that this very spot was less than a quarter of a mile from the Boundary. The trail led uphill. There was no longer any doubt where Renaud hoped to cross.

If they could get over the hump between Penobscot Lake and Lac Portage, they would be safe—at least from me. Pursuing them into Québec without sanction, and toting prohibited firearms to boot, would be a major violation of international laws. My status as a

Maine law enforcement officer mattered not at all after I crossed the slash into the sovereign nation on the far side. I might well be prosecuted for my incursion.

Fuck it.

If I was going to end my career, then I would end it saving a child. I might live to regret what I was about to do; but I would regret it even more if I let Paul Renaud escape to continue abusing his daughter when they were mere minutes ahead of me.

The trail became easier as it climbed—a Cub Scout could have followed it. I had to remember that Renaud was also hurting, from that truck crash and his fight with Pratt. The trio of escapees didn't have the time, energy, or endurance for advanced evasion techniques.

Halfway up the hillside, the realization hit me.

I don't have to follow them.

I can get ahead of them.

I might have been soaked, shivering, and borderline hypothermic, but I was pumped with so much adrenaline that I felt as if I could run from here to Montreal. The two men ahead of me, by contrast, were badly injured and dragging along an exhausted child.

Under most conditions, it would be a stupid move, leaving an easy-to-read trail to attempt a flanking maneuver. But I had a shot at catching them before they reached Lac Portage in Québec.

More to the point: If I were in Renaud's place, would I prepare against the possibility of a pursuer using this nutso tactic?

No.

Not knowing me, Paul Renaud had to assume that I valued my career. I'd clearly worked hard for my position as an investigator with the Warden Service. Why would I throw it away sneaking into a foreign country?

I turned left where the escapees' footpath circled around a glacial moraine. I felt a surge of blood to my glutes and quads as I summited the ridge. Provided I didn't make too much noise, I could cross the corridor and beat them to Lac Portage. I might even set off one of the hidden sensors or motion-detecting cameras that guarded the slash. If I did, it would attract an armed force of border agents to assist me at the final confrontation.

There was no view at the top, but through the mostly bare branches I glimpsed a burning ember in the sky. It was Mars, I realized. The storm had passed, the clouds were thinning to gauze, and the red planet had appeared to guide me into battle.

I'd barely begun to descend before I stumbled, almost without realizing it, into the corridor.

The border was hardly well marked, especially in the near-worthless starlight. It was a twenty-foot-wide clearing that stretched endlessly away to my right and left. The ground between the walls of trees was soft and tussocky. Every summer, a bushhogger must have driven the length of the slash, clearing away any upstart plants that might render its significance ambiguous.

I'd worked the corridor before. Like most wardens I'd participated in a federal program code-named "Stonegarden." It had been created as a force multiplier to allow local law enforcement agencies stationed along the border to work extra shifts and gather information to assist the feds.

On those occasions, I'd reflected on the gross disparities between how this border was policed versus the line that separated the United States from Mexico. There were no walls or barbed wire here. No families fleeing war zones. No coyotes except the kind that ran on four legs and didn't abandon their marks to perish in the desert at the first sign of La Migra.

Would Paul and Chloé Renaud have been able to slip so easily into this country if they'd come from the south rather than the north? Maybe no. Maybe yes. The question was moot in any case.

Red Mars caught my eye again, and I remembered the promise I'd made to Pratt. Standing in the open, beneath clearing skies, I tried the phone again.

Two bars.

A signal.

And a notification: *Welcome to Canada. Talk, text, and data rates*

are not included in your domestic plan. Additional charges apply for
international roaming.

If I ever made it home, I thought cynically, I would have to add
the fees to the reimbursement form I submitted with my report.

Then an unfamiliar male voice spoke from the darkness.

"Je pense que la balle a sectionné un nerf."

It had to be Renaud's accomplice, the hooded, wounded man
Charon was muttering some complaint in French.

The trio entered the slash a hundred yards to the south of me.
I had been right about them having abandoned stealth in their
weariness and eagerness to cross into Canada. Two high-powered
flashlights—one nearly a spotlight—marked their positions as they
stepped from the tree line into the cut.

If forced to guess, I would have said they were searching for a
known gap in the surveillance: a mousehole through which they
could squeeze into Canada unnoticed.

If only I had crossed the corridor first! Then I could have waited
in the cover beyond and lined up potential kill shots. But because we
were parallel to one another, I had no advantage at all.

I dropped into the weeds and began scrambling forward through
the puckerbrush. If I triggered a hidden sensor myself—an "Oscar"
I'd heard a border patrol agent call one of these devices—all the
better. I desperately needed backup.

Halfway through my snake's-eye journey across the slash, I came
upon an obstacle. It was a granite monument on a granite pedes-
tal. The stubby obelisk was one of hundreds—maybe thousands—of
identical stones strung along the border from Maine to British
Columbia.

I remembered seeing one for the first time in full sunlight and
thinking how quaint and amiable it seemed, this little marker in the
woods. I hadn't realized that, despite the profusion of weeds at my
feet, I was standing in a semi-militarized zone of sorts. It might look
like a mowed clearing, but there were men and women on both sides,
armed with automatic weapons, to prevent bad actors from crossing.

I hadn't planned on hiding behind the obelisk.

But I hadn't planned on a gunshot, either.

From behind me and to the left came the report of a pistol. One of the flashlights jerked toward the American side of the slash. The other, brighter light dropped to the earth. I was certain I saw Paul Renaud fall.

"Papa?" Chloé's voice was a shriek now. "Papa?"

"It's all right," answered the voice of a man who most certainly was not all right. "Come here, chickpea . . ."

"I don't want to."

For a moment, I couldn't move my muscles; my mind hadn't yet processed what was happening.

Then I understood. It was Pratt, of course. Once I'd left the bounty hunter, he had ceased his playacting and come staggering along behind us. I'd said the trail was easy enough for a Cub Scout to follow. And Pratt had claimed that he'd worn one of those blue uniforms in his long-ago youth.

But where had he managed to pick up a gun?

And then my mind found its way to the answer. I'd stuffed his CZ into my rucksack. Then in the sinking boat, I'd tossed the pack to him. He might not have found a cup useful for bailing water from the boat, but he had managed to pocket his old pistol.

Now he fired twice more in the direction of where Renaud was lying supine.

I rose to my knees, using the obelisk for cover, not knowing what might happen.

"Stop firing, Pratt! You'll hit the girl."

Then I heard Charon speak again in French.

"*C'est bon, Paul,*" and then words I didn't recognize ending with one I did: *sécurité*. He would make sure Chloé was safe.

Renaud called from the ground, "*Non! Non!*"

"Toss out your guns, asswipes," snarled Pratt from his place of concealment. "Toss them out, and I may let you live. But no guarantees! I don't take kindly to being shot in the gut."

"For Christ's sake, Pratt!" I shouted back. "This isn't TV!"

"*Viens avec moi, petite Chloé—*"

"*Non!*" Renaud barked again.

Was he addressing Charon? He seemed to be. He didn't want his daughter to accompany the other man.

I had one flare remaining. Whether it would fire after having been dunked was an open question. I pulled the trigger of the plastic gun, and miracle of miracles, the projectile ignited as it arced high above the narrow corridor in the forest.

I will never forget what I saw in that glow: Renaud, on his knees, reaching for his daughter with his crooked, broken arm while he held the other arm outstretched, clutching that cannon of a revolver. Only he wasn't aiming in Pratt's direction, and he sure as hell wasn't aiming at me.

He was trying to find Chloé in his gunsights.

The stunt he'd pulled at the sugarhouse hadn't been an empty threat, I realized with horror. He was genuinely prepared to kill the girl before he died.

"*Paul? Que fais-tu?*" asked his mystified accomplice.

Now Charon interposed himself between Renaud and his daughter, seeking to safeguard the vulnerable girl. He'd thrown off his hood to reveal a face I didn't recognize. In the dying glow of the descending flare, he offered a reassuring smile to his comrade. He had dropped his own gun and was holding his hands aloft to show he meant no harm.

Charon didn't know what was about to happen.

But I knew.

Paul Renaud shot his accomplice dead with a perfectly placed bullet to the brain.

33

The flare landed and sputtered in the wet bushes, but not before I saw Renaud turn his shaking gun hand toward his daughter. Chloé was backing toward the Canadian edge of the slash: a perfect hedgerow of evergreens, all the same height, all clearly planted in the same year. Then Ammon Pratt came charging out of the near woods, as big as a grizzly and moving with the same surprising speed as those ungainly animals.

And suddenly, we were again in darkness.

"Don't you hurt her!" It was Pratt, guttural and enraged.

I heard shots fired in succession, at least five from the CZ, one from the Colt. Followed by a heavy thud.

I leaped out from behind the obelisk and began rushing forward heedlessly in the direction of the thud.

"Police! Drop your weapons!"

Then a familiar voice rose boomed from the ground ahead. "Did I get him? Did I get him, Mike?"

I dropped to one knee. "Pratt?"

"Tell me I got the motherfucker."

There was nothing, no sound, from Renaud's last location.

Maybe Pratt had killed him. I hadn't expected the gruff, bumptious, self-promoting bounty hunter to trade his life for a girl's. But he must have known that was the deal. He must have seen the revolver in her father's hand as clearly as I had, and understood what it portended. And he must have anticipated that the revolver would be turned on him if he chose to charge Renaud's position.

I heard labored breathing several yards ahead of me. I clicked on the Nitecore.

The beam showed Ammon Pratt lying on his side, one arm thrown over his head, his knees bent a little. He looked like a man restless in bed and unable to sleep. His eyes were half-open. But he had died.

I had missed his death rattle.

Instantly, I swung the light toward where Renaud had been. It first caught the crumpled form of Charon against the gray-green undergrowth. Then it found an impression in the weeds where a man had dragged himself toward the far evergreens. Fresh blood, bright red with oxygen, glistened on the bent grass.

I flicked the light off and rolled sideways in case Renaud was somehow still alive.

But there was no shot.

Nor did I hear Chloé across the corridor. Was she waiting there? Or had she dashed deeper into the trees to escape her murderous father?

From my new angle, I tried the light again.

This time, the beam found him.

Paul Renaud was lying on his stomach, arms outstretched in a posture that I wouldn't want to dignify with the word *crucified* but which described his position better than any other. His legs were pressed together at the knees as if he'd lost use of them. Perhaps he had. Maybe one of the 9mm rounds from the CZ had severed his spinal nerve.

I saw two black spots in his coat: one below the left shoulder blade, the other inches from a kidney.

His left hand was purple and swollen from the break he'd suffered when he'd crashed into that boulder.

His right hand gripped the handle of that deadly revolver.

He looked as if life had left him. He looked harmless.

"Don't presume you ever have the drop on him," my father-in-law's voice reminded me.

Without a moment's hesitation, I threw myself across his bullet-riddled body and caught hold of his right wrist.

Even before I landed on him, he was already twisting to fire the Colt at me.

I would have thought my weight alone would have been sufficient to explode the air from his lungs. And yet this relentless man somehow had the strength to fight. As I twisted his wrist, digging for the pressure point that would force the muscles in his hand to release the gun, he tried to drive the back of his skull into my chin.

"Son of a—"

I finally found his radial nerve and dug my thumb into the soft tissue. Then I snapped his wrist back, not hard enough to break it but with enough force that a breath hissed from between his teeth. With my left hand, I reached for the handcuffs in their holster on the back of my belt.

I cuffed Paul Renaud in one swift, crisp motion. As soon as he was secured, I found myself wanting to twist the bracelets, to inflict that extra edge of pain. But I resisted the base and shameful instinct. Instead, I released one hand and took hold of his shoulder and flipped him roughly onto his back.

His face reminded me of a Japanese theater mask: chalk white and contorted in an exaggerated depiction of agony. More than grotesque, demonic. He had his eyes squeezed so tightly shut that tears were gushing down his bloodless cheeks.

Standing over my enemy now, holding the light on him and the Browning, too, I could tell at once from his knock-knees that he had lost the ability to move his legs. One of Pratt's bullets had caught him in the spine.

He parted his bluing lips. Blood gleamed red on his tongue.

"Renaud?"

Without opening his clenched eyes, he spat a word: "Killer."

"I'm not the one who shot you, asshole. It was Ammon Pratt. And, congratulations, you got him. If there's a murderer here, it's you. Pratt brings your score tonight to three."

The faintest shake of his head. "No."

"Almost four if he hadn't stopped you."

His eyes snapped open. Shock had caused his pupils to dilate until the cornea, too, had vanished.

"No."

His insistence made me want to laugh. "I saw you kill them. Josie, your buddy over there, Pratt. You're a fucking murderer, Renaud. But even so, I'm going to do my best to save your worthless life."

It was a meaningless pledge, of course. We both knew he would be dead in minutes.

I was reaching for my phone when he repeated with great difficulty the word *killer*.

Were his multiple injuries causing the neurons in his brain to misfire? "I told you I wasn't the one who shot you."

"Kill . . . her."

I wasn't sure I had heard him.

"Kill Chloé?"

"Dangerous. Too dangerous."

He wasn't delirious. He was as cogent as ever. He was trying to tell me something, pass along some final warning.

My memory flashed back to the minutes before Josie had died, the last words Renaud and I had spoken to each other before he'd left us tied to those trees. I'd told him to think of his daughter, and he'd responded with more real emotion than he'd expressed in my presence.

"It's all I've ever done, you idiot. Isn't it obvious by now?"

I remembered what Ammon Pratt had told me about how father and daughter had come to be on the run. He'd claimed to be sitting on several big secrets. One of them was now being revealed. Without giving voice to the horrific idea in my head, I wanted the dying man to disavow it.

"What are you saying? What are you trying to tell me?"

"You can't let her . . ."

Pratt had described in gory detail how Paul Renaud had supposedly killed his ex-wife.

"The brutal SOB shot her through the heart, and not even cleanly. The Mounties said it took her fifteen minutes to die. The guy really hated her, is all I can think. He wanted that lady to suffer."

The description went against everything I had come to know about Renaud over the night. His precision and decisiveness, his immunity from panic.

Paul hadn't shot Selene.

Chloé had.

It explained the self-harm. It explained the continuing mood swings between fear and outrage and glee. It explained why she'd become more and more unhinged as the night had gone on.

And I, in my ignorance and naive belief in the innocence of children, had failed to see the truth in front of me.

Because Chloé had been the one who'd put the drugs in our coffee, too.

Which meant her conscience wasn't just writhing with the knowledge she'd killed her own mother. Intentional or not, she'd murdered her surrogate grandmother as well. Josie Jonson had been kind to her, and Chloé had taken her life.

I dropped to one knee. Renaud was losing consciousness fast. His eyelids had begun to flutter.

"Did Chloé kill Selene, Paul? You need to say it for me. I need to hear the words out loud."

"You can't . . ."

"Yes or no?"

His eyes closed. I pressed two fingers to his carotid artery.

There was a pulse, very faint, very slow.

Never in my life had I met a man who clung so stubbornly to life. How was he not dead?

"Paul? Paul?"

I kept my fingers on his throat until I no longer felt blood flowing.

I didn't know why I had wanted him to confirm what I knew to be the truth. The past years on the run had never been about *his* escaping justice. Paul Renaud had only wanted to protect his murderous daughter. He had wanted to safeguard Chloe from being put away in some walled hospital. He'd given himself entirely to this cause.

But he couldn't protect her against self-knowledge, however much he might have tried, not through books or through lessons in woodcraft. He must have known the torture that was her existence. He was too smart not to have known.

But how could he have seen death as a better option?

His own daughter?

How many times has he stood with a loaded gun over her in her sleep?

He'd been planning her murder and his suicide probably from their first day as fugitives. The man planned everything, Charley had reminded me.

I glanced toward the tree line where Chloé had taken cover. I needed to lure her out. But at the moment I was too stunned, too confused, too unsure what I could possibly say.

Stalling for time while I formulated a plan, I turned out Renaud's pockets. I found two sets of passports: American and Canadian. Both looked genuine to my eye.

In the Canadian document, Paul Renaud was bearded and long-haired. His weight was listed in kilos, which my brain had a hard time reckoning in pounds. But he'd been heavier once. Renaud was the muscle-bound mountain man I had been led by Josie to expect.

Mark Redmond, by contrast, had done his best to appear bland, nondescript, and unthreatening in his passport photo. Here was a man at whom a Border Patrol agent wouldn't glance twice. His birthplace was given as Meadow Lakes, Alaska. He was three years younger than his other self.

How had he obtained a genuine U.S. passport? It might have been a convincing forgery that could fool the eye of a nonexpert, but the documents produced by Customs and Border Protection came with secret technological safeguards. The days of printing fake IDs to travel abroad were as dead as James Earl Ray.

Renaud must have had powerful allies, and not just in Canada. But who?

There was movement now in my peripheral vision.

Chloé Renaud blinked when I raised my flashlight beam. She'd half emerged from the evergreens as quietly as a woodland creature. With her face muddy, her jacket shredded, and her hair coming loose from its braids, she looked like one of those feral children from Indian folklore.

"It's all right!"

Even as I uttered the words, I thought that among the many lies I'd told that night, this was the worst of them, because nothing would ever be all right again for Chloé Renaud.

Somehow, though, my next lie was even more egregious.

"I can help you, Chloé."

She didn't speak. She remained suspended in the wet boughs as if being clutched by them. I thought she must be in severe shock. How could she not be after everything she'd done and watched being done?

But she wasn't in shock, not in the sense that I'd thought. She'd heard me. And she'd most definitely seen me. Because as I holstered my gun and took several steps in her direction, crossing the invisible border at my feet, she had the presence of mind to draw my own weapon and fire a shot at me that was louder than any cannon.

Part III

It's a life's work to see yourself for what you really are and even then you might be wrong.

—Cormac McCarthy, *No Country for Old Men*

34

The round grazed the lowered hood of my poncho. The bullet passed within millimeters of my jugular and ripped the fabric bunched around my neck. Even though it missed my throat, it was still one hell of a shot.

I hit the ground beside Renaud's corpse. We lay side by side, as close as an elderly married couple sharing a twin bed.

Being shot at with my own service weapon only added insult to the injury I was feeling.

"Chloé, stop!"

But she hadn't fired more than that first round. No doubt her father had taught her not to waste ammunition shooting into the darkness. As I drew the Browning again, in case she planned on rushing my position, it seemed that I tasted the bloody coffee I had vomited up earlier.

I can't shoot a child.

And if she knew that about me or merely suspected that my scruples would cause me to hesitate before I fired, then she had me at a potentially fatal disadvantage.

On television and in movies, you see pretend cops shoot to wound. But this is nothing any real law enforcement officer is ever taught. We learn the opposite, in fact: never draw your weapon unless you have no other choice and are prepared to take a life—either to protect yours or someone else's. Any bullet, even fired by a sharpshooter who has aimed for a part of the body devoid of major arteries or essential organs, has the potential to be fatal. Firearms, by design, are meant to deal death.

As I lay on my back, clutching the pistol with both hands, ready to roll and take aim (even if I doubted I could bring myself to squeeze the trigger), I noticed that Mars was fading. The color of the sky was closer to charcoal now than black.

Dawn was coming: a clear and cloudless dawn.

Think, Bowditch. You need to reach her.

Paul Renaud had brainwashed his daughter into believing that every cop posed an existential threat to them. At the same time, her "papa" must have loomed constantly in her waking and sleeping mind as the likely agent of her destruction. Did she feel abandoned and alone now? Or was she feeling liberated from a lifelong fear? Either way, the girl must have been stressed to the very edge of sanity.

I rolled away from Renaud. I wanted Chloé not to know where I might be.

Only when I was ten feet clear of my former position did I dare raise my head.

The Canadian side of the slash was a jagged line of balsam firs. She might have been hidden there, squatting amid the wet boughs; she might have fled. Chloé Renaud had been taught to remain quiet, and it was impossible for me to guess.

Where would she go?

My gut told me she knew that her father's evacuation route led through Lac Portage. But Paul would never have provided her with instructions on what to do if they were separated, for the obvious reason that his plans never embraced that possibility. Chloé's night had always been destined to end in escape or execution.

At the same time, I was certain that Charon wasn't Renaud's only accomplice. Pratt had said there were others, perhaps many others, in the Services frontaliers, the Royal Canadian Mounted Police, and maybe even U.S. Customs and Border Protection. Charon had been their designated guide into the borderlands of Québec. I strongly suspected another confederate was waiting at Lac Portage or beyond to escort the father and daughter on the next leg of their journey.

So Chloé was alone, for the time being.

But she was smart, too. Much smarter than I had been at her age. Smart enough for me to be as wary of her as I had been of her father.

I scrambled on my belly to the confederate Renaud had shot and killed. Despite the mythological nickname I'd given him, Charon was just another middle-aged guy with the bad haircut and hard features of a law enforcement officer. His eyes were wide open, as if death had chosen to preserve the shock and disbelief he'd felt watching his accomplice become his murderer.

I patted him down but discovered no badge or identification. Not even a wallet. He'd been carrying a Mora bushcraft knife on his belt and his own sidearm, a Springfield 1911 Garrison, in a generic Kydex holster.

I brought out my phone again and saw three bars now and the notification on the screen welcoming me to Canada. Over the preceeding hours, I'd had several cells in my possession and lost all but this one: my personal iPhone. I had hidden it from Renaud and protected it from his confiscation. And in the end, it was the only one I needed.

I hesitated as I ran down a mental list of everyone I might call for help. I had no idea whom I could trust. I had even less of an idea how to explain the events that had led to this moment.

The Maine Department of Public Safety: the nexus of law enforcement in the state I'd left behind.

The Warden Service colonel.

The Jackman office of U.S. Customs and Border Protection.

The nearest headquarters of the Services frontaliers, southwest of Prentiss Pond in Armstrong.

But there was only one person I ever considered calling.

"Mike?" said Stacey, answering at once despite the lateness, or rather the earliness, of the hour. "Where are you?"

"Canada. Right on the slash northwest of Jackman. I've been chasing Mark Redmond and his daughter all night. Their real names are Paul and Chloé Renaud, and they're fugitives and murderers from Canada. They killed Josie, Stace. I'm so sorry."

She didn't miss a beat. "Where's my dad?"

"He's OK. I think he's at Josie's cabin—if he hasn't already walked out to Route 201."

"So you were right about Redmond—"

"Not right enough. But he's dead now. His daughter, Chloé, is still at large, though, and I'm going after her into Québec. She's a killer, too, Stace, and maybe even more dangerous than her father because she's unbalanced and unpredictable. I'm sending you my coordinates so you can contact the colonel and he can alert the U.S. and Canadian border agencies."

"You can't cross into Canada without authorization, Mike."

"I know I can't. But I'm doing it, anyway. The girl is a killer. I'll never be able to live with myself if she hurts someone else."

"What did she—?"

"It's a long story, and I still don't know the half of it."

Just then, I heard three sharp blasts on a survival whistle. The sound came from the west. I couldn't judge the distance.

"That's her!"

"That whistling in the background?"

"I've got to go. Call the colonel. Tell him where I am and what I'm doing."

"Which is what exactly?"

"I wish I knew. But I love you, Stacey."

"I love you, too."

By now, I was already on my feet, knowing that Chloé Renaud had left the edge and wasn't waiting to pot-shoot me from within the nearest trees.

One thing held me back. While speaking with Stacey, my gaze had wandered back to the big man whose arrival had started me on this hunt. I stood over the body of Ammon Pratt, feeling almost like

I should speak a few words in memoriam. For all his bombast and buffoonery, the big gorilla had been a good private investigator—if a piss-poor woodsman.

It wasn't much of an epitaph, but it was the best I could do.

The last stars were dimming overhead. Search planes and helicopters would be able to take off now, and with luck, the colonel could mobilize the border agencies to take immediate action, converging on Lac Portage a quarter mile to my west.

I'd told Stacey that I wished I knew what I was doing. But in my heart, I had no doubt.

I was going to lose my job for breaking not just the state laws I'd sworn to obey and the regulations I was obliged to uphold. I might lose my freedom, too, for violating Canadian laws controlling entry into their nation. However dangerous Chloé Renaud might be, the bureaucrats in Ottawa wouldn't grant me a special dispensation. My status as a Maine warden investigator had ceased to matter. I had never been more on my own.

Still, I didn't hesitate. This ride had to end sometime.

I was unafraid of what was coming and prepared for the unpreparable.

As I crashed through the Canadian conifers, no different from those across the cut, a question intruded into my thoughts.

Why was Chloé blowing a whistle?

Three blasts is the international signal for help. With me on her tail, she wouldn't be giving away her location unless—

She had seen someone out on Lac Portage and was trying to get their attention. Was it another of her father's unsuspecting accomplices or some innocent bystander, a fisherman out early for squaretails? By all appearances, Chloé Renaud was a helpless girl, alone at the edge of a howling wilderness. Anyone with a conscience would rush to rescue a lost and vulnerable child. They couldn't possibly imagine that a mud-spattered waif might be the agent of their death.

I had to get to the lake before the boat reached her.

35

Once I'd gotten through the wet wall of firs, I found that the forest on the Canadian side of the corridor was wetter than the higher ground above. Young ferns unfurled amid the matted maple and beech leaves, and there were muddy pools from which mounds of skunk cabbages and their poisonous cousins, false hellebore, sprouted. Fresh deer prints showed in the black, ill-smelling mud. You never appreciate how small their hooves can be until you see them in soggy ground.

I chanced using the Nitecore to follow Chloé's trail. She'd given her location away at the edge of the lake. I might as well use the flashlight if it meant I could move faster through the swamp.

Hurrying through a landscape of widowmakers and deadfalls can feel like running one of those gauntlets the Native tribes had made their captured enemies pass between. Lines of warriors armed with sticks and clubs on all sides. The way the woods beat me up made me empathize with the prisoners of the Wendat and the Haudenosaunee.

I didn't pick up Chloé's trail but kept forging steadily west. In time, I saw light bleeding between the trunks and heard a phoebe offering its high-pitched, two-parted song to the dawn. The birds are flycatchers that prefer treelines and chase bugs hatching out of lake bottoms. I must have been nearing the shore.

As soon as I emerged from the woods, however, I realized I had come out too far to the south.

Before me was a cove littered with sun-whitened stumps and logs—the bones of once-submerged trees. Mainers called these desiccated hunks of wood *dri-ki*. And now they constituted something like a spiky barrier between me and the water's edge. I looked for indications that Chloé had come this way but concluded she had veered to the north where a forested point jutted into peaceful Lac Portage.

In the twilight, the water was gray and calm except where fish were rising to take gnats on the surface. Circles appeared and expanded in rings where brook trout and chubs sipped the small black bugs. It would have been a beautiful morning to be in a boat with a fly rod.

As I was breaking trail to avoid the dri-ki, Chloé blew the whistle again: three sharp blasts. I marked the location, just around the tip of the point and therefore out of view. From her map, I recalled that this arm of the lake was called Baie du Penob. The exoticness of the French name had left an impression. I remembered, as well, that there were no roads or trails on this side of Lac Portage—at least when the land had been surveyed and the map drawn many decades ago.

I had no idea to whom Chloé might be signaling, if anyone. I spotted no boat or the wake of a boat. But my view was blocked by the timber running along the point.

Chloé, panicked, might have been blasting away in vain. I hoped that was the case.

For the moment, I had no choice but to fight my way through the small saplings—alders, poplars, and willows—growing above the impenetrable dri-ki. I needed to reach the tip of that point, and this bushwhacking was easier than retreating into the swamp.

Luckily for me, I stumbled on a moose trail leading out to the peninsula. There were cloven tracks punched as deep as postholes in the mud. They had been left by a monster bull. Its size didn't entirely help me. As big as moose are, they can slip through shockingly narrow passages in the understory.

Then I heard it: a man's shouted voice coming from around the point. The words were unintelligible. They might have been in French, probably were French.

I didn't pause to catch the girl's reply.

But it seemed as if the man was calling, beckoning to her from an unseen boat.

I thought of firing three shots from the Browning as a warning. But I was learning enough about Chloé Renaud to suspect she'd tell her rescuer that a man with a gun was chasing her. And if I were in that hapless boater's place, wouldn't I have believed her, too?

Now: the distant scraping of wooden paddles against rocks. Or maybe it was the keel of a canoe being pulled up onto a ledge. More excited conversation in French.

My heart was heaving in my chest. My pulse beat overloud in my ears.

But before I could reach the end of the point, an outboard sputtered to life. I wasn't more than a minute away, but I was too late to prevent Chloé's escape.

When at last I broke free of the timber, I found myself at a picnic site. A wooden table was tucked beneath a crude roof of sorts and surrounded on three sides by red oaks and striped maples. Four bleached logs served as the supports for the shelter.

Before me stretched a long, wide ledge, streaked red with oxidized iron. At the very end of the rocks was what, at first, I took to be a cairn before realizing it was a makeshift firepit. In the summer, people must have come here to grill their day's catch.

And beyond that pile of stones, a fast-departing boat.

It was a fishing craft with a green hull, made for multiple passengers, some of whom might wish to stand to cast, and it carved a spreading *V* in the flatness of the lake.

Aside from the man holding the tiller, Chloé was the only passenger. He had put her in the bow, facing backward, and there was no doubt she saw me come blundering out of the trees. The distance was already too great for me to read her expression, but how could she not be feeling triumph at her unlikely escape?

Again, I considered firing a few shots into the air. But doing so would condemn Chloé's rescuer, I realized. Her father had surely taught her how to operate a motorboat, and what need would she have of the boatman now that she had his boat?

I began to pace in a circle on the striated ledge.

The picnic area had the feel of a place you can reach only by water. As a game warden, I had visited similar shelters on similar lakes. I looked around the table for a trail map but found nothing. I was stranded.

In my frustration, I started kicking apart the rock pile that made up the firepit. A rusted grate tilted over the sodden ashes. Bears must have routinely licked charred grease from that iron grill.

I was surprised not to see other fishermen. Was it possible the lake wasn't yet open? I had no idea about Canadian fishing seasons.

Who was the boater, then?

Not another of Renaud's accomplices. My impression of his body language said he was a civilian. The unfortunate man more likely had been a bystander out for an early cruise on Lac Portage.

Think, Mike.

What would Renaud and Charon have done if there hadn't been a convenient boater to hail when they arrived at the lake?

They had left the Grand Laker behind on the Maine side of the border, but that was always going to happen. There is no water passage from Penobscot Lake to Lac Portage, and they couldn't possibly have carried the motorized canoe through the swamp. This ledge—or somewhere near this ledge—had to have been their destination.

"There's another boat!" I said aloud.

And in less than five minutes, I found it, pulled up into some hobblebushes: a canoe with a raised bow and stern, the same design favored by French voyageurs and their Native guides. Inside, under a canvas cover laden with rain, were three long-bladed paddles. But I only needed one.

36

I didn't bother with stealth but paddled in a straight line, following the motorboat toward the western shore of the lake. Chloé had already spotted me, anyway. She continued to watch my canoe from her catbird seat.

Alone in a long canoe, you are always better off sitting backward on the bow seat, making the stern the front, so to speak, because it positions you closer to the center of the craft, where you have more control and greater balance.

Minute by minute, the sky was brightening from lead gray to slate blue. I couldn't yet feel the warmth of the sun on my neck, but I could see the shadow of the canoe stretching ahead of me—my own shadow, too.

A loon surfaced to starboard, its head sleek and black, its bill spear-shaped and gripping a medium-size trout, which it tossed back in one fluid motion and swallowed whole.

I was sweating heavily, my back especially, and breathing as if I'd run a half marathon. I did my best to remained focused. Nothing slowed me faster than thinking. And the western shore was miles away.

Now the sun was above the Boundary Mountains. The conifers on the ridges ahead of me popped with sudden and spectacular greenness. A moment later, the rays caught some reflective object—a window, perhaps—that could only be human-made. A cabin, at the water's edge. I made for the structure.

There was no wind nor any waves; the canoe glided through the top water as if the keel had been greased. Even so, I couldn't do better than four miles per hour. I kept waiting, too, for a gunshot to break the quiet. I couldn't help but imagine Chloé Renaud turning on her rescuer as soon as she stepped ashore—unless she had a scheme to get more use out of him.

My destination revealed itself in pieces. First as an indistinct cluster of docks. Then as a large golden building rising seemingly straight up from the bedrock at the water's edge. Only as I drew near did I see that the lodge, or whatever it was, sat on a high field-stone foundation that dropped from the porch into the indigo lake. The weathered logs that made up its walls had merely appeared gold in the sunlight.

The motorboat with the green hull was tied to one of the docks. It was the only boat present.

So the recreational fishing season hadn't opened yet. If it had, I would have seen other boats on the water or tied to the dock.

The first sounds I heard coming from the shore were staccato foot-steps. They were the unmistakable echo of young feet running. I saw the boy at once. He cried something in French, his voice high-pitched and excited—and also a little frightened. Then he went sprinting back to the lodge and safety.

So Chloé has already spoken to these people about me.

Who did she tell them I was?

What did she say I had done?

Best to keep paddling. Try to appear unthreatening. And hope the boatman spoke English and would hear me out before opening fire.

But I did not get my wish. The boatman had come down to the lakeshore and, not taking his chances, was standing in shadow at the landward end of the long dock. He was wearing a leather hat and a red overshirt. He was toting a scoped hunting rifle. Its shoul-der sling dangled from under his arms.

I could feel him squinting at me as I closed the distance. I had a fluttery feeling he was waiting for me to come within shooting distance, and I was right.

A hundred yards out, he brought the gun up fast and aimed it at me, using the magnifying scope to examine me and make a threat assessment. The mere fact that he was staring down the length of a rifle barrel told me that Chloé had spun one lie at least. A seasoned woodsman would never aim a firearm at another person unless he might have to kill them.

I stopped paddling, set my paddle across the thwarts, and let the momentum carry me in a line across the frictionless surface.

In a deep, rough voice, the man in the leather hat shouted at me in French, just a handful of words, only a couple of which I recognized.

He wanted me to keep coming—but slowly.

My late mother had been of French-Canadian descent, and her parents, my grandparents, had occasionally lapsed into their native tongue when we'd visited the family house. My mom had never taught me the language; she'd considered her working-class culture ripe for rejection. Nor had I studied French in high school or college. But I'd picked up a pidgin version through my work. I'd encountered many loggers from Canada, and a few moose poachers, in my travels through the Maine woods.

"*Je suis un policier américain!*"

Removing his hand from the stock of his rifle, the man beckoned me forward and spoke words I recognized.

"*Continuez de venir.*"

I wanted to show him my badge but couldn't remember the word for it. As I reached toward my belt, he jerked his rifle up.

"*Continuez de pagayer ou je tire!*"

I got the gist of this: keep paddling or he would shoot me.

An unseen current in the lake was slowing the canoe and turning it sideways. In the process, I was becoming an easier target.

Under the short brim of his hat, he stared through the scope at me as he advanced in careful steps down the dock.

I was having trouble recalling the Québécois term for *game warden*. My recreational reading tended toward history and natural history, as well as criminal law and investigative procedures. If I got out of this mess, I needed take a crash course in French, I decided.

And possibly parenting books, too, Mike, a niggling voice reminded me.

"Do you speak English?"

"Continuez de pagayer!"

Among the Québécois who lived on the farmland and in the villages between New England and the St. Lawrence, bilingualism couldn't be assumed. I'd discovered as much on the handful of trips I'd taken to Québec City and Montreal, the time when my Bronco had broken down being the most memorable.

I took hold of the paddle again and, twisting my torso, dug the blade into the water, making the slightest of J-strokes to correct course and bring me on a line toward him.

Soon I was close enough to see him clearly. He was squat, unshaven, with a complexion that some might have described as olive-toned. His bare hands were more deeply tanned than his face and neck. He looked to be in his late forties.

He must have been the lodge caretaker, I decided, probably here to begin or to continue opening the place for the season. That might be good or bad for me, based on his past encounters with Canadian wardens.

I brought the canoe parallel to the dock.

"Keep your hands where I can see!"

So he did speak English, albeit with a heavy accent.

"I'm an American police officer. Let me show you my badge."

"Non! Continuez de pagayer." Then added, "I want to see your hands. Understand?"

As soon as the bow came within reach of the dock, he grabbed hold of the gunwale. He kept his other hand on the rifle so that his index finger remained curled within the trigger guard. The man was confident and experienced with this firearm.

When his other grasping hand found the bowline, he yanked it from the canoe and, without looking, secured the rope to a cleat as he'd done thousands of times before.

"My name is Mike Bowditch. I'm a game warden—umm, *un garde-chasse*—"

"*Vous êtes garde-chasse?*"

"*Oui*—from Maine."

"Hands on the paddle!"

"I can show you my badge."

"*Savez-vous que vous êtes au Québec?* You have no authority here."

"The girl you picked up across the lake—"

"*La patrouille frontalière arrivera.* We will wait until they come. Understand? We will wait?"

"No."

He blinked at me over the scope and his rough voice became almost light with amusement. "No? No? I have the gun, you see? You do as I say."

"I'm going to stand up slowly and get out of the canoe."

Looking somewhere between amused and concerned, he brought the rifle up toward my legs but no higher.

"*Non!*"

"I am who I say I am, monsieur. I will wait for the border patrol to arrive, but not in the canoe. You can hold me at gunpoint while we wait. But I'm getting out of the boat."

"*Non! Non! Non!*"

I was testing him. He already had me at his mercy. The only way I could determine whether he was part of Renaud's scheme or an innocent bystander—the only way I could determine whether he was prepared to shoot a man in cold blood—was by seeing how he reacted to my provocation.

Despite his commands for me to halt, he backed away, feeling with his feet for any obstacles on the dock over which he might trip.

The floating wharf swayed beneath me. "What is your name, monsieur?"

"Stop there!"

"You are the caretaker of this lodge?"

"*L'auberge.* Yes."

"The girl you rescued, where is she?"

"Inside. She said you killed her father. She said you chased her."

"And you believed her?"

"I wait for the authorities. They decide. You must stop. Don't make me shoot. I don't want to shoot."

By now, I knew the caretaker didn't have it in him to kill me. But I wasn't going to spook him, either. I paused with my hands raised. He couldn't see the Browning in my belt beneath the shredded poncho, but he must have suspected it was there. He was very scared, I could tell. He'd never been in a position like this before. How many people had?

"She lied to you, monsieur. I'm willing to wait. But you must understand, she only looks helpless. She is very dangerous. Did you see that she has a gun herself?"

He didn't answer that question, but from the way he blinked at me above the scope, I knew for certain that he hadn't seen she was armed with my stolen SIG.

"Monsieur? That boy I saw before? Is he your son?"

"*Mon petit-fils.*"

"Your grandson. Where is he now?"

"*Dans l'auberge.*"

Shit. He was with Chloé.

The girl who'd already killed twice in sixteen hours now had a hostage.

37

I will walk ahead of you into the lodge with my hands raised," I said calmly and evenly. "But you need to take me to the girl now."

"*Non*. We wait here. You understand?"

"What is your name, monsieur?"

"Gaetan."

"What is your grandson's name?"

His face above his beard shone with perspiration, and yet the tension he was feeling must have been causing his mouth and throat to grow dry. It was a natural response in a fight-or-flight situation. When Gaetan finally spoke, he all but rasped, "Étienne."

I thought of asking him to call the boy outside, but I worried how Chloé Renaud might respond. She'd know I was trying to separate her from her potential hostage. And she was smart enough to understand why.

"I am going to walk toward you now so you can take me to the girl."

"I will shoot," he said again, croaking now. But he must have realized that I understood his threat was empty, and he was merely repeating it out of desperation. His fear was edging into panic. I didn't want him to become any more nervous than he already was, lest his finger reflexively pull the trigger.

I tried to use the gentle tone and deliberate cadence I might have employed with a child. "Monsieur, I promise I won't hurt her. I'm not here to hurt her. I am happy to wait for the border agents, but I am concerned for Étienne's safety."

He made a smacking noise as he tried to coax moisture from his uncooperative salivary glands.

The loon called on the lake behind me.

The yodeling cry echoed ever so slightly. There were no cliffs around Lac Portage from which it could reverberate. The noise stopped without fading.

It was in the quiet that followed that I heard the truck. A vehicle was approaching along the road that connected the lodge to the paved highways of Saint-Théophile.

"They are arriving," Gaetan said, half smiling with relief. "The Services frontaliers. You understand?"

Renaud had multiple accomplices in the Canadian Border Service and potentially in its American counterpart as well. If the fugitive had been making for Lac Portage, it made sense that the first agents to arrive at the lodge might be his allies.

Did I play dumb about what I had learned? Did I tell them the truth about Renaud being dead? Did I temporize until I could speak with higher-ups who might be less likely to assassinate me in this remote, if idyllic, location? And how might my words change Chloé's fate? Had the meticulous planner left instructions with his cronies on how to dispose of his daughter in the event of his death? He might have left behind a financial incentive. But would his accomplices have the will to follow through?

The approaching vehicle was obviously big and powerful—a pickup or an SUV with an engine designed for high-speed police chases—and as it roared toward the lodge and its cluster of outbuildings and docks, I could hear its tires kicking up gravel.

I wasn't sure what to make of the absence of sirens.

On the one hand, it signaled the agents didn't believe they were rushing into an armed standoff. On the other hand, shouldn't they have assumed they might be rushing into an armed standoff? I would have if I'd been in their place.

Gaetan's widening smile revealed stained teeth. I'd deeply frightened the poor *bûcheron*—Charley had taught me the French word for *lumberjack*—and I regretted the damage I'd inflicted on his nerves.

The white SUV that skidded to a stop bore the now-familiar insignias of the Canada Border Services Agency. The Ford Explorer appeared identical to the one Officier Nadeau had been driving when he'd visited Josie. In fact, it was more than identical. Through the smeared windshield, I saw Nadeau himself behind the wheel. His passenger, another uniformed enforcement agent, was a stranger.

Both grim-faced men emerged from the patrol vehicle but did not step immediately out from behind the modest protection of the doors. I didn't have to see their hands to know they were clutching the grips of their service weapons.

Nadeau, in his parched voice, called commandingly in French to my friend with the hunting rifle. Gaetan nodded, lowered the old Marlin, and stepped aside as if to provide a clear firing lane should the agents require one. I raised my hands higher.

"What are you doing here, Warden?" Nadeau demanded. His face was flushed, beet red in the ears, and a little puffier than I remembered from the day before. The man looked like he had been up late drinking.

Do I trust him?

Hadn't Nadeau been friendly with "Mark Redmond," seeking cabin-building tips from the man? But surely the Services frontaliers had photos of fugitives and alerts at every checkpoint and posted in every regional office. Unless he was dull-witted and unobservant—neither of which Nadeau had struck me as being—he must have recognized he'd been dealing with one of Canada's Most Wanted.

Nadeau *had* to be another accomplice. There could be no other explanation for him.

But what about his partner?

The other agent was lanky-limbed, thin in the chest, and almost as tall as Nadeau. But his coloring, unlike that of his fair-skinned partner, was closer to that of my mother's clan of Québec émigrés:

olive-toned and dark-eyed, hair somewhere between brown and black, with eyebrows so heavy they might've been applied with a Sharpie.

Even with my excellent eyesight, I couldn't make out the name tag on his bulletproof vest.

"I asked, what are you doing here?" Nadeau demanded again. Two red spots, one on each cheekbone, brightened as he glowered at me.

"I was pursuing a man I saw commit murder on the other side of the corridor."

Nadeau peered sideways at his partner; it was definitely a look of concern, maybe even suspicion.

"Where is he? This man?" asked the officer with the eyebrows.

But Nadeau broke in before I could speak. "Are you armed, Warden?"

"Yes."

He stepped clear of the vehicle and raised his semiauto. It was a Beretta PX4 Storm, the full-size version of a futuristic pistol I often carried off duty. His sudden motion prompted the other man to do the same.

"Bring it out slowly."

I played a card that I knew would never work. "I am a law enforcement officer, guys."

Nadeau remained unmoved. "But you violated Canadian sovereignty crossing the border without permission and bringing in a weapon. You must know the shit you're in."

"I told you I was chasing—"

"Then you should have alerted the CBS," snarled the agent with the eyebrows.

"I had no signal until I reached the slash. I was only able to contact your agency an hour ago. Isn't that why you're here? In response to my call for assistance?"

The other agent tossed a bewildered glance at Nadeau. They hadn't received the call for backup I'd asked Stacey to put through channels. They'd sped out here on another mission. Perhaps Gaetan had called them about the bedraggled girl he'd rescued from the edge of the wild.

"You can explain everything when you put the gun down on the dock," said Nadeau. "For the moment, we must treat you as a criminal. You understand that, right?"

"I understand."

His lack of interest in the murderer I'd claimed to be pursuing couldn't have been more worrying. It almost seemed as if Nadeau was doing his best to keep me from uttering Renaud's name in front of his partner. If I wasn't careful, he was going to concoct a reason to discharge his weapon. Even if I moved as slowly as a snail, he might claim I'd been raising my pistol when he was forced to shoot me.

As I withdrew the Browning and squatted to set the pistol on the planks, I thought of the hidden Ruger .38 LCR revolver in its ankle holster. I sure as hell wasn't going to produce my backup gun, which I'd seized from Pratt. Not yet, anyway. Not until more agents arrived and I felt assured that Nadeau hadn't come up with a pretext to execute me.

Both agents wore black vests over their navy-blue uniforms. Both had mic handsets clipped to their shoulders above the bullet-stopping plates in their vests. With a simple click of a button, they could communicate with their dispatcher or any law enforcement officer tuned to their frequency.

"You need to call your headquarters," I said.

"We will," said the other agent. The sun had shifted, and I could read the name tag on his chest now. It was Proulx. The name rhymed with *crew*. "Step back, please."

"Any farther and I'll be in the lake."

"Step back."

I did my best to comply. Gaetan, meanwhile, had retreated to the safety of the nearest trees. He'd pushed the dented leather hat clear of his sopping forehead. He appeared nervous again; he had picked up on the escalating tension. At one point, he looked up at the lodge. He must have been wondering about his grandson. Neither Étienne nor Chloé Renaud had appeared in a window to watch the unfolding drama.

Which was itself strange, I thought.

In French, Nadeau commanded Proulx to retrieve my handgun. The lanky, dark-haired agent grinned for some inexplicable reason. He looked to be about my age and carried himself with the confidence of an experienced officer.

After a long pause, he offered a response in French that I didn't understand. It seemed offhand. Like, "*Sure I'll do it.*"

But before he could move, both of their mics crackled. The voice of a female dispatcher issuing a district-wide announcement came through the speaker. Whatever the French-language version of an all-points bulletin was, this was one of those calls.

"*Le pistolet,*" Nadeau said to his partner. Keeping his own gun pointed at me, he brought his free hand up to use the mic. "*Poursuivez.*"

Grinning, Proulx strode down the wobbly, wooden dock, jamming his own duty weapon back into its holster. We were less than ten feet apart when he squatted on his long haunches. He closed his hairy hand around the grip of the Browning.

"Where is your murderer?" he asked again in lightly accented English.

I dropped my voice. "Dead. Back on the corridor."

My answer seemed to freeze him in place. He remained squatting. "But you said you were chasing him. That is how you came to be here, *non*?"

"I was chasing his daughter. Chloé Renaud. You must know the name?"

His maple-brown eyes widened. He cocked his head slightly as if he hadn't heard me clearly. He held the Browning.

"What did he say?" Nadeau called.

"Renaud has accomplices in the CBS," I whispered. "Nadeau—"

"What is he saying?" The senior officer's hand hovered by the On button of his radio microphone.

Proulx straightened to his considerable height. He didn't turn. Except for darting movements of his eyes, he made no expression. I found the man remarkably difficult to read.

"The girl is here, then?" he whispered. "*Dans l'auberge?*"

I nodded.

Nadeau's patience was about to break. "What did he say, Proulx?"

"*La fille de Paul Renaud est ici à l'auberge.*"

"*Quoi?*"

Nadeau seemed genuinely confused. Proulx rolled his eyes at me, almost in amusement, and sighed. Then he turned toward Nadeau.

"*La fille de Paul Renaud—*"

He left the sentence unfinished. He wanted Nadeau to be listening closely and off guard as he brought up the Browning and fired a round through his partner's unarmored neck.

38

Nadeau staggered back against the door of the Explorer. His blue eyes wide with terror and bewilderment, he dropped his own weapon onto the gravel and brought his hands up to his bleeding neck. The bullet had caught him near his Adam's apple. He clutched desperately at the gushing wound and slid against the SUV until he was on one knee, like a knight taking a vow of fealty.

Meanwhile, Proulx was spinning toward me. He tossed my Browning into the lake and reached for his own sidearm.

I threw myself onto my back, knocking my head against the raised edge of the dock. I brought up my left knee.

Proulx was as experienced as I'd guessed; he recognized immediately that I must have had another gun concealed on my ankle. He gripped his Beretta and tried jerking it from its holster. But in his haste, he didn't depress the thumb guard. The pistol stuck in the leather for a microsecond before he could disengage the safety mechanism and draw it free.

His clumsy hesitation gave me the time I needed to pull Pratt's revolver loose. The handgun was an inexpensive little Ruger, but it came with a laser dot that engaged when you gripped the handle. I didn't even need to aim. As soon as the glowing red bug landed between the agent's eyebrows, I squeezed the trigger.

His head didn't jerk back as you see on TV. Instead, he crumpled. He dropped as if the force of gravity on his person had increased by umpteen orders of magnitude. Even the sound of his body hitting the dock was different from a televised portrayal. The noise was less like a bag of gravel than a sack of soft flour.

I found myself sitting upright, looking at Proulx's dead body between my bent legs. My right hand, gripping the Ruger, rested on my knee. The air wafting off the warming lake now smelled of gunpowder.

"Help! Help!"

It was Gaetan. The caretaker, rushing to Nadeau's aid, had lost his leather hat, revealing a mostly bald scalp over which thin hairs had been combed. He'd added his hands to the border agent's, trying to staunch his wound. But blood oozed between their combined fingers and spilled down their wrists and forearms.

I jumped to my feet and rushed up to the Explorer.

Nadeau had a wild, half-crazed look. Why shouldn't he be terrified? His life was draining away.

The bullet had missed the carotid artery—there would have been spray if it hadn't—but it might have clipped one of his jugular veins. The blood was nearly brick colored, indicating it was carrying very little oxygen. The jacketed 9mm round had exited the back of his neck without mushrooming. Nadeau had been lucky in several ways, but most of all in the fact that Bob Stombaugh hadn't chosen to load his Browning Hi-Power with hollow points. The wound might or might not be fatal, in other words. If Nadeau continued to bleed out at the present rate, he would be dead in minutes. But I wasn't resigned to that outcome. I knew there must be a first aid kit in the Explorer; every patrol vehicle carried one.

I told Gaetan to keep pressure on Nadeau's neck as best he could—to use all his strength. But I wasn't sure how much the Québécois understood. He shouted something unintelligible as I went around the SUV to access the first aid kit through the passenger's door.

All this time, I had thought the worst of Nadeau because the man had rightly disdained my murderous father and had treated me rudely. He hadn't been the first officer to view me with mistrust, and he wouldn't be the last, but his bad manners hadn't excused my irresponsible speculations. Instead of an accomplice, he seemed to have been working to locate Paul Renaud. He was a senior officer in his service; his assignment might even have included identifying the key individuals who had assisted the fugitive to escape justice in Canada. Perhaps it was why he'd been partnered with Proulx.

All these years on the job and I was still making assumptions about people that I was eventually forced to disavow. I needed to do better. I needed to *be* better.

When I returned with the trauma kit, Nadeau's gaze became as expectant and innocent as a child's.

"You can—?"

"I don't know. But I'm going to try."

Nadeau remained conscious through it all even as shock set in through his body. His lips became frothy with spittle, but no blood was rising into his mouth, which seemed a promising sign. As I leaned close to him, I smelled that he'd lost control of certain muscles. It wasn't unexpected under the circumstances.

"Girl . . ." he burbled.

"I'm going to find her."

"She shot . . ."

"Chloé shot her mother, I know." I ripped a bandage loose from its packet. "I promise I won't let her hurt anyone else."

He pawed at my stubbled face with his red hands. He seemed to want to communicate some other piece of information, but he'd lost his voice. His lips moved soundlessly.

"Baby . . ."

Did he mean there was a baby inside the lodge? I didn't think so. His face was losing color except for the threaded capillaries in his cheeks.

The trick was taping the compression bandage to his neck. There needed to be pressure to slow the bleeding. But if it was too tight, it would cut off either the air through his windpipe or the flow of blood to his head. Stacey would have known what to do. I'd had her teach me how to treat gunshot wounds, but we hadn't dealt with the exceedingly rare scenario of a through-and-through to the neck.

"Try to breathe normally. In through the nose and out through the mouth."

The packed gauze was reddening but not soaking through instantly. The blood flow was being contained—to a degree. In emergency medicine, you always take the small wins.

Nadeau was losing consciousness, though, but before he went under, he needed me to understand something. He tried to pull me close. I got a dermatologist's view of his veined nose.

This time, he forced the word out: "*Baby.*"

"What baby?"

Then I became aware of a plane passing overhead. When I glanced up, I saw only birch branches, some budding, others green with emergent leaves. Hopefully, it was a floatplane sent by the Services frontaliers. Nadeau needed to be evacuated immediately. Even then, I doubted he would survive the flight to the nearest ER.

Behind me, I heard the echoing clatter of Gaetan running down the dock. I caught sight of him waving his small hands like a man stranded on a desert island, afraid of being missed by a passing freighter. But the floatplane had already set down on the lake and was taxiing in our direction. It was a golden-yellow de Havilland Beaver. Charley had told me that Josie had owned one of those big bush planes. But this couldn't be hers, of course.

Could it?

Maybe a local pilot had volunteered to assist the first responders massing along the border. Maybe he'd borrowed Josie's trusty de Havilland. In a different universe, it would have been she at the controls.

In a better universe.

I glanced over my shoulder and saw Gaetan, hatless, still dancing and waving, as the de Havilland cruised ever closer behind the power of its slow-spinning propellor.

Then I looked back at the contents of the first aid kit spilled across the leaves. My gaze passed absently over the three CPR masks in the kit: one sized for an adult, one for a child, and one for an infant.

"*Baby.*"

What baby?

The only two people I'd seen around the lodge were Gaetan and his grandson. Perhaps a woman was also there—Étienne's mom? Perhaps she had an infant whom I hadn't yet glimpsed?

But how would Nadeau have known about that baby? And more to the point, why would he have felt it vital to tell me before he passed out?

He'd been trying to impress on me some crucial fact.

I'd planned on staying with the wounded man until the plane arrived at the dock.

Now I found myself following with my eyes the stone foundation of the lodge up from the lapping waters to the structure above. It had a porch on the land side that wrapped around the building as far as a monumental chimney. To the lake, the lodge presented a weathered wooden face, broken here and there by windows. A triptych of glass let light into what must have been the dining room. One of the small panes was broken: a casualty of a winter storm, no doubt.

Chloé was kneeling there, watching me through the gap.

We made eye contact. She disappeared.

I'd left the little Ruger revolver on the dock. Proulx had dropped Bob Stombaugh's Browning into the lake, so I removed the Beretta from the ground where Nadeau had dropped it before I backed away from his supine body. Gaetan was chattering in rapid-fire French to the men in the de Havilland as he tied up their plane.

How many guns had I appropriated over the past twenty-four hours?

Add one more to the list. With Nadeau's service weapon in hand, I hurried around the SUV, making for the trail of pine needles that led to the lodge above the lake.

39

From the gravel forecourt, I took the first flight of stairs up to the porch. Some of the steps were missing, as if Gaetan might have been replacing rotting boards. A winter's worth of snow had also pushed over the lattice beneath the balcony. Every backwoods lodge requires weeks of repairs and cleaning before the season opens and the guests arrive.

From the porch, I could see one of the men from the plane rushing up the dock behind Gaetan to attend to Nadeau.

"Where's Bowditch?" I heard him ask in an accent that told me he was American. He was dressed in a wool coat and waxed canvas jeans tucked into Bean boots, but I didn't get a good look at his face and didn't know who he was. Definitely a volunteer from the far side of the border, though.

Maybe that is *Josie's plane?*

Could Charley be with them?

The thought was too much to hope for, and I was too intent on finding Chloé to give the possibility any consideration.

The door at the end of the porch was unlocked and admitted me into the great room, where guests warmed themselves while they sipped whiskey and swapped fish stories on furniture currently draped beneath winter coverlets. The sun shone in through the unwashed windows onto the dusty pinewood floor.

I paused to listen and get my bearings. A chandelier in the shape of a wagon wheel, with bulbs contained in sconces like hurricane lamps, was strung with cobwebs. Mounted above the fireplace was a taxidermied loon that would have been illegal to possess in the United States under the federal law protecting most migratory birds. That single detail—one dead, dusty loon—was the only thing that differentiated L'Auberge Lac Portage from the Maine sporting camps I'd known east of the border.

A push door separated the great room from the dining room. I stood to one side, protected by a timber support, as I eased it open. But when I peered inside, I saw only a long table with its dozen chairs stacked upside down atop it. Another door on the far side entered the lodge kitchen. I heard nothing from that direction but took a quick look to be sure.

No one else was here.

Through the near window, I saw a single vehicle: a mint-green pickup with the resort logo painted on its door. Gaetan's truck, presumably.

If there was no mother here, what had Nadeau meant when he'd warned me about a baby?

Who had he wanted me to protect?

Even succumbing to shock, he wouldn't have used *baby* to describe Étienne. I'd barely gotten a look at the boy, but he had to be at least eight years old.

The south side of the lodge looked out on a flooded lawn with picnic tables littered with the little wood chips red squirrels leave behind after they have devoured a pine cone. And when I stepped out onto the boardwalk behind the building, one of the rodents, caught off guard, began scolding me from a white pine standing sentinel above the property.

Springtime meant that the grass was mostly withered, but turning green where it received plentiful sun, and there were even a few crocuses and snowdrops popping up from the moist soil, purple and white.

The ground was uneven from buried roots, and the soil was thin, but I located two sets of small footprints in the soft, wet turf near the flower beds. Even in her haste, Chloé had known not to cross the yard but had skirted it the way a house cat does its territory. She had the boy, Étienne, with her. And my experience as a tracker told me, from the placement of their feet, that she was forcing him to walk ahead of her.

Why?

What is she so afraid of now?

Did her dad instill in her that much terror of what the police might do to her for killing her mother?

I double-checked to see if there was a round chambered in the Beretta. The pistol had a double-action trigger. I didn't have to cock it to fire.

I paused again to listen. In the distance, now I heard sirens approaching, and then an airborne drone passed low overhead. The Services frontaliers, along with the Royal Canadian Mounted Police and all its sister agencies, was descending on Lac Portage. Maybe even the U.S. Border Patrol, too.

But would they be too late to save little Étienne?

The drone hovered over me with the intensity of a horsefly at the beach. I paid it no mind.

To the pilot guiding it, I must have looked like a wild and dangerous threat in my torn and weather-stained poncho, my face scratched from branches, and gripping what any border agent would have recognized as one of their standard-issue Berettas. I had to have stolen the gun. I had to be stalking the girl and boy now.

The situation was all chaos. How long did I have before a bunch of Mounties closed in around me with Colt C8 carbines? Another floatplane swung in over the lake. Its fuselage, like the underbelly of a fish, flashed white in the sunlight.

I took off at a trot, following the footprints.

The drone pursued me.

Chloé was leading Étienne away from the lodge and the surrounding cabins and outbuildings.

In the trees beyond, the sun made every new green leaf look like it was lit from within: the chlorophyll electrified. Newly hatched mayflies—blue-winged olives—drifted in nebulous swarms. A phoebe darted in to grab an unlucky bug.

The road from Saint-Théophile into Lac Portage tracked in from the northwest. Chloé Renaud was skirting the south side of the point, hiding in the green-and-gray cover of the spring woods. Her father had taught her so much bushcraft, but to what end?

I reduced my speed as I slipped into the shrubs and saplings along the tree line. Charley had taught me to stalk deer—the hardest way to hunt those skittish creatures—and his first piece of advice had been, "As slow as you think you can move, try moving half as slow as that."

Behind me, I could hear more trucks and SUVs racing in along the rocky road.

The drone had moved off as soon as I'd ducked under the boughs of the pines. I heard it whining ahead and to my right. The pilot had spotted Chloé and Étienne. I turned and saw a vast cut in the forest. A beauty strip of woods separated the weedy clearing from the well-manicured grounds around the lodge.

On Charley's orders, I was moving slowly, soundlessly toward the cut when I heard the all-too-familiar crack of a gunshot. Few rounds are as distinctively loud as the .357 SIG. I imagined Étienne falling lifeless.

Instead, Chloé Renaud had used my pistol to fire at the drone. She'd hit it squarely, too. The uncrewed aerial vehicle dropped like a goose shot dead on the wing.

I couldn't see them yet, but Étienne let out a wail that was immediately muffled, as if by a hand being clamped over his mouth.

"Shut up," Chloé hissed. "Shut up or I'll shoot you, too."

I had reached the perimeter of the field and saw them, roughly fifty feet ahead. The girl and boy were nearly the same height, although he must have been four or five years younger than she was. But while she was skinny and ethereal, he was squat with unusually short legs and unusually long arms. A fleeting thought went through my mind that he might be suffering from some developmental disability.

I'd done my best to regulate my breathing, but the sight of Chloé pressing my pistol against Étienne's temple, just as her father had done to her, caused my heart to beat time against my sternum. Instinctively, I'd tried to acquire a target. I was staring with both eyes open through the rear sights of the Beretta at Chloé's unruly head.

If the Mounties and the border agents came crashing through the trees now, she would fire out of sheer surprise and alarm.

I needed to defuse the crisis first. It took a tremendous act of will, but I lowered the gun.

"Chloé," I called. "It's over."

She swung around fast—she hadn't heard me approaching over all the shouts and sirens—and thrust the boy in front of her. Only when she'd hidden behind him did I see his flattened face, his undersized ears, the distinctive slant of his eyes. Étienne had Down syndrome.

Her voice became as shrill and high-pitched as a falcon's. "I'll kill him."

"You don't have to do that. You don't want to do that."

"Why not?"

"Because you don't need to run anymore."

"You killed my papa!"

"It wasn't me. The man chasing you shot him."

"*You're* the man chasing us."

She wasn't wrong. "Your father is dead, Chloé. You can stop running. It's over."

"No, it's not."

I'd previously had only the briefest glimpses of her rage, but now her reddening face was consumed with the emotion. There wasn't the faintest hint of fear in her bulging eyes. That worried me. She should have been afraid.

I was afraid.

"Your father's dead, Chloé. He can't hurt you anymore."

She laughed at that, or rather her mouth twisted into a shape like a laugh. When she removed her hand from Étienne's mouth, he let out another wordless wail. The noise only made her madder. She dug the end of my SIG into his temple again. It was as if she was trying to drive the barrel through the thin skin along his hairline.

"Put the gun down, Chloé."

"Why?"

"Because you don't want to hurt that boy," I said. "He's innocent."

"He's defective!" Then she pressed her face close to his ear and shouted, "Stop crying, you baby! Stop *fucking* crying."

The outburst brought me up short. It wasn't just the forbidden profanity, the word I'd never heard Paul Renaud's daughter speak before. It was what she'd called Étienne, too.

Nadeau had told me to protect the baby.

Or so I'd thought.

"Fucking baby!" she said. "Fucking, fucking baby."

The realization caused me to reel. In my innocence, I had thought I understood what I was dealing with in Chloé Renaud. But the image of her that I'd assembled—meek, abused, and in need of protection—had been entirely false.

The baby.

The baby, I thought, with increasing dread. Her little brother had supposedly died before birth.

I had to fight the urge to raise the gun again and take the head shot.

"Tell me about your brother, Chloé."

She snapped her head away from Étienne to glare at me. Rage became confusion. "How did you . . . ?"

"Your little brother wasn't stillborn, was he?"

She began to blink rapidly. Her eyes welled with tears. She was on the verge of disintegrating before my eyes.

"He was born alive," I said.

"How did you know? Who told you that?" Then her voice rose to a shout. "How did you fucking know?"

No wonder her mother had had a nervous breakdown. No wonder she'd started using drugs to mute the pain of what her daughter had done to her baby brother. And no wonder Paul had dreaded what would become of his weird, brilliant, deeply disturbed daughter if the truth came out.

"Chloé . . ."

"Why wouldn't he stop crying? Why wouldn't he ever shut up?"

Renaud had foreseen this moment in the clearing. Without knowing about Étienne, he had understood that sooner or later Chloé would kill an innocent person again. And that was why he'd wanted her to die—to protect her next victim, because there was always going to be another victim—to prevent what was about to happen to this poor little boy.

"Chloé, please."

"No!"

She twisted the gun into Étienne's head, drawing blood from the edged sight.

I had no choice but to raise the Beretta. I aimed over the boy's shaking shoulder. I had a clean shot at Chloé's forehead.

I can't do this.

"I'm going to!" she shouted. "I'm going to!"

I hadn't heard the officers come up behind me. I was so focused on my target I missed their blind crashing through the forest until a chorus of harsh male voices ordered me to put the gun down.

And if I did, what would happen next?

They didn't know what I knew. They didn't understand who she was.

I can't do this. I can't do this.

Chloé let the barrel of the SIG wander a few inches away from the sobbing, shaking Étienne. But it was a feint, I could tell. She would bring it back any second.

The men were shouting at me to drop the pistol. I could almost feel their laser sights gathering at the back of my skull.

I can't do this. I can't do this. I can't do this.

Even if it means saving Étienne?

No.

I lowered the pistol. I stretched out my arm to my side where they could see the gun. And then I let it drop.

Even as they rushed me, one of them called to Chloé in French. I wasn't sure of the exact words. But I think the armed and armored officer wanted her to know that she was finally safe.

Two bodies hit me hard from behind. I could feel their body armor. It was like being tackled by two brothers of the Knights Templar.

I was on my way to the ground when I saw Chloé Renaud, wild-eyed but grinning now in triumph, turn my service weapon from the boy and fire a bullet into the side of her own mussed and muddy head.

40

In my ten-year career as a game warden, I had seen the aftermath of many suicides. A few of them were from lacerations to the wrists or cuts across the throat. More were the results of ligature strangulation: bodies hanging from shower rods and closet rods or from the limbs of lonely trees. But most of the self-inflicted deaths I'd witnessed had come from gunshot wounds to the heart or, more often, the head.

As with every other subject, the internet offers disturbingly detailed information to troubled people who are contemplating taking their own lives. Websites tell us that, if you plan on using a gun, be sure to put the barrel in your mouth. You must by all means fire up and back to ensure the bullet destroys your brain stem.

Why the mouth and not the temple? Because even the most committed soul, intent on ending their existence, is likely to flinch as they curl their index finger around the trigger.

Chloé Renaud flinched.

I only learned this later; I was in no position to see anything at the time, having two large men pinning me to the earth and twisting my arms into place to apply handcuffs to my already raw wrists. The impact of the men tackling me hadn't knocked the wind from my lungs, but I felt very much as if my lungs had been flattened. No matter how hard I gasped for air, I couldn't refill them.

I assumed Chloé was dead. I was certain she must be dead.

Only as the first officers closed in around the bleeding girl did I gather—in my imperfect French—that she was still alive.

"Elle a raté! La balle n'a pas pénétré le crâne."

When the agents had me cuffed, they hauled me to my feet as if I weighed no more than Chloé Renaud. I marveled at their strength, as I was feeling ponderously heavy. The accumulated exhaustion of the past twenty-four hours—the adrenaline highs and the adrenaline lows—had turned my muscles to lead. My heart most of all.

A man wearing the navy uniform of the Canada Border Services Agency came dashing into the cut bearing a serious trauma kit, not unlike the one that Stacey and her partner kept in their ambulance back home. He carried himself like a man trained in emergency medicine. A litter, suitable for backcountry rescues, appeared minutes later.

Then a man in tactical gear interposed himself between me and the medical crisis unfolding in the field twenty feet distant. He was heavily armored in the dark khaki combat uniform of the RCMP Emergency Response Team. A C8 carbine hung on a sling across his chest with spare mags in the pockets of his vest. He glared at me from beneath his Kevlar helmet, looking very much like a warrior trying to assess whether the man before him was or was not a terrorist. The irises of his eyes were the color of raw tobacco.

"Who are you?" he demanded.

"Mike Bowditch, investigator with the Maine Warden Service. My badge is on my belt."

Another Mountie had already begun to pat me down from behind, rifling my pockets as Chloé herself had done when I'd been tied to the hemlock, and he found the shield—which he showed his partner.

"You are a U.S. citizen, and you crossed the border without authorization?"

"Yes."

Wait until you find the two guns I illegally brought with me.

I was tired and traumatized in ways that went beyond the physical. Despite my own best efforts and the work of the medics on scene to save Chloé Renaud from herself, she might yet die. And I had ceased to care what would become of my career after this day was over.

In my rookie years, when I had acquired the reputation for being a misfit and a maverick—a reputation I'd mostly left behind as I'd grown up—I had often felt this way. It surprised me that this emotion, which I'd thought I'd exorcized, had merely been lurking, biding its time, hiding in some shadowy rift in my brain. But we don't leave our past selves behind so easily; unlike Peter Pan, we cannot be severed from our own shadows.

"Just arrest me already," I said.

Neither of the poker-faced Mounties reacted immediately. Then the man who'd addressed me, the one with the tobacco-colored eyes, produced a laminated card and began informing me of the specific reasons he was arresting me, as well as my rights under the Canadian Charter of Rights and Freedoms. He read the words carefully and clearly so no defense attorney could claim he'd omitted a key phrase. Maine wardens, too, were trained to read Miranda rights for this same reason. I carried a similar card in my lost wallet.

With that, the two men moved me roughly toward the lodge, although I wasn't resisting, and I lost sight of what was happening to Chloé. Not that I could have seen her in the scrum.

When we reached the gravel drive, I glimpsed Gaetan on his knees, weeping as he embraced his still-wailing grandson. Their reunion produced a moment of satisfaction in me: a spark bright enough to dispel the inner darkness. At the same time, I thought of the remorse I'd be feeling if Chloé had shot Étienne instead of herself.

You didn't deserve to get that lucky, Bowditch.

Somehow, Gaetan must have seen me being frog-marched toward a waiting vehicle because he leaped to his feet and rushed over, gesticulating almost violently, his voice overloud and bouncing back and forth between French and English.

"*Qu'est-ce que vous faites? Cet homme a sauvé Étienne!* He's a hero, this man."

One of the armored Mounties interceded. "*Monsieur, monsieur—*"

"*Vous ne devriez pas le traiter de cette façon. C'est honteux!* Let him go, I tell you! He's a hero, this man, I tell you."

"*Monsieur—*"

"He saved the life of Officier Nadeau."

The Mounties stopped pushing me. The one with the brown stare asked what Gaetan meant by this. The caretaker told him that I'd shot Proulx after he'd fired on his partner.

This statement didn't strike me as necessarily helpful. It caught the tactical officers off guard, too. Here was another, more serious charge on which to arrest me. Never mind for now the circumstances or whatever justifications I might have had; I had killed a member of the Services frontaliers.

But Gaetan kept rattling on, talking as much with his hands as his tongue. He called Proulx an attempted murderer. He praised my quick work with the med kit; how I had stabilized Nadeau's critical wound.

The other armored Mountie, the junior of the pair, asked Gaetan if he would give a sworn statement. Gaetan pronounced he would do so eagerly, now, on the spot, but was told that, no, he would need to come to the IBET Detachment in Saint-Georges-de-Beauce.

I recognized the name of the city, having driven through it on trips to Québec City, but the acronym meant nothing to me.

Gaetan asked if he might shake my hand before they took me away.

"*Non, monsieur.* It's not possible."

"*C'est honteux!*"

The word, I later learned, meant *disgrace*.

The two Mounties then escorted me to a white SUV emblazoned with slogans and insignia marking it as an official vehicle of the RCMP. My eyes fixed on a little blue image on the rear. It was the outline of a man on a horse carrying a flag. I'd met members of Canada's signature law enforcement agency before—at meetings to discuss cooperation along the border—but I had never noticed Dudley Do-Right's silhouette on their patrol vehicles.

One of the officers now pressed his hand to the top of my skull just as wardens are trained to do, to keep me from bumping my head as he placed me in the back seat. I sat separated by a cage from the officers up front. The junior man—he had the air of being second-in-command—moved to attach my manacles to a D ring on the floor at my feet. It seemed I would be spending the drive to Saint-Georges hunched forward.

But at the last moment, the other Mountie pulled him aside. They stepped away to discuss the situation, then quickly returned.

The brown-eyed officer released me from the D ring. He cuffed me again, but this time with my hands in front of me, so I could rest them on my lap. It was something cops do only when they are convinced the individual they are transporting poses no danger to their persons.

For the first time, the man seemed to notice the abrasions and bruises around my wrists. I sensed he might want to ask about them. But his professionalism made no allowance for personal curiosity.

"You understand we must keep you restrained?" he said.

"I do."

"You won't give us trouble?"

"All I want to do is sleep," I said. "How far a drive is it?"

But he didn't answer. Whatever courtesies he might be extending me, he wanted me to know that I remained under arrest for serious crimes against the people of Canada.

I had been cautioned.

41

I slept without dreaming and awoke an hour later to find that we were pulling into the parking lot of a midsized building with a brick-and-concrete façade. The pavement was mottled from the recent rain, and a Canadian flag hung limp from a pole in a lawn already overdue for mowing. It was disturbing to see grass so vividly green at this latitude in the first week of May.

The acronym IBET, a sign in the lawn announced, stood for INTEGRATED BORDER ENFORCEMENT TEAM, which explained the presence of SUVs from the Services frontaliers among the motley civilian vehicles.

Two black patrol trucks belonging to the Maine Warden Service were already backed into spaces, side by side, in front of the station. But it was the unmarked pickup beside them that caught my eye. It was my duty vehicle: the same GMC Sierra I had driven to Jackman.

Charley leaned against the hood of my truck, talking on a cell phone that he must have borrowed from one of his former colleagues. My father-in-law had obviously retrieved my vehicle from Josie's farm. *But how had he started my pickup without my keys?* I realized Charley had many more tricks to teach me.

I could imagine the words that must have been going through his bristling, white-haired head.

"Leave it to that young feller to start an international incident."

Charley paused his conversation and raised a hand in greeting. I welcomed the gesture of hope and solidarity, but the old man's expression—sad, solemn, weary—told me he had a clearer idea of what was waiting for me inside the grim building than I did.

The Mounties drove around back to an automatic door that rolled upward to admit us to a fortified bay used to bring prisoners into the facility. Except for the bilingual signage, it appeared identical to every large jail in Maine.

Instead of locking up their weapons in the lockers in the bay, the arresting officers handed me off to another Mountie, a woman dressed in a standard gray-and-black uniform. She wore her brown hair pulled back in a bun, the tightness of which also seemingly pulled at her face, which was squint-eyed and lipless. I wasn't sure if I'd meet the arresting officers inside, as they belonged to a SWAT team. More likely, the remainder of my day would be spent in an interrogation room with detectives.

Instead, I was surprised to be led into a small white-and-gray room with a one-way mirror on a wall and a table with four chairs, two on each side, and a camera mounted in a corner of the ceiling.

The female officer removed my cuffs and told me she would need my clothes for potential evidence. She offered me a prisoner's jumpsuit and slippers to change into. Before she left me to undress, she asked if I wanted water or coffee. When I replied, "Both," she didn't smile—her face was too tight for that—but when she disappeared through the door, I had the distinct sense that I would be brought the beverages I'd asked for.

I was waiting for her to return when the door opened and a dapper man in a remarkably well-fitting chalk-stripe suit entered. His hair was blond and silky, and he wore a mustache a shade darker. His shirt had cufflinks instead of buttons, and his striped tie was secured in a perfect Windsor knot. The smell of sandalwood cologne rose around his person in an invisible cloud.

"Good morning, Mike. May I call you Mike?" he said in lightly accented English. "I'm Daniel Labelle, and I've been sent by your consulate in Québec to provide you temporary legal representation. My understanding is that your people are lobbying hard for you to be released—"

"My people?"

"Representatives of the state of Maine in coordination with the U.S. Consulate General. To be honest, I am not totally sure what discussions are happening where and with whom, but your actions over the past hours are causing quite the ruckus. I'm the local talent sent to advise you of your rights prior to your interview by the RCMP. I can't be in the room for the conversation, by the way."

I laughed for the first time in hours. "Conversation? That sounds so pleasant and civilized."

"Canadian police are down on the term *interrogation*."

He spoke like a man who'd spent significant time in the States; his easy colloquialisms.

"Thank you." I had developed a kink in my neck muscles, which proved resistant to my attempts at self-massage. "But I want to know how Chloé and Nadeau are doing."

"That's understandable, but I'd suggest focusing on your own situation for the time being. Detectives will be here momentarily, and—"

"Do you know how they're doing?" I asked. "Chloé and Nadeau."

He nodded his golden, well-coiffed head. "The last I heard, they were both in surgery. She is stable. His condition is critical. But I strongly suggest that we discuss how you might choose to answer the detectives' questions. Now it goes without saying that you must agree to my representing you first before I can offer counsel."

There was a knock at the door, and the female Mountie with the pinched face returned with water and black coffee in identical paper cups. The debonair attorney smiled at her in a way that made me think he had an eye for the ladies.

After she'd left, Labelle said, "Mike, you really are in deep shit here. I believe you can claim extenuating circumstances, but the police are alleging you violated multiple Canadian laws, and your status as a game warden in Maine is immaterial in that regard. Now, it's my understanding that the caretaker at L'Auberge Lac Portage will be making a statement on your behalf. And if Officier Nadeau recovers and recalls the events, that should also help your case."

"Nadeau wasn't just a Border Services agent, was he?"

"What?"

"Paul Renaud obviously had help from a number of people in the Services frontaliers. Nadeau was tasked with identifying those individuals, I suspect."

"What makes you say that?"

"Because if he only wanted to arrest Renaud, he had multiple opportunities to do that. Canada Border Services knew where Paul and his daughter were hiding in Maine. The fact that they were never arrested suggests someone was after bigger fish."

"The biggest fish," Labelle said, rolling the term around his mouth as if it gave him pleasure. "Renaud's stepfather is a current member of parliament and the former minister of public safety. In that role, he oversaw the Services frontaliers."

"Ah," I said.

"My understanding is there is no proof he assisted his stepson while he was a fugitive."

"But it explains why Selene Renaud's family felt compelled to hire an American PI—because they had no confidence your government would bring their daughter's and grandson's killer to justice."

"Grandson?"

"How much do you know about the Renaud case, Mr. Labelle?"

"Beyond the courthouse rumors surrounding the minister, only what I've read in the news."

"There's been no speculation in the tabloids that Paul and Selene's second child, a baby boy, had not in fact been a stillbirth?"

"I'm not following you, and I really think we should discuss how you might consider answering—or rather not answering—the RCMP's questions. If you did shoot and kill an officer of the Services frontaliers, you'll be going on trial, whatever agreements our two governments might make on the other charges. The politicians in Ottawa can't give you a pass on that. They'll be too terrified of how any deal might play out in the media, and how Canadians on the left will react to stories of a renegade American police officer—"

There was another knock at the door. This time, a sturdy-looking man in plain clothes entered. He had a wine-colored birthmark on his broad forehead and was obviously the detective who'd come to "converse with" me.

"Thank you, Mr. Labelle," I said before my interrogator could speak. "But you can go."

"But I haven't informed you of all your rights, Mike, including your rights under the charter to remain silent." The prim attorney swiveled in his chair to address the mute detective. "Can we have another five minutes, please?"

"That won't be necessary. I'm prepared to answer every question the detective wants to ask me."

"I'd strongly advise you to reconsider—or at least wait for new counsel—before you make that decision."

"I did what I did," I said.

"Mike?" he implored.

"I take full responsibility for my actions. Everything I did, I would do over again in a heartbeat. My defense is that I did what I felt was right. I'll accept the consequences. I'm not Paul Renaud. I'm not running away from anything."

42

Early that evening, I received the surprise of my life. The Mounties announced they were not charging me after all. Rather they were reserving the right to charge me at a later date. I was no longer under arrest.

At my request, Labelle had continued to act as my counsel. He said the Americans had struck an unprecedented deal not to fight extradition if the Canadians reversed their decision and insisted on trying me.

"In my entire career, I have never seen anything like this happen," he said. "They have you dead to rights."

"How did I get so lucky?"

"Firstly," he said, "you are the only surviving material witness to the killing of Paul Renaud on the American side of the border, as well as his assassination of his accomplice—a former member of the Services, by the way. The Department of Justice is going to need your statement to stand up in court, which means they can't undercut your credibility by prosecuting you as a border-jumping cowboy. Hence the deal they're offering.

"Secondly, the RCMP and the Canada Border Services have spent years pursuing an investigation into Renaud's stepfather and the network of corrupt agents who assisted Paul in avoiding capture. There's concern that if the focus shifts to you, it will provide an opening for the big fish to escape. You risk muddying the narrative the Department of Justice has been constructing for the courts. You must have been born under a lucky star, Warden Bowditch."

At this, I laughed. Labelle joined me at first until I kept on laughing long past his comfort level.

The Royal Canadian Mounted Police were not pleased by my deliverance. Nor did they have any intention of releasing me on my personal recognizance. Instead, after they'd returned my clothes to me, they drove me back to the border in handcuffs. Putting me in bracelets was meant to signal the displeasure of the local officers at my politically motivated release.

But they must have recognized that their own discretion mattered little against the expediencies of the federal government. It didn't help them that Nadeau had come out of surgery with a complete memory of Proulx's shooting him and my subsequent actions. I'd saved his life, and he wasn't going to keep quiet if the prosecutors flip-flopped and threw me back into the clink to await an appearance before a magistrate.

The birthmarked detective who removed my cuffs at the border checkpoint growled that I had better not get complacent—I should prepare to be indicted for my crimes in Canada and face extradition back to Québec. I wasn't sure if the threat was real or if he was voicing his frustrations at not being able to charge me with the criminal acts I had confessed to committing.

All cops are like this. I had no doubt that, in his place, I also would have felt aggrieved at the special treatment of a maverick game warden with no regard for sovereign borders.

I almost wanted to reassure him that I wasn't getting off scot-free; I would be facing another investigation back home. I had shot Charon, as I kept calling him, on American soil, even if my bullet hadn't been the one that killed him. The Maine attorney general would be compelled to open a use-of-deadly-force case. The odds were that I would skate, though. I had identified myself as a police officer; it had been a righteous shoot.

At the U.S. border crossing, half a dozen agents on duty emerged from their complex. Every one of them wanted to shake my hand for running Paul Renaud—the killer of their friend Josie Jonson—to ground. I didn't want their congratulations, but what could I do but smile and be gracious?

I suspected that Renaud had accomplices among their ranks, and I wondered if one of the men or women praising my perseverance and courage might be among their number.

Charley, it turned out, had made his way out to the Stombaughs' and was there when Brandon Barstow and two other wardens arrived to arrest them—the state troopers having gotten stuck in the mud.

Bob and Rose had been removed to the Somerset County Jail, where they would be charged with being accessories to felony murder, I predicted. I pitied the gullible couple and considered offering a statement on their behalf for reduced sentences if it came to it. In the scheme of things, their holding me at gunpoint seemed a minor inconvenience at best.

Chiefly, I was preoccupied with what would become of Chloé Renaud now that doctors had pronounced she would survive. The bullet had passed harmlessly between the hypodermis and her skull. She would suffer no long-term damage beyond a scar, which she could have surgically repaired when she reached adulthood.

Assuming she doesn't spend the rest of her life locked behind bars.

"Can a child be evil, Charley?" I asked as we drove back into the welcoming arms of my native land.

He was driving my truck because I lacked the energy. When he'd seen my scratched face after my release, he'd told me I looked like I'd lost a wrestling match with a briar patch.

His eyes widened for effect. "Can a child be evil? I'm going to leave that question for the priests and rabbis. I'm just an old fart who lives in the woods and flies planes."

"She killed her baby brother because he wouldn't stop crying."

"Do you have proof she did?"

I hadn't yet told him everything Chloé had said as she'd pressed my service weapon to the head of a boy with Down syndrome. I was too shaken to tell the story, even to my father-in-law, but in my mind, I had all the proof I needed.

Meanwhile, Charley was giving my philosophical query some thought.

"I suppose it depends on your personal definition of evil," he said.

"Does it?"

"I wouldn't let the question tie you up in knots, son. Nothing good will come of it. And Renaud's worst fears are going to come true in any case. That little girl will be institutionalized, maybe for life."

"That wasn't Renaud's worst fear," I said. "His worst fear was that she would kill again if she left his protection. He was fully prepared to murder her, Charley. I saw it with my own eyes."

His voice became gentle. "I'm sorry that was something you had to witness."

"If you were her dad, what would you have done?"

"Hell, son, you really are putting me on the spot tonight. I wouldn't have contemplated taking her life, that's for damned sure."

"Even if you feared she would hurt people in the future? In Renaud's mind—and I'm not saying I agree—he was taking ultimate responsibility for the child he had created."

"That isn't fatherhood. That's not being a father."

No, I thought. *But the fear he'd felt for her was.*

That was something I hadn't known before I'd left for Jackman. That horrible, never-ending sense of personal responsibility for the human life you have created.

It was nearly dark again, and Charley's craggy face had grown green from the dashboard lights.

"Stacey may be pregnant."

That statement shocked him into a long silence. I watched his expression and saw emotions come and go. He tried to hide the last one, but I recognized it as pure happiness.

"Is that what she told you on the phone before we left Saint-Georges?"

"She bought a test yesterday and was waiting until I got home to take it, and then I never came home. She still hasn't taken it."

"What are you hoping?" he asked, trying to keep his voice flat and disinterested but unable to conceal his deepest wishes.

I didn't answer.

Stacey and I had talked on the phone for half an hour, maybe longer, after I'd been released by the Mounties. By unstated mutual agreement, neither of us had brought up the pregnancy test. The story I had to tell her about the Renaud family was too full of ill omens.

My own career situation was direr than I had confessed to Charley. But I'd felt obliged to share it with my wife.

"The colonel drove to Canada to support me," I'd told Stacey, "but when I asked him what it might mean for my job—the unsanctioned actions I'd taken—he said there would be a formal hearing with my union rep."

"They're not going to fire you, Mike," she had said. "You're the best investigator they have."

"If the Canadian media makes a stink, they might have to. Or suspend me without pay for some period. Or demote me, even. I might have to go back on patrol."

She had paused to consider this. "What'll we do?"

"We'll be fine with whatever happens. I'm not afraid of any of it. I won't be controlled by fear."

Like her dad, my wife was a speaker of blunt truths, and I could tell she wanted very much to dispute me on this point, that there were good reasons to be concerned. Whatever bravado I might have expressed in that moment, my job as a warden investigator was central to my identity. Stacey didn't believe that I could blithely accept its loss.

I had been working in law enforcement long enough to know that you can't deny your emotions after traumatic events. Sooner or later, they will hit you like a hammer to the heart. But watching Josie die and Pratt die and hearing Paul Renaud's strangled confession in his last moments—and especially contemplating the tragedy of Chloé Renaud—had made my current predicament seem trivial.

"Are you sure you're all right?" Stacey had asked.

"I have some scrapes and bruises, but I've been through a lot worse."

"You know that's not what I mean."

"How's the brute?" I had asked, meaning Shadow.

"He was a bad boy last night. He was growling and jumping and scratching big gouges in the door. I honestly wondered if someone was lurking around the house. But he seemed to want out. It was because you weren't here, I think. He didn't like not knowing where you were. Maybe he sensed you were in danger."

Unlike me, Stacey tended to believe she could get inside the wolf's head from time to time. She was a former wildlife biologist and a scientist, but she held superstitious beliefs when it came to Shadow. She needed the wolf to be a semi-magical being.

"What did you do with him?"

"Put him out in his pen. I worry he might never be tame enough to live with us like a dog. What will we do when we have a baby—"

"You haven't taken the test?" I'd asked abruptly.

"I told you I wouldn't until you were home." Then she'd added in a soft, almost pleading voice, "Unless you want me to take it now. I could call you back with the results."

For someone who'd seemed skeptical about the possibility of being pregnant the day before, she seemed to have had a change of heart. I couldn't blame her. Once again, I had put myself in mortal danger. Any child of mine faced the possibility of growing up fatherless.

"I'd rather you wait."

She let seconds pass before she answered.

"OK. I will."

I fell asleep again in the passenger seat, but this time, I dreamed.

I was in an unfamiliar house at night. Shafts of cold moonlight came in through the windows, but the rooms were otherwise dark. Somewhere down the hall, a baby was crying. I made for the sound, thinking the infant needed to be picked up, but the halls and staircases were like a maze, and before I could locate the room where the baby was, the noise stopped suddenly.

"We're home," Charley said.

I sat up and rubbed my eyes, feeling disoriented from my dream journey through Paul and Selene Renaud's house.

My father-in-law had parked alongside his old Ford Ranger pickup. The headlights from my truck shone down the hill to the gate of the fenced pen where Shadow was serving his detention. Before Charley cut the lights, I saw the wolf's eyeshine as he approached the wire. I would need to chide the animal for his bad behavior—right before I fed him a venison steak I'd been saving in the freezer.

"Do you want to come in for a cup of coffee?" I asked.

"After what happened to Josie, I think I might switch to tea for a while."

"We have English Breakfast."

The door to the porch opened, and Stacey stood at the top of the steps, waiting. Her hair was up for once, and she was wearing a sweater that hugged her body and slacks instead of jeans, and I thought she looked beautiful.

"I expect you and my girl might want some time alone."

He was right, of course. Stacey came down to kiss and hug me so hard, she compressed my rib cage. Then she did the same to her dad. She repeated my invitation to him to come inside, but Charley said he was eager to get back home to see Ora, which happened to be the truth. My mother-in-law had also suffered a long thirty-six hours of not hearing from her man and then, of course, had received the news about Josie.

My father-in-law was such a mule in terms of his ability to withstand punishment that even I had forgotten that he might have died as easily as his friend had. Ora, I was certain, had thought of nothing else.

When Charley joked to Stacey, "Leave it to your husband to start an international incident," I wanted to hug him.

Part of loving someone is knowing them so well you can predict their responses. We'd been through a lot together, the old geezer and I. Our relationship had truly become that of a father and son.

"Keep me posted," were his last words before leaving.

He might have meant about the inquiry in Canada or about the review of my shooting by the attorney general or the tribunal I would be facing at the Warden Service's headquarters. But I knew what he really meant was that he wanted to hear whether his daughter was pregnant as soon as we had a test result. I doubted there was anything he or Ora prayed for more than Stacey and I becoming parents.

We stayed outside, waving to him, while he backed the little truck up and turned around and idled toward the paved road—the rear lights of the Ranger growing smaller and smaller in the warm night.

When we could no longer hear his engine, the wolf let out a plaintive whine.

"Do we dare let him back inside?" I said.

But Stacey had thrown her arms around me again and pressed her head against my shoulder. I didn't realize she was crying until I felt tears on my neck. I folded my left arm around her and kissed the top of her head where she'd piled her hair. Then the realization came to me why she had dressed up and why she seemed so upset.

"You didn't wait," I said. "You took the test."

"I'm sorry."

"It's all right. I should have trusted you to know your own body, anyway. I know you're disappointed."

She raised her lovely face, and I saw her blinking rapidly as if to stem the tears streaming down her cheeks.

"Mike, you don't understand. The test came back positive. We're going to have a baby."

I stared dumbly into her wet, joyful eyes.

Stunned by the news, I waited for the emotions to arrive. But it was as if I were standing outside my body. And then, when I was finally pulled back into myself by the need to draw a breath, I heard above my thundering heartbeat and the electrical humming of my nerves a voice not my own.

You are going to be a father.

Down the hill, Shadow cried in the darkness.

Acknowledgments

A novel might begin with an author working alone to bring an idea to life, but by the time it is published it has become a collaboration reflecting the insights, talents, and hard work of many people.

Among those who helped me with this one were my agent Ann Rittenberg, editor Charles Spicer, publisher Andrew Martin, associate publisher Kelley Ragland, publicist Sarah Melnyk, marketing vice president Paul Hochman, and social media wiz Stephen Erickson.

For sharing their time and tremendous knowledge, I wish to thank Judy Camuso, Commissioner of Maine Inland Fisheries and Wildlife; Warden Colonel Dan Scott; Sergeant Scott Thrasher; Master Maine Guide Greg Drummond; wildlife biologist Ron Joseph; and all-around expert Jessica Hollenkamp, who always answers my questions no matter how obscure or nonsensical they might seem.

My wife, Kristen Lindquist, is always my first, best reader. I am grateful to Mat and Nancy McConnel for reviewing the manuscript and am in special debt to Elizabeth Pierson whose editorial acumen kept me on schedule.

And what kind of a son and brother would I be if I didn't thank my beloved family? Thank you all for supporting me in my life's dream.

About the Author

PAUL DOIRON, a native of Maine and bestselling author, attended Yale University, where he graduated with a degree in English. *The Poacher's Son*, the first book in the Mike Bowditch series, won the Barry Award and the Strand Critics Award for Best First Novel, and has been nominated for the Edgar, Anthony, and Macavity Awards in the same category. He is a registered Maine guide specializing in fly-fishing and lives on a trout stream in coastal Maine with his wife, Kristen Lindquist.